Sex Lives

LE BON PAPE.

Sex Lives
of the
Popes

An irreverent exposé of the Bishops of Rome
from St Peter to the present day

Nigel Cawthorne

PRION

First published in Great Britain in 1996 by PRION
32–34 Gordon House Road,
London NW5 1LP

Copyright © Nigel Cawthorne 1996

A catalogue record of this book can be obtained
from the British Library

ISBN 1-85375-207-X

Front cover image by Bourdet from
Historie des Papes, c1870

Back cover image by M.Greuber, from
Illustrierte Sittengeschichte by Eduard Fuchs, c1910

Picture opposite title page: *Le Bon Pape*
by Grandville, from *Chansons de Beranger*, c1840

From Mary Evans Picture Library, London SE3

Typeset in 11/13 Baskerville
by Books Unlimited (Nottm)
Printed and bound in Great Britan by
Biddles Ltd., Guildford & Kings Lynn

Contents

Introduction

Even in an age when priestly misdemeanours regularly hit the headlines, it would be hard to imagine Pope John Paul II being ministered to by a mother superior, while the college of cardinals looked on. However, such a spectacle would not be without historic precedent.

Plenty of previous popes have got up to all kinds of mischief. Many have been married. More, while making a show of celibacy, have installed their mistresses in the Vatican and promoted their illegitimate sons – or 'nephews' as they are known in the Church – to high office.

There have been gay popes who have made their catamites cardinals. There have been grossly promiscuous popes of both persuasions. Orgies were not unknown in the papal palaces. One pope ran a brothel out of the Lateran Palace. Several have increased their income by taxing the whores of Rome. Others sold indulgences to the clergy in the form of a sin tax that allowed them to keep their mistresses, provided they paid an annual fee.

1

The Catholic Church has gone to great lengths to hush this sort of thing up. Virtuous popes, on their election, have taken the same name and number as earlier popes to cause confusion. Radical Protestants in the sixteenth and seventeenth centuries had a field day evicting skeletons from cupboards. One pamphleteer of the period blithely lists which popes were poisoners, murders, fornicators, whoremongers, drunkards, lechers, gamblers, necromancers, devil-worshippers and atheists, and includes a special section for those that had committed incest.

Many popes have been accused of simony – the selling of offices in the Church for gain.

Up until the fifteenth century, the Church occasionally split, so there was more than one pope at a time. Rival popes would excommunicate, imprison and even murder each other. The loser in the power game – the one who did not maintain himself on the direct line from St Peter to our present pope – was called an anti-pope. In the eyes of Church historians, anti-popes were allowed to be a bit more risqué. The real popes – according to official sources – could, of course, do no wrong, even though poisoning their predecessor in order to seize the papal chair was not unknown.

With the wealth, power and position the papacy brought, it is not really surprising that popes regularly found a balm to the cares of the world in the arms of their lovers. Few would dare criticize. It was established early on in the history of the Church that the pope was answerable to no one but God, and he, presumably, was expected to turn a blind eye.

These days we tend to think of all popes as being old. After years of service to the Church, one would expect a

2

pope to have left the hot-bloodedness of youth far behind. But through the stratagems of scheming families, some have been crowned pope when barely in their teens. With such unlimited wealth and power at such a young age with no one who dared tell you that anything you did was morally wrong, the potential for debauchery was equally unlimited.

Although some of the allegations are somewhat overstated, many have a firm foundation. Celibacy was not required of priests until 1139, and even after that, clerics continued to take concubines. The Catholic Church was the wealthiest institution on the face of the earth. Religion was a lucrative career, and rich men must have their pleasures.

What's more, papal excesses were easy to cover up. From 1557, publications detailing the popes' misdemeanours could be kept from the faithful by putting them on the Index of Forbidden Books. The official histories make the popes out to be impossibly innocent. All but one of the first thirty popes were described as martyrs, but there is no evidence that they died for Christ.

Since the earliest times, sex and religion have been bound closely together. Many pagan cults included explicit sexual acts among their rituals. Even after Christianity had become firmly established, it found itself up against a much sexier religion – Islam. This is what Muslims entering paradise can expect:

Seventy-two Houris, or black-eyed girls of resplendent beauty, blooming youth, virgin purity and exquisite sensitivity, will be created for the use of the meanest believer; a moment of pleasure will be prolonged to a thousand years, and his faculties will be increased a hundred-fold to render him worthy of felicity.

Compare that to the Christian idea of heaven – psalm-singing, sermons, sunshine and celestial architecture.

The history of the Christian Church, however, is not nearly as staid as it makes out. The popes particularly have been debauched. So do not be too surprised if you wake up one morning to the headline on the front page of the *Sun* or *The New York Post*: 'Pope in love-child shock!'

1

The Bishop of Rome

The first pope, St Peter, was a married man. The Gospels of Mark, Matthew and Luke all mention the fact that Simon Peter had a wife when Jesus met him.

Scholars have generally disagreed about whether the other Apostles were married, though there is a consensus that John was not. Early writers almost unanimously described him as a virgin. They also agree that Peter had a house in Galilee, where he lived with his wife, his mother-in-law and his brother Andrew.

According to the Gospels of Luke and Matthew, Peter said: 'Lo, we have left our homes and followed you.' Jesus replied: 'Truly I say to you, there is no man who has left house or wife or brothers or parents or children for the sake of the kingdom of God, who will not receive...eternal life.'

But, while Peter did say he had left his home, he did not say that he had left his wife. Indeed, they were still together after Christ's crucifixion. In his first Epistle to the Corinthians, St Paul talks of Peter taking his wife with him on his travels during his apostolic ministry. He may have taken his children with him too. The body of St Petronilla, which is buried in Rome, was long venerated as St Peter's daughter.

When Jesus said that Peter was the rock on which he would build his Church, he must have known about Peter's marital status. And he certainly would not have asked him to divorce. Christ's disapproval of divorce was well known. In the Gospel according to Matthew, he declared: 'It was said, "Whoever divorces his wife, let him give her a certificate of divorce." But I say to you that everyone who divorces his wife, except on the grounds of unchastity, makes her an adulteress; and whoever marries a divorced woman commits adultery.'

That is pretty clear.

Jesus would not have expected Peter to have a sexless marriage either. Despite the teachings of the Catholic Church, Jesus was certainly not an advocate of celibacy. Again in *Matthew* he said: 'Have ye not read, that he which made them at the beginning made them male and female... For this cause shall a man leave his father and mother, and shall cleave to a wife: and they twain shall be one flesh.'

In other writings, Jesus seems almost pro-sex. According to the *Gospel of Thomas*, one of the apocryphal gospels excluded from the Bible, Jesus said: 'When like little children you take your clothes off without shame, when you make the two become one, when you make the male and the female into a single unity, then you will enter the kingdom.'

So Jesus took a fairly broad-minded attitude to sex. For some time there has been speculation that Jesus himself was married. Certainly, the Bible does not state clearly that Jesus is not married. It is silent about the matter, which is odd. At the time it was usual, almost compulsory, for a Jewish man of his age to be married. Except among strict Essenian sects, celibacy was condemned. One Jewish writer of the period even compared celibacy to murder. It was as obligatory for a Jewish father to find a wife for his son as it was to ensure that he was circumcised.

More importantly, Jewish Mishnaic Law says: 'An unmarried man may not be a teacher.' Jesus would not have been allowed to go around the Holy Land preaching to the people if he had not been married. If Jesus was married, it begs the questions: when was he wed and to whom? Possibly in Cana, when he turned water into wine? Possibly to Mary Magdalene? There have been many speculations.

According to Matthew's gospel, Jesus was of royal blood – that of the house of David. He would therefore be expected to produce heirs. The book *The Holy Blood and the Holy Grail* contends that Jesus and Mary Magdalene had a child, who was taken to France and his descendants went on to form the Knights Templar. The authors say that this terrible secret led to the bloody suppression of the Templars in the thirteenth century.

The Holy Blood and the Holy Grail is not the only book that argues that Jesus was a married man with children. In *Jesus the Man*, the author Barbara Thiering maintains that Jesus actually had three children by Mary Magdalene, two sons and a daughter. Thiering says that Jesus did not die on the cross. He was only on it for a comparatively short time – people often survived several days before they finally succumbed. Jesus was taken down and, Thieling says, revived. That is why his tomb was found empty.

There are even indications that he may not have been faithful to Mary. The *Gospel of Thomas* says that Jesus often shared the couch of Salome and the Coptic *Book of the Resurrection of Christ*, attributed to the disciple Bartholomew, mentions that Mary Magdalene was not alone when she discovered that Jesus was gone from his tomb. With her was 'Salome who tempted him'. From accounts of the dance of the seven veils, there is little doubt that Salome knew just how to tempt someone.

Thieling believes that Jesus and Mary Magdalene were divorced in AD 44, and that in AD 50 he married Lydia, a female bishop of the Thyatira 'virgins'. When Lydia became pregnant, many of Jesus's followers disputed the validity of the offspring. Those who doubted the legitimacy of Jesus's new child, says Thieling, 'were associated with sodomy'.

The first century theologian Clement of Alexandria, who wrote on Christian sexual ethics, mentions that St Peter was married. During his apostolic ministry, Peter and his wife would have visited Alexandria.

Some of the more straitlaced Catholic historians insist that St Peter was a widower by the time he reached Rome. He was met there by St Paul who did so much to shape the sexual behaviour of the Church. The majority of Catholic writers claim that Paul was a strict celibate. But it seems more likely that he was a widower who had suffered a long and unhappy marriage.

However, in his first letter to the Corinthians, Paul writes: 'Have I not the right to have a Christian wife about with me, like the rest of the apostles?' Later he claimed that his relationships with Christian sisters were purely platonic. Even in marriage, St Paul maintains that a man does well 'to preserve his partner in her virginity'. But it was Paul who said: 'It is better to marry, than to burn.' The 'burn' here has often been thought to mean 'burn with passion' rather than 'burn in hell'.

He also said: 'If you marry you do not sin.' And he urged husbands and wives to give each other their conjugal rights and cautioned against any prolonged continence. In his Epistle to the Ephesians, he presents conjugal love and marriage as a sublime conception. Yet in his first Epistle to the Corinthians, he warns: 'It is well for a man not to touch a woman.'

Obviously, when it came to sex, Paul was a bit mixed up.

Christianity was up against some pretty stiff opposition when it reached Rome. The most important state religion there celebrated celibacy – the priestesses of the goddess Vesta were, of course, the Vestal virgins who tended Vesta's sacred fire. But in fact, these six 'virgins' had the devil's own job hanging on to their virginity.

When the Romans were defeated by Hannibal at Cannae, for example, it was blamed, not on military incompetence, but on erring virgins. Two were denounced and condemned. Later all six were accused of going astray. They were tried and three of them were found guilty of surrendering their virginity. The penalty was a lingering death. They were sealed in an underground chamber with a bed, a lamp and a few days' food.

In first-century Rome, the goddess Venus was still worshipped in the age-old fashion, as was the god Liber. He was the Roman equivalent of the Greek god Priapus, the god of the erect penis.

However, the authorities were trying to clean things up a bit. They had already clamped down on the worship of Bacchus, the god of wine, madness and sexual liberty. Traditionally, women worshipped Bacchus three times a year in secret ceremonies. But when men got involved and began 'forcibly debauching' young initiates, the Roman Senate stepped in. Official permission had to be given for Bacchanalian celebrations that involved more than three women and two men.

The Roman authorities also cracked down on the worship of Isis in AD 19, when a gullible young matron named Paulina, spent a night of what she thought was holy intercourse with Isis's associate, the god Anubis. She later discovered that the part of the god had been played by one of her earthly admirers. The scandal surrounding her discovery triggered a vicious suppression of the sect. The priests of Isis were crucified and worshippers were deported to the mosquito-infested island of Sardinia.

But this did not stop other unscrupulous clergymen taking advantage of their flocks. A priest of Saturn named Tyrannus told the husbands of beautiful women that Saturn himself had asked for their wives to spend the night in the temple. The women would feel honoured and turn up at the temple beautifully dressed and carrying gifts. They would be seen to be locked inside by Tyrannus. He would then slip round the back and enter by a secret tunnel that led into the statue of Saturn. From there, he would speak. The woman would be so flattered that the god was talking to her that she would do whatever he said. When Tyrannus had got his victim sufficiently aroused, he would blow the candles out, enter the chamber and have his way with Saturn's willing devotee.

He managed to get away with this for some time, until one of the women recognized Tyrannus's voice. She went home and told her husband. Tyrannus was arrested and tortured. He confessed and a large number of Roman families found themselves dishonoured by adulterous wives and illegitimate offspring.

Christianity's message of sexual restraint no doubt struck a chord in ancient Rome. Marital infidelity was rife. Claudius was emperor when Christianity first reached Rome. Claudius's own wife, the lascivious Messalina, had numerous affairs. She was so insatiable that she would leave the Imperial palace at night in disguise and go to a brothel where she prostituted herself under the name Lycisca. In her dank cell, she would expose her vagina and her nipples 'naked and gilded'. She would then satisfy all-comers. The indecisive Claudius was finally persuaded to have her murdered after she performed a wedding ceremony in public with one of her many lovers. Claudius then married Agrippina. She was little better. It is almost certain that she had an incestuous relationship with her own son, Nero. They frequently travelled together in a closed litter, and when they emerged it was noted that their clothes were often stained and dishevelled.

When Nero became Emperor, he deliberately antagonized his mother by taking up with a freed slave named Acte who was Agrippina's spitting image. He tried to have his mother killed when she opposed his affair with the beauteous Poppaea.

Poppaea, unfortunately, was already married, but Nero got rid of her inconvenient husband by appointing him governor of Lusitania. He got rid of his own wife, Octavia, by accusing her of adultery with a slave and divorced her on the grounds of sterility. She was sent into exile, where she was murdered, probably on Nero's orders. She was just nineteen when she died.

Although Nero married Poppaea, the Roman writer Suetonius says that to the end of his days, he 'never gave up drinking or changed his indulgent way of life...or the manner of his entertainments'.

When St Peter and St Paul arrived in Rome, Nero's corrupt regime was at its height and every type of exotic vice was on offer. Nero had built a princely garden in the Vatican Field, where some of his finest orgies took place. The early Christian settlement in Rome was practically within earshot. Peter and Paul must certainly have known what was going on only a hundred yards from their own front door.

Curiously it was claimed by early Christian scholars that Nero's second wife Poppaea was a Christian. With or without the blessing of St Peter, she certainly participated in these orgies.

'The most notorious and profligate of these entertainments,' Tacitus wrote,

were those given in Rome by Tigellinus [joint head of the Praetorian Guard]. A banquet was set out upon a barge on a lake in the palace grounds. This barge was towed about by vessels picked out with gold and ivory and rowed by debauched youths who were chosen in accordance with their proficiency in libidinous practices. Birds and beasts had been collected from distant countries, and sea monsters from the ocean. On the banks of the lake were brothels filled with ladies of high rank. By these were prostitutes, stark naked, indulging in indecent gestures and language. As night approached the groves and summer-houses rang with songs and were ablaze with lights. Nero disgraced himself with every kind of abomination, natural and unnatu-

ral, leaving no further depth of debauchery to which he could sink.

It was not just the emperor and the upper classes who indulged in promiscuous sexual practices. When St Peter came to Rome, the games were very popular. Around the great circuses or arenas, there were taverns and booths where prostitutes plied their trade. They were specially trained to give men the sort of sexual satisfaction that their wives could not give. Due to the declining Roman birth rate, wives were encouraged to use more restrained positions which were thought most likely to result in pregnancy.

The games themselves were no spectator sport. In his *Art of Love*, Ovid (43 BC–AD 17) writes:

> *Many are the opportunities that await you at the circus. No one will prevent you sitting next to a girl. Get as close to her as you can. That's easy enough, for the seating is cramped anyway. Find an excuse to talk to her... Ask her what horses are entering the ring and which ones she fancies. Approve her choices... If, as is likely, a speck of dust falls on her lap, brush it gently away; and, even if no dust falls, pretend it has done and brush her lap just the same. She will certainly let you have a glimpse of her legs... The deft arrangement of a cushion has often helped a lover... Such are the advantages which a circus offers to a man looking for an affair.*

According to Nero's tutor Seneca, homosexual men used the bathhouses to measure each other up. Sometimes men and women would bathe naked together. Newly invented magnifying mirrors were the latest sex toys. And at dinner, entertainment would be provided by naked Spanish dancing girls.

See-though clothes that exposed both the breasts and the genitals were all the rage. The problem was, Seneca said, 'our women have nothing left to reveal their lovers in the bedroom that they have not already shown on the street.'

Something of St Peter's attitude to the sexual mores of Imperial Rome can be garnered from one apocryphal tale. While St Peter was in Rome, the leader of another gnostic sect, Simon the Magus, turned up. He was known as 'The Standing One' because he headed a priapic cult that worshipped the erect male member. Although he was baptised a Christian, his passion for 'strumpets' was well known. Simon the Magus challenged St Peter to a battle of magic in front of the Emperor. As an opening shot, Simon levitated himself, but Peter fell to his knees in prayer, weakening the potency of Simon's spell and Simon came crashing to the ground, breaking his thigh.

This story demands an allegorical reading. And if it truly reflects St Peter's anti-sex attitude, he and Nero were bound to come into conflict.

To get rid of the Christians, Nero blamed them for the fire which burned down much of Rome. Contrary to common wisdom, Nero did not fiddle while Rome burnt. He actually tried to put the fire out. But he did take time off from directing the firefighting, when the flames were at their height, to appear on the stage and sing a song comparing the fire to the sacking of Troy.

After the fire, St Peter was arrested and crucified. St Paul was martyred at around the same time, probably by beheading.

Peter was, of course, canonized later, but this gave the Paulite anti-sex wing of the Church problems. How could Peter have the stuff of sainthood if he had defiled

14

himself with a woman? One celibate zealot found a neat way out of this problem. He excused Peter of the sin of unchastity by declaring that 'Peter washed away the filth of marriage with the blood of his martyrdom'.

Despite the martyrdom of Peter and Paul, the citizens of Rome were not fooled by the scapegoating of the Christians. The Senate passed a resolution condemning Nero to the death of a common criminal. He was to be stripped naked, tied to a stake and flogged. When he heard the sentence, Nero decided to commit suicide, but he could not summon up the courage. It was only when he heard the hooves of the horses of the soldiers who were coming to arrest him that he finally picked up a dagger. Even then, he needed assistance to stick it into his throat.

The death of Nero did not end the persecution of the Christians, which continued, on and off, for the next few centuries. When it was at its worst, they literally went underground, hiding in the catacombs under the city.

But slowly Christianity began making headway. What impressed the Romans in particular about the new religion was the extraordinary ability of some Christian priests to remain celibate. One young devotee even applied to the Emperor for permission to be surgically castrated so that he would not be tempted. The Emperor Domitian (died AD 96) had outlawed castration. The lead in Rome's water supply and excessive drinking had caused a perilous drop in fertility and Rome needed all the new citizens it could get. The Emperor Hadrian (died AD 138) had extended the law. Even voluntary castration attracted the death penalty. Permission was denied to the young devotee.

From the earliest times, the popes seem to have been

divided by their attitude to sex. Pope Soter (AD 166–174) reprimanded Dionysius, Bishop of Corinth, for his lax attitude to sexual continence and his tolerance of sinners. But Pope Victor I (AD 189–198) seems to have shared many of Dionysius's attitudes.

Victor I was the first pope known to have dealings with the Imperial household. His go-between was Marcia, mistress of the depraved Emperor Commodus (AD 180–192). Victor supplied her with a list of names of Christians condemned to work in the mines of Sardinia, and during pillow talk, she persuaded the Emperor to have them released.

Marcia was quite a woman. Like many unwanted female infants in Rome, she had been 'exposed' – that is, left out in the open to die. She was saved from her fate by a Christian named Hyacinthus. He was said to be a eunuch and may have been a priest. He certainly brought Marcia up as a Christian.

However, Hyacinthus made his living in a not very Christian way. He would save female children who had been exposed, rear them to maturity, then sell them into harems or brothels. When Marcia reached puberty, she was duly sold as a slave-concubine into the household of a Roman nobleman. The nobleman, however, was involved in a plot to kill Commodus, instigated by the Emperor's sister, Lucilla. When the intrigue was discovered, he was put to death and his property – including Marcia – was confiscated by the Emperor. She was put into the Imperial harem with three hundred beautiful women and three hundred of the fairest boys Commodus's pimps could find in Roman society.

By virtue of her beauty and erotic skills, Marcia quickly

rose to become one of Commodus's favourites. She presided over orgies which, it is said, 'in their wildness and obscenity surpassed those of Nero'. She loved to show off her opulent figure and frequently wore very revealing clothes when Pope Victor visited her.

Having done her Christian duty by getting her fellow believers released from Sardinia, Marcia spent three more years orgying. Then she joined a successful plot to murder Commodus, and Marcia saved her soul by marrying the chief murderer.

In what turns out to be a routine piece of papal spite, Victor I omitted the name of one Christian, Callistus, from the list that he gave to Marcia. Callistus had been sent to Sardinia because of his involvement in a financial swindle rather than because he was a Christian. He nevertheless managed to convince the governor of the mine that a mistake had been made and was released. He went on to become Pope Callistus I (AD 217–22).

To have returned from the mines of Sardinia was something of a miracle. The slaves there were treated appallingly. Most lasted between six and fourteen months.

Back in Rome, Callistus had much more trouble than his immediate predecessors in maintaining a Christian influence in the Imperial household. And there was a new religion to compete with. In AD 218, the fourteen-year-old Elagabalus had become Emperor. He was a follower of the Syrian sun-god El-Gabal, whose cult worshipped a conical black stone said to have fallen from heaven. As part of the rites of El-Gabal 'a chorus of Syrian damsels performed lascivious dances to the sound of barbarian music'. Elagabalus was a high priest in the sect. Even the Roman senators were shocked at the orgies that took place in the Imperial palace. Concubines and catamites disported themselves on cushions stuffed with crocus petals while the Emperor, dressed as a woman, made mockery of high Roman officers.

He would go to the baths with his women and rub psilothrum, a depilatory, all over their bodies. He liked his bodies smooth and perfectly polished. His own body was purged of hair in the same way. But he would shave the genitals of his male lovers with the same razor that he would use on his own beard.

He spent his life finding new and creative ways to satisfy his lusts. Lovers of both sexes were given the top jobs. But he went too far when he broke the most sacred laws of Rome by violating the Vestal virgins. The Praetorian Guard mutinied and killed him.

Under the reign of Elagabalus, Pope Callistus ran a rather liberal regime. He ordained men who had married two or even three times, let priests marry and even let a bishop guilty of 'grave offences' stay in office.

He also knew how to attract sinners to his flock. In a time when the penalty for adultery in Rome was still death, he announced: 'I will absolve even those who are guilty of adultery and fornication, if they do penance.' This naturally attracted new converts.

Some churchmen were against Callistus's lenient attitude and they elected an alternative pope, the stern and unforgiving Hippolytus (AD 217–235), who became the first anti-pope. He was outraged at Callistus's broadminded membership policy, especially when it came to women, complaining that Callistus 'even permitted females, if they were unwedded and burned with passion at an age in all events unbecoming, or if they were not disposed to overturn their dignity through a legal marriage, that they might have whomsoever they would choose as a bedfellow, whether slave or free, and that they, though not legally married, might consider such a person as their husband.'

Callistus also allowed free women to marry slave men, something against Roman law at the time. This brought even women of senatorial rank into the Church.

Hippolytus was against sex in any shape or form, with or without the sanctification of marriage. However, he ended up on the 'island of death', Sardinia, with Pope Pontian (AD 230–235), one of Callistus's successors, when the Emperor Maximinus Thrax got tired of their squabbling.

Slowly but surely, Christianity was taking over the Roman Empire. The Emperor Diocletian married a Christian and protected them from persecution for eighteen years, until Galerius convinced him that they were a fanatical sect plotting against him.

The Emperor Constantius the Yellow had a concubine who was a Christian. She had been a maid in a roadside tavern where he had stopped. He was so taken with her that, when he left the inn, he took her with him as his mistress. Their son Constantine became the first Christian emperor of Rome. He was converted from Elagabalus-style sun-worship by his mother. When he invaded Italy in AD 312, he discouraged the more licentious sects, though he never gave up the title Pontifex Maximus, head of the Roman state's pagan cult.

The Pope at that time, Silvester I (AD 314–335), must have had some ideological problems with his patron, Constantine. The Emperor married twice, murdered Crispus, his son by his first wife in AD 326, and had his second wife killed in her bath. He also murdered his brother-in-law, after promising him safe conduct, and his eleven-year-old nephew. Constantine waited until the end of his life, when he had no more strength left to sin, before he was baptised.

The Church's teachings were not nearly so strict back then. It was only in AD 314, at the Council of Ankara, that having sex with animals was outlawed. Besides, Constantine and his family showered the Church with lavish gifts – gold, silver, precious stones and fabrics. The Pope was moved out of his dingy lodgings into the splendid palace of the Laterani family.

In exchange, the Church bent over backwards to indulge Constantine. In an attempt to accommodate the generous Emperor's sexual inconstancy, St Augustine wrote that if a man finds himself married to a barren wife, it is perfectly okay to take a concubine. There was no reason to believe that either of Constantine's wives was barren, nor did he confine himself to one concubine. But the Pope said nothing.

It dealt the Roman Church a great blow when he quit Rome and moved his capital to Byzantium, which was renamed Constantinople. Constantine died there in AD 337, leaving the empire to his family who promptly fell out. The succession was decided by homicide.

First, all of his male relatives, with the exception of his three sons, were murdered. Then the eldest son was murdered by the youngest who, as Emperor, was said to rival Elagabalus in his vices. When he too was murdered, the second son, Constantius took over.

Unfortunately, from Rome's point of view, the victor was an Arian – that is, he denied the divinity of Christ. This split the Church, with much of the Eastern establishment following the new Emperor.

Although the Church was split by Constantine's family, Rome could at least claim his granddaughter, Constantia. She consecrated her virginity to Christ and offered herself for martyrdom at the age of twelve. As a reward, the Catholic Church made her a saint.

2

Fathers and Sons

Women were very powerful in Rome. To maintain power there, it helped to be a ladies' man. Liberius (352–366) was a pope who recognized this. In 355, he was banished to Thrace – modern-day Bulgaria – by Constantine's son Emperor Constantius II, and his place was taken by the anti-pope Felix II (355–365). Felix simply did not have the same rapport with the womenfolk. When Constantius visited Rome from his capital in Constantinople in April 357, he was lobbied by rich women who demanded the return of Liberius. And they meant business. Constantius was quickly convinced that he would be unable to maintain public order in Rome unless Liberius was reinstated. So the women got their way and Liberius returned.

Strictly speaking, Liberius and Felix reigned jointly after Liberius's return. But Felix moved out to the suburbs and left all the serious work, and the handling of Rome's militant womanhood, to Liberius. However, it was Felix who was canonized. Liberius never became a saint.

When Liberius died on 24 September 366, Ursinus, his deacon, was elected pope. But Damasus, a priest's son who had worked for both Liberius and Felix, was not happy with this. An ambitious man, he was not going to let such a trifling detail as an election get in his way. So he simply hired a gang of thugs and stormed the Julian Basilica. A three-day massacre of the supporters of Ursinus followed. On 1 October 366, Damasus's men seized the Lateran Basilica and the priest's son was consecrated Pope Damasus I (366–384). The fact that Damasus was married did not stand in his way – he simply renounced his wife and children.

The bloodshed between Damasus's supporters and those of Ursinus only ended when the prefect of Rome, Praetextus, a pagan, stepped in and forced Ursinus's remaining followers out of the city. Even that was not the end of the fighting. Some of Ursinus's men holed up in the Liberian Basilica. Damasus's partisans attacked and 137 Ursinians were slaughtered. For the rest of his life, Damasus needed protection from the Ursinians.

A pagan historian of the period, Ammianus Marcelinus, was not surprised that men should go to such lengths to secure the papacy. He wrote:

> No wonder that for so magnificent a prize as the Bishopric of Rome, men should contest with the utmost eagerness and obstinacy. To be enriched by the lavish donations of the principal females of the city; to ride, splendidly attired in a stately carriage; to sit at a profuse, luxuriant, more than imperial table – these are the rewards of successful ambition.

Damasus I certainly enjoyed the favours of 'the principal females of the city'. He entertained lavishly and was nicknamed by gossips 'the matrons' ear tickler'.

Damasus's secretary, the ascetic St Jerome, did not approve of the Pope's goings-on, or of the men surrounding him, looking more like bridegrooms that clerics. He warned a dozen or so virtuous ladies that the Roman Church, clergy and laity, was monstrously corrupt. His comments about their sexual practices were so explicit that, sadly, academics will not translate them. But Jerome's general line of argument was that priests, monks, professional virgins, widows and Christian women were all debauched.

In a letter to an aristocratic old maid called Eustochium, he warns her to avoid Damasus's flock altogether. Christian virgins 'fall every day', he said. Christian widows were hooked on drink and drugs. He wrote of 'love-feasts' – orgies – in churches on saints' days. Other early Christian writers, such as Ambrose of Milan and Augustine of Hippo, confirm this. In consequence, Jerome told Eustochium that she must 'avoid the society of matrons and not go to the houses of noble ladies... [They] pass as chaste nuns and then after supper they sleep with the apostles.' Under Damasus, men became priests and deacons 'so that they may see women more freely'. Priests who have curled hair, scented robes and jewels on their fingers and who spend all their time visiting rich women – like Damasus – must be regarded 'as husbands, not clerics'. Some priests were obeying the ordinances that discouraged marriage, Jerome conceded, but instead they surrounded themselves with slave girls and spent their entire life in female company.

Jerome warned another Roman maid never to remain alone in a room with a priest. If she found herself in such a situation she must 'plead that either her bowels or her bladder needed relieving'. Christian women were to be avoided too. 'Never enter the house or be in their company alone.' As for monks who go barefoot and nuns who wear old and tattered clothing, shun them. They fast during the day, but at night and on feast days, they 'gorge till they vomit'. The only virtuous women to be seen on the streets of Rome, soberly dressed and looking pale and ascetic, according to Jerome, were pagans.

Intellectually, Pope Damasus was very much on Jerome's wavelength. When it came to sex, Damasus said, he was against it. He wrote Latin prose and poetry on the virtues of virginity. 'Intercourse,' Damasus wrote, 'is a defilement.' There has been a long-running debate about exactly what he meant by 'defilement'. Some argue that he meant defilement in the sense of sin; others that he meant a defilement of the law. Either way, he did not practise what he preached. In 378, a converted Jew named Isaac brought a 'disgraceful charge' against him. Damasus was tried for the crime of adultery by a synod of forty-four bishops.

After hearing the evidence, the bishops had no doubt that the Pope was guilty and were about to depose him and condemn him to death when the Emperor Gratian stepped in to prevent it. Not only was Damasus acquitted but, after he died, he was canonized – though this was largely because he had converted Gratian's successor Theodosius I, who adopted Christianity as the official religion of the Roman Empire.

On the death of Damasus, Ursinus tried to make a come-back. He put his name forward to become pope once again, but he was howled down and Siricius (384–399) was elected unanimously.

Although Siricius was one of Damasus's deacons, he was not of Damasus's liberal persuasion. He renewed the decrees against the marriages of priests and deacons and enforced the canons which prevented females dwelling in presbyteries. He also excommunicated Jovinian, a monk living in Milan who was a critic of fasting and celibacy. Jovinian had had the audacity to suggest that the Blessed Virgin Mary had lost her virginity when she gave birth to Christ! The Bishop of Naissus was similarly condemned when he suggested that Mary had had other children after Jesus.

Siricius was against sex in any shape or form. Married priests must give up their double beds, he said. He was very upset when he heard that the clergy in Spain were continuing their marital relations. Bishops, priests and deacons, he believed, should not indulge 'in such immorality'. 'Those that remain in the flesh cannot be acceptable to God,' Siricius maintained. If they had sinned through ignorance and now put away their wives, they would be pardoned but never promoted. Sex had irretrievably soiled them. But the Spanish bishops would not give up their wives. They argued that God should be able to sort out the 'whoremongers and adulterers' among them.

Someone else who came up against the strictures of Siricius was that old stickler St Jerome. While no libertine, he praised marriage because it produced virgins for the Church.

Jerome also pointed out a foul practice that was current in the Church at the time. Women, it seemed, were living under the same roofs as men under a vow of sexual continence. St Jerome asked with typical directness:

From what source has this plague of 'dearly beloved sisters' found its way into the Church? Whence come these unwedded wives, these new types of concubines, nay, I will go further, these one-man harlots? They live in the same house with their male friends; they occupy the same room and often the same bed; and yet they call us suspicious if we think that anything is wrong.

This sort of talk was too much for the blessed St Siricius. He contrived to have Jerome banished from Rome, the old ascetic finally being driven out when a Roman noblewoman died under the extremely austere regime he championed.

The other great guardian of sexual morality, St Augustine, was more in tune with the pontificate of Pope Siricius. He began the Church's condemnation of contraceptive devices. He called them the 'poisons of sterility' and regarded a wife who used them as 'her husband's harlot'.

Unlike Jerome, Augustine actually knew about such things. As a youth he had visited prostitutes. At the age of eighteen he had fathered a child. He had lived with a woman for eleven years without marrying her and took a second mistress while waiting for his chosen wife to come of age. 'I was in love with loving,' he confessed. 'Like water, I boiled over, heated by my fornications.' When he converted to Christianity at around thirty, he knew his limitations. 'Give me chastity,' he prayed to God, 'but not just now.'

However, his memory of illicit loves left him with a sense of guilt and misery. 'Nothing,' he wrote in his *Soliloquies,* 'is so powerful in drawing the spirit of a man downwards as the caresses of a woman and that physical intercourse which is part of marriage.' In his sermons he warned: 'Husbands, love your wives but love them chastely.

Insist on the work of the flesh only in such measure as is necessary for the procreation of children. Since you cannot beget children in any other way, you must descend to it against your will, for it is the punishment of Adam.'

In later life, he would not let a women – even his older sister – set foot in his house or speak to him without witnesses being present in case lust overwhelmed him.

Augustine gives a fascinating insight into the Rome of the early popes. While Siricius was on the papal throne, Augustine left Carthage, in what is now Libya, which he called 'a cauldron of dissolute loves'. In his religious quest, he headed for the Rome of the straitlaced Siricius. But he did not find a holy city founded on celibacy and sexual abstinence – far from it.

Augustine was particularly struck by Roman marriage ceremonies. These began in the temple of Priapus where the bride had to sit on the god's enormous, ugly phallus – though Augustine pointed out that this only robbed the bride of her modesty, not her virginity or her fertility. He was also struck by a number of other gods that were involved in the business of marriage, all of whom accompanied the newlyweds home for the wedding night. There was the god of marriage, the god who brought the bride to the marriage home and another god to keep her there. Once the wedding guests had gone, there were a horde of other gods and goddesses who trooped into the marriage chamber for the deflowering. Augustine marvelled at how a man could be aroused and a virginal young woman throw off her sexual inhibitions with so many people around.

With this sort of thing going on, it is no wonder that Siricius's dictums on a celibate priesthood did little good. Even his successor Pope Anastasius I (399–401)

28

had a son who became his deacon, then succeeded his father as Pope Innocent I (401–417).

Innocent I established the primacy of the Roman See and is often thought of as the first true pope, but the ascendency of Rome during his pontificate came about by pure accident. During Innocent's reign, Rome was sacked by the Goths. The Pope fled to the safety of the degenerate court of Emperor Honorius – who had a hankering for young girls – at Ravenna. Innocent was said to share his tastes. Meanwhile the Goths looted Rome, beating and violating noble ladies, matrons and nuns in the streets. When Innocent returned, he found that the old Roman order had collapsed. The noble families who had maintained the old pagan practices were gone and he was the first Pope to sit in a wholly Christian Rome. Innocent I was canonized, but then so was his father, Anastasius.

Boniface I (418–422) was another priest's son who became pontiff. He had a rival for the papacy, Eulalius. Both were duly elected and consecrated pope on the same day, 27 December 418. Boniface's claim succeeded because he was close friends with Galla Placidia, sister of Emperor Honorius.

Things hit a new low when, in 440, Pope Sixtus III (432–40) was tried for the seduction of a nun, but as there were no eyewitnesses, his accusers were unable to substantiate the charge. In his defence, Pope Sixtus told the biblical tale of the woman caught in adultery, which could be seen as a tacit confession. None of his prelates sought to cast the first stone.

Pope Leo I (440–61) cleverly used sexual corruption to expand the political power of the Church. The Emperor Valentinian III was a man much given to licentious adventure and his mother, Boniface's old friend Galla Placidia, would do anything the Pope asked. She encouraged Valentinian in his excesses, so that she and Pope Leo had a free hand in running what remained of the Roman Empire.

However, in her growing devotion to the Holy See, Galla Placidia made a disastrous mistake. She pledged her daughter's virginity to God, only to find that her daughter was pregnant. The unfortunate girl was walled up in a convent, but she found a way to send a letter to Attila the Hun, promising half Italy as a dowry if he would come and rescue her. Attila answered the call, but his raping and pillaging army was exhausted by the time it reached Rome and Leo managed to persuade him to go back.

Valentinian III was murdered by one of his own officers for raping his wife. The wife died soon after and the officer demanded that Valentinian's widow sleep with him in recompense. She sent a message to Gaiseric, the leader of the Vandals, asking him to come and save her. Leo tried to persuade Gaiseric to turn back too, but the Vandals were fresh from the conquest of Sicily and determined to loot Rome. However, Leo spoke out so persuasively against rape that the Vandals mostly left Roman womanhood alone when they sacked the city in 455. Valentinian's widow was saved from the bed of the officer her husband had dishonoured, but she was robbed of her jewels, and she and her daughters were shipped to Africa in the Vandal fleet where, no doubt, a worse fate befell them.

Leo I behaved pretty honourably throughout all this. But he was a strange man. He was a stickler for the virginity of women and demanded that a woman be tested in her virginity for sixty years before she could take the veil and become a nun. However, bishops were allowed to keep their wives, provided they treated them 'as a sister'.

He was also a warped and sadistic torturer. When he started suppressing Manichaeanism, a Christian sect that incorporated the last vestiges of paganism, he brutally tortured its followers. What he wanted to hear from his victims was very specific. They were forced to confess that they mixed semen with the sacrament and used young girls at the altar for the purpose. Leo was the first Pope to claim the right to put heretics – that is, anyone who disagreed with him – to death. Pope Felix III (483–92) was more well adjusted. He was another son of a priest. Like his father, he did not practise celibacy. He was a widower when he became Pope and had at least two children, one of whom was a forebear of Pope Gregory I (590–604).

Gelasius I (492–96) and Anastasius II (496–498) were both priests' sons. But Anastasius represented a new, more independent papacy. In the writer Volaterranus's quaint phrase, he 'voided his own bowels at stool' – he went to the lavatory without assistance. (By this time, the Roman pontiff had become so imperial that like an emperor or king he had a 'gentleman of the stool' to assist with such things.)

The next pope, Symmachus (498–514) was not the son of a priest. In fact, he was born and brought up a pagan and he never shook off this early influence. He won a bribery battle to become pope against anti-pope Lawrence (498–99 and 501–06), but in 501, Symmachus was called to appear before Theodoric, the Ostrogoth king of Italy, and charged with 'unchastity', adultery and the misuse of Church property. Symmachus immediately fled back to Rome and took refuge in St Peter's, which to many seemed like an admission of guilt. Three times Symmachus was called before a synod to be tried. The first time, he refused to give evidence; the second time, he did not turn up at all; the third time, he argued that, as pope, no human court could judge him. During the trial, a struggle broke out in the Roman senate. The upshot was that many Christian men were killed and 'even dedicated women and virgins were displaced from their monasteries or houses', stripped and whipped through the streets.

Against this background, the synod found that they had no alternative but to let God be the judge of Symmachus. King Theodoric, far from satisfied, installed Pope Lawrence in the Lateran Palace, while Symmachus was confined to St Peter's by street violence. Symmachus spent his time forging documents to show that there were precedents supporting his position that the pope can be judged by no man. After five years it was decided that two popes was one too many. Theodoric backed down and Lawrence retired to a farm belonging to his patron Festus, where he died in 507/8.

Many of the clergy were never reconciled to Symmachus because of his continued misconduct. Nevertheless, like many misbehaving pontiffs, Symmachus was rewarded after his death by canonization.

Pope Hormisdas (514–523), another saint, was also a father, not in the priestly sense. He was married before his ordination and had a son who became Pope Silverius (536-537). Agapitus I (535–536) was the son of Gordians, a priest who had been killed by followers of anti-pope Lawrence in September 502.

3

Ladies' men

I n the sixth century, two immensely powerful women got their hands on the papacy, beginning with Pope Vigilius (537–55) who obtained the papacy 'by means of Theodora, the Empress, and Antonia, wife of General Belisarius'.

Theodora particularly had the most notorious reputation. She came from a circus family and had been put on the stage as a child. She also played maid for her older sister Comito, who was a famous courtesan. Theodora, too young for intercourse, would perform oral sex or masturbate the slaves of the men who came to see her sister.

When Theodora grew up, she too became a full-time courtesan, working with the so-called 'infantry', the lower end of the market. Later, she became an actress and was famous for exposing her body shamelessly on stage, even though it was against the law. She performed lewd acts with the actors. Once, on stage, she had slaves sprinkle grain on her pudenda and had geese peck it off.

She was also renowned for inventing new sexual techniques and would seduce anyone who took her fancy, especially 'beardless young men'. At her dinner parties she would exhaust as many as ten athletic young men; then she would take on up to thirty servants.

In 527, she married the Emperor Justinian in the church of Hagia Sophia in Constantinople. In an excess of hypocritical zeal, they set about cleaning up Byzantium, closing down the brothels and shipping the prostitutes out to convents. Sometimes the punishments that Theodora had devised for them were so extreme that the women killed themselves rather than undergo the process of reform.

Vigilius was sent as papal nuncio to Constantinople by the then Pope Boniface II (530–32). There, Theodora set about corrupting him, lavishing expensive gifts on him and promising to make him pope. An avaricious and ambitious man, Vigilius readily accepted her proposals.

When Agapitus I (535–36) died, Theodora sent Vigilius back to Rome, but he got there too late and found that Silverius (536–37) had already been installed. Theodora, in great anger, persuaded Justinian to send Belisarius to depose Silverius and instal Vigilius in his place. Silverius was charged with treason, stripped of his papal robs, demoted to the rank of a monk and deported. Justinian thought that was a little harsh and ordered that he be given a fair trial. If he was found guilty, he would be given another see; if innocent, he would be restored as pope.

Vigilius simply could not let this happen. He rigged the trial and when Silverius was exiled again, connived in his murder. According to the ecclesiastical historian

Milman, Vigilius was 'the most doubtful character who had ever yet sat on the throne of St. Peter' – which is saying something – and that he was rightly punished for his 'crimes'. What this punishment was is not explained. True, Vigilius fell out with Theodora and had to flee to Sicily, but after a couple of years Justinian forgave him but he died on the voyage back to Rome.

On Vigilius's death, another of Theodora's and Antonia's favourites, Pope Pelagius I (556–61), was installed. He too had served in Constantinople, and his successor John III (561–74) also got the seal of approval from the East.

Under Pope John, the Council of Tours (567) endorsed the Benedictine rule that monks should never sleep two in a bed. Several centuries later the same rule was applied to nuns. It also decided that any cleric found in bed with his wife would be defrocked and excommunicated for a year. But since the Council admitted that there was hardly a cleric in Christendom who did not have a wife or mistress, the effect of this ruling was negligible. Bishops and priests continued to live openly with their wives and mistresses. If anyone was punished, it was the women. Many were given a hundred lashes for the sin of fornicating with a priest.

Pope Pelagius II (579–90) more or less turned a blind eye to clerical unchastity, provided married priests did not hand any Church property over to their wives and children. Detailed inventories were taken of the Church's assets. The Church under Pelagius II was so corrupt that, when Italy was hit by floods, rumours spread that a second deluge was coming.

Gregory I (590–604) was a worldly man. In his youth he was the prefect of Rome and he spent eight years, from 578 to 586, representing the Catholic Church in Constantinople. He was the son of a family that had already provided two popes, Felix III and Agapitus. But on the death of his father, he turned the family home into a monastery. Then he retreated into the contemplative life and ruined his health by fasting.

In 590, under protest, he was elected pope. He soon passed an edict enforcing the celibacy of priests, reasoning that if he could do without sex, so could everyone else. Those who offended against the celibacy rules were deposed. He was particularly strict on monasteries where women had open access and the brothers openly played 'godfather' to their children.

However, Gregory I was not quite as resolute as it may seem. He was the first pope to grant indulgences and pardons. So if you were in the Pope's favour, or were rich enough, you could get yourself a licence to sin. This led to the little rhyme:

> *Poor curates only keep Gregory's laws*
> *And fish in rills, or river's surface sweep;*
> *Whilst fatter Jacks and Carps escape their paws,*
> *Our prelates sink St Peter's larger net*
> *And in the bottom what they find they get.*

In other words, the bishops could get away with anything they liked, while lowly priests and monks were forced to put away their wives and families. Later, it is said, Gregory discovered that his edict had caused the needless deaths of many children whose clerical fathers had been forced to disown them. According to a letter from Huldric, Bishop of Augusta, to Pope Nicholas I (858–67), Pope Gregory had ordered his servants to empty a fish pond. At the bottom of it, they found the skulls of 6000 children, drowned or otherwise murdered. Immediately, he revoked his edict. Huldric observed that, far from obeying Gregory's dictum, the priests had 'not only not abstained from virgins and wifes, but not even from near relations, nay, not from males and even brute beasts'.

None of this would have surprised Gregory, who saw himself as a great authority on sex and wrote a number of books covering all manner of sexual behaviour. In these learned tomes he spent a great deal of effort adjudicating on the vexed question of whether it was sinful for a man suffering a build-up of semen to ejaculate spontaneously. With enormous care, he set out the various degrees of sinfulness resulting from the exact circumstances surrounding the emission. For example, if a priest suffered a nocturnal emission while asleep due to overeating, Gregory said, he should not be allowed to officiate a Mass, but he could take the communion if another priest was present. If he helped the emission along at all – manually, say – he should be denied communion altogether.

Gregory also put a great deal of thought into the entire vexed question of what has to be done when a man has defiled himself with the act of sex itself. A man, he said, must not enter a church after having intercourse with his wife unless he has washed himself first. The intercourse had to be for procreation, not pleasure, of course, otherwise it would be a sin and he should not enter the church at all.

Gregory made judgements on homosexuality, bestiality and periods when sexual abstinence was required. It seemed quite an obsession.

'Unnatural intercourse in marriage' was singled out for special condemnation. And *coitus interruptus* was a worse sin than fornication or adultery – worse even than a man having sex with his own mother. Incest was described as 'natural' because it could lead to procreation, whereas anything that prevented conception meant that the sex was just for pleasure and, therefore, inherently evil.

One could conclude from this that Gregory was something of a hypocrite. That view would certainly be borne out by his letters. On the massacre of Emperor Maurice and eleven of his family, Gregory wrote to the murderer, the new Emperor Phocas: 'Glory be to God on high... Let the heavens rejoice and the earth be glad.' He also sent a letter loaded with servile compliments to Phocas's wife, Empress Leontia, whom he called 'a second Pulcheria'. Empress Pulcheria was a model of virginity, piety and refinement, while Leontia, it is commonly agreed, made Theodora look like a nun.

Gregory's obsession with sexual practices set off a debate in the Church which tried to systemize penances for carnal sins. For centuries, theologians picked over every aspect of human sexuality in an attempt to affix a proper punishment to it. In the Middle Ages the involuntary emission of semen earned seven days' fasting. If it was hand assisted, the penitent got twenty days. A monk who masturbated in church would be sentenced to thirty days' fasting; a bishop caught doing the same thing would have to fast for fifty days. *Coitus interruptus* earned two to ten years' penance. 'Poisons creating sterility' – that is, using contraceptives – anal intercourse and oral intercourse (called in Latin *seminem in ore*, 'semen in the mouth') earned three to fifteen years' penance on bread and water, and with no sex. The precise length of the penance depended on the circumstances of the offence, which the penitent would have to reveal in graphic detail to his confessor. One would have thought that would have been punishment enough. Corrupting a virgin was seen as a lesser offence and earned just three years' penance if the girl became pregnant, and only one if she didn't. Women who were poor generated lesser penances.

Penances only applied to the lower orders, of course. Popes and Emperors need not bother themselves with that sort of thing. Boniface III (607), for example, gained the papal throne by forming an allegiance with the Emperor Phocas – who is regularly described in history as an 'adulterer, parricide and tyrant'. Some commentators say that Boniface and Phocas shared 'certain tastes'.

Phocas declared Boniface, as Bishop of Rome, head of all the churches, seeing off a rival claim by the bishops of Constantinople. In return, Boniface had a gilded statue erected to Phocas, with an adulatory inscription.

Despite the backing of the Emperor, the popes of Rome found they could not exert their authority over the patriarchs in Constantinople, who were becoming an increasingly degenerate lot. One had himself castrated in public, to end all possibility of fornication. Another exposed himself in open court in an attempt to prove that he had not raped a nun.

Roman clerics were little better. Repeated edicts exhorting priestly celibacy did no good. Adeodatus I (615–18), canonized as St Deusdedit, was the son of a subdeacon, while Theodore I (642–49) was the son of a bishop. Sergius I (687–701) tried to reassert clerical

celibacy in the West, while the Eastern church abandoned it altogether. However, Sergius found that trying
to ban marriage resulted in other forms of sexual misbe-
haviour. In 693, the Council of Toledo described
sodomy as being 'prevalent in Spain'. The Council
decided: 'If any one of those males who commit this vile
practice against nature with other males is a bishop, a
priest, or a deacon, he shall be degraded from the dignity of that order, and shall remain in perpetual exile,
struck down by damnation.' A hundred lashes, a shaven
head and banishment were the penalties for guilt by
association. The King of Spain added castration to the
list. This would have ended any church career. In
accordance with the old law from the Book of Leviticus,
a priest must be sexually intact.

Pope Gregory III (731–41), a firm believer in the monas-
tic life, remained obsessed with the fight against sodomy.
He proclaimed it 'a vice so abominable in the sight of
God that the cities in which its practitioners dwelt were
appointed for destruction by fire and brimstone'. He
harked back to the vivid descriptions of sin supplied by
the first century historian Philo of Alexandria, who said:

The land of the Sodomites was brimful of innumerable iniqui-
ties, particularly those arising from gluttony and lewdness...
[The inhabitants] threw from their necks the law of nature, and
applied themselves to deep drinking of strong liquor and dainty
feedings and forbidden forms of intercourse. Not only in their
mad lusts for women did they violate the marriages of their
neighbours, but also men mounted males without respect for the
sexual nature the active partner shares with the passive; and so
when they tried to beget children they were discovered to be inca-
pable of any but sterile seed.

The problem was, of course, that sodomy and other forms of vice were more deeply rooted in the clergy than in any other part of society. In Germany, St Boniface found such depravity among the bishops and priests that he begged Gregory III to wash his hands of the lot of them.

However, for the protection of the Church, Gregory III was forced to make a pact with the King of the Franks, Charles Martel, who, in exchange, used convents as his brothels and spent his leisure time corrupting bishops.

Reporting to Gregory's successor Zacharias (741–52), St Boniface claimed that all the German clergy were wildly promiscuous. Men who had spent their youth in rape and adultery were rising to the highest ranks. Priests, Boniface said, slept with four or five women a night, then got up to celebrate Mass.

4

Latin lovers

Zacharias was the first pope to camp it up. He introduced new vestments adorned with gold and jewels. His successor Stephen II (752–57) was the first pope to become truly rich, thanks to the devotion of the King of France, who liked to kiss his feet. Stephen was also the first pope to be carried on men's shoulders. Humility had been the thing up until then.

Stephen made another breakthrough. He allowed free men to marry slave girls, if they were both Christians. This was something of a rogue's charter as such marriages could be dissolved, allowing the man to marry again. The girl, however, would never be free.

Leo III (795–816) was another pope not thought to be celibate. Although he was elected unanimously, he was not popular with the Roman aristocracy. One day, on his way to take Mass, he was ambushed by a gang who slashed him around the face and tried, unsuccessfully, to cut out his eyes and tongue. After being formally deposed, he was locked up in a monastery. With the help of friends, he managed to escape and sought safety with Charlemagne, King of the Franks. When representatives of the rebels turned up at Charlemagne's court and charged Leo with adultery and perjury, the charges were thought to be well founded. Leo used the same defence as St Symmachus, claiming that no earthly authority could try a pope. Charlemagne was not about to fall for that feeble line of defence. He took Leo back to Rome and set up an assembly of Franks and Romans to examine the charges against him. However, when Leo repeated the Symmachus line, the assembly refused to sit in judgement on him.

While Charlemagne was in Rome, he took the opportunity of having himself crowned Holy Roman Emperor (800). Leo, diplomatically, went along with it, and after he had put the crown on Charlemagne's head, knelt before him in homage, the first and last pope to kneel before a western emperor. Throughout the rest of Charlemagne's reign, Leo tried to keep his nose clean, although Charlemagne, the Church's great protector, was not really in much of a position to lecture anyone on sexual morality. He had divorced his first wife, had six children with his second wife and dropped her too. A third wife provided him with two daughters, and he had another by a concubine. His fourth wife died childless, but he consoled himself with another four concubines.

However, after Charlemagne died in 814, Leo got up to his old tricks again. When a fresh conspiracy to have him deposed and assassinated was discovered, Leo charged the conspirators with treason, tried them personally and condemned scores of people to death.

He spent huge sums of money on a new banqueting hall in the Lateran Palace and generally did up the place in lavish style. A great mosaic depicted him with Charlemagne and St Peter. In 1673, Leo was canonized on the spurious ground that a miracle had restored his eyes and tongue to him. He was also given a feast day, 12 June, but it has now been suppressed.

Under Leo and his successors in the ninth century, many monasteries became the haunts of homosexuals and convents were brothels where unwanted babies were killed and buried. The Council of Aix-la-Chapelle in 836 openly admitted this. However, some effort was made to clean up the public image of the Church. The clergy were forbidden to have their mothers, aunts or sisters living in their houses as the sin of incest was so rife. French prelates recorded that this, too, resulted in unwanted children and infanticide.

Not all ninth-century popes were sexually corrupt. Benedict III (855–58) was, by all accounts, a saintly man. But his journals are full of fevered accounts of the activities of Hubert, the Abbot of St Maurice, who went about France with a troupe of mistresses, desecrating monasteries and convents with his orgies.

Hubert's sister Theutberga was married to King Lothar of Lorraine. Lothar, who wanted a divorce so that he could marry his mistress Waldrada, accused his wife of incest with her brother, the Abbot, and of procuring an abortion to terminate the offspring of the match. Although Theutberga passed trial by boiling water, she was pressured into signing a confession.

Benedict's successor Nicholas I (858–67) 'forbade all Christians hearing mass celebrated by a whoring priest'. But despite this the seventeenth-century critic Cypriano de Valera is hard on him. 'Now the Pope's horns began to sprout forth,' he wrote in his book *Popery*, but only

44

because Nicholas sacked John, Bishop of Ravenna, for not bowing to him and for allowing Mass to be celebrated in Polish and Slovene. Nicholas also 'swaggered with Michael [the Drunk], Emperor of Constantinople' who was renowned for the orgies that he and his mistress held in their Byzantine palace.

Nicholas got involved with Lothar's divorce when Theutberga asked for his help. One synod had sanctioned the divorce. At a second, the papal legates were bribed and ratified Lothar's new marriage to Waldrada. Even though it was clear that Theutberga suffered some malformation that prevented her enjoying sex, Nicholas overturned the previous decisions and deposed and excommunicated two bishops for conniving at bigamy.

Unfortunately, the Emperor Louis II took up their cause and marched on Rome. Nicholas took refuge in St Peter's. Louis eventually relented, the bishops accepted their sentence and Lothar returned to Theutberga, temporarily. Hadrian II (867–72) finally sorted things out. He let Lothar have his passionate Waldrada again, but only after Lothar and his followers swore an oath at Mass that he had never committed adultery with her. Stoutly, they lied to a man.

There was a good reason for Hadrian being a more understanding man than his predecessor when it came to sexual matters. He was married himself and his wife, Stefania, was still alive when he was elevated to the papacy. They lived with their children openly in the Lateran Palace, but Hadrian was already in his seventies when he was elected pope and Catholic historians claim, perhaps with some justification, that their continued cohabitation was entirely chaste.

Pope Marinius I (882–84) was another son of a priest

to make it to St Peter's chair. Despite repeated attempts to impose celibacy on the clergy, things were looser than ever. The Bishop of Vercel, for example, had to reprimand his clergy in these terms:

> *Several among you are such slaves to passion that you allow shameless courtesans to live in your dwellings, share your food, show themselves with you in public. Subjugated by their charms, you allow them to direct your households, make settlements on their bastards... In order that these women may be well attired, the churches are despoiled and the poor made to suffer.*

Marinius's successor, Hadrian III (884–85), tried to impose his authority by having the wife of a Roman dignitary, who opposed him, stripped naked and whipped through the streets of the city. But when he opposed the succession of the Emperor Charles the Fat's bastard son, he was murdered. His successor, Stephen V (885–91), took a more liberal line. He stopped the 'purging of witchcraft or adultery by casting the person suspected into water'.

5

Pope Joan

*S*tories of a female pope began to circulate in the middle of the thirteenth century. This is one of the early accounts:

> *She first was called Giberta, but counterfeiting the virile sex, in the habit of a man went to Athens with a monk; her sweetheart after her great proficiency in the arts and the death of her friends, she returned to Rome in disguise, and in all disputations earned the garland, being admired for her eloquence and her acute answers, gaining the esteem of all her auditory. Leo being dead, she was chosen pope and sat two years and six months in Peter's Chair; during her popedom she was got with child by her chaplain and in a solemn procession fell in travail in the midst of the city; before all the people she brought forth a son and died.*

She was said to be an English woman and her boyfriend's name was thought to be John. The Leo referred to is Pope Leo IV, so this would put her accession at 855, the year Benedict III was consecrated.

No one was quite sure when Pope Joan, as she is usually called, had sat on the papal throne – in the ninth, tenth or eleventh century – but the idea that she had existed was almost universally accepted. Catholic historians only began to backtrack on the tradition in the nineteenth century, when militant protestants and other papal critics used the story of Pope Joan to attack the papacy.

The first recorded story appeared in the *Universal Chronicle of Metz*, around 1250. The author was a Dominican friar, Jean de Mailly. He maintained that Victor III (1086–1087) was succeeded by a talented woman who had disguised herself as a man. With her sex well hidden under clerical garb, she had worked her way up to the position of cardinal before being elected to the papacy. In de Mailly's version, she was found out when mounted on a horse. It was then that she gave birth to a child. Her punishment for this gross impertinence was to be tied to the tail of the horse and dragged around Rome until she was dead.

Another Dominican, Stephen de Bourbon, and a Franciscan monk from Erfurt who was the author of the *Chronicon Minor* gave similar accounts of a female pope. But they could not agree when she had lived. De Bourbon thought it was around 1100; the Erfurt monk put it at 915.

Martin of Troppau, a Dominican from Poland, gave what is usually considered the definitive version of the story at the end of the thirteenth century in his *Chronicle of Popes and Emperors*. He calls her John, which is the only name given to her in the earliest accounts. Later historians, therefore, began calling her Joan or Joanna. Troppau said that a John Anglicus succeeded Leo IV

(847–55). He reigned as pope for two years, seven months and four days, until it was discovered that he was really a woman.

However, other earlier accounts place the female pope around 1099 or 1110, which may be a more accurate date, as they are closer to the time when the story was first told. The nineteenth-century historian Professor N.C. Kist claimed ingeniously that Pope Joan was, in fact, Leo IV's widow who served jointly as pope with Leo's successor Benedict III.

According to the early tales, the future female pope was born in Mainz, Germany, probably of English parents. As a girl she went to Athens dressed as a man with her lover. There she became a student and showed brilliant promise. Later she moved to Rome, still accompanied by her male lover. A later version, discovered in a Benedictine abbey in Bavaria, insists she was from Thessaly and that her name was Glancia. Several versions say that she taught at a Greek school in Rome, famous for its connections with St Augustine. Distinguished Roman audiences turned out to hear her speak and, as she seemed to be less debauched than most clerics around that time, she was unanimously elected pope.

In Martin of Troppau's version, she is found out when she gives birth prematurely while riding in a procession from St Peter's to the Lateran Palace along a narrow street between the Colosseum and St Clement's. She died in childbirth and was buried where she lay. After that, popes studiously avoided using that street.

Intriguingly, there really is a street in Rome which popes avoid. In his account of the coronation of Pope Innocent VII in 1404, the Welshman Adam of Usk, who was in Rome at the time, says: 'After turning aside out of abhorrence of pope Agnes, whose image in stone with her son stands in the straight road near St Clement's, the Pope, dismounting from his horse, enters the Lateran for his enthronement.' This statue is mentioned in the various editions of the *Mirabilia Urbis Romae* (a guidebook to Rome on sale throughout the Middle Ages) from 1375 to 1500 and in other guidebooks. Johann Buchard, the papal master of ceremonies under Innocent VIII, Alexander VI, Pius III and Julius II also mentions it in his account of the Pope's coronation: 'In going as in returning, the Pope came by way of the Colosseum, and that straight road where the statue of the female pope is located, in token, it is said, that John Anglicus gave birth there to a child,' Buchard writes in his *Liber Notarum*. 'For that reason, many say the popes are never allowed to ride on horseback there. Therefore, the Lord Archbishop of Florence, the Bishop of Massano and Hugo de Bencii the Apostolic Subdeacon, delivered a reprimand to me. However, I had words on this subject with the Lord Bishop of Pienza, who told me that it is foolishness and heresy to think that the popes are prohibited from travelling by this street, no authentic document or custom being known which would prevent it.'

Some have suggested that the custom grew up because the street was too narrow. The street was certainly widened by Sixtus V (1585–90), but Buchard does not mention that the procession had any problem using the street. There was a statue nearby which showed a woman in what could be papal vestments suckling a child. The legend on the plinth may have referred to Pope Joan. Unfortunately, the statue was removed during Sixtus V's road widening, though there is a similar figure in the Vatican gardens.

Boccaccio called Pope Joan Giliberta. The fifteenth-century Bohemian heretic John Huss called her Agnes and she appears as Jutta in Dietrich Schernberg's play *Ein Schön Spiel* in 1490. Other accounts simply leave her unnamed. Her lover is called Pircius in the Bavarian manuscript and Clercius in the Schernberg play. In one or two accounts, he denied being the father of her child. One early account says that the baby was the child of the devil. Others say a chaplain or 'a certain deacon, her secretary' was responsible. One woodcut even shows him in the vestments of a cardinal.

There are also several versions of her fate. As we have seen, Martin of Troppau suggests that she died in childbirth or was killed once her secret became general knowledge. Boccaccio says that she was tempted by the devil into the sin of lust, so she was imprisoned by the cardinals and stayed in jail until her death. An early version of *Mirabilia Urbis Romae* says that she was buried 'among the virtuous' in the Basilica of St Peter's. But this was deleted from subsequent editions.

A Benedictine monk writing in Malmesbury Abbey in the west of England in 1366, says that Pope Joan attained the papacy in Rome in the year 858 because 'so many were the fools in the city that no one could compare with her in learning'. He goes on to say that 'when she had reigned for two years and a bit, she became pregnant by her old lover, and while walking in procession gave birth, and thus her sin was revealed and she was deposed'.

Again her crime seems not to have been deceiving everyone into thinking that she was a man, but giving way to lust and being discovered in such a dramatic way. Of course, many male popes gave way to lust but the evidence of their incontinence was never as palpable as giving birth in a public thoroughfare. The only situation comparable was when popes were actually caught in *flagrante delicto* – and they seem to have be despatched by irate husbands.

So what happened to the child? Most accounts take it for granted that it died at birth. However, in a copy of Martin Polonus's *Chronicon*, which appeared in 1400, it says: 'She was deposed for her incontinence, and taking up the religious habit, lived in penitence for such a long time that she saw her son made Bishop of Ostia. When, in her final days, she perceived her death approaching, she instructed that her burial should be in that place where she had given birth, which nevertheless her son would not permit. Having removed her body to Ostia, he buried her with honour in the Cathedral. On account of which, God has worked many miracles right up to the present day.' Others maintain that the child was the antichrist in person.

Early accounts despatch the soul of Pope Joan, her lover and the baby to hell. Many say that she made a pact with the devil or studied devil worship using the *Book of Necromancy* to attain the papacy, but during the dark ages that accusation was regularly thrown at popes who had anything more than a rudimentary education.

Later writers started taking a more compassionate view. After all, Joan's behaviour had been pretty mild compared to many medieval popes. In 1490, Felix Haemerlein wrote that 'she gave birth for the remission of her sins'.

The edition of *Mirabilia Urbis Romae* compiled in 1500, in the reign of Alexander VI, the Borgia pope, takes a similar view:

We then proceed to a certain small chapel between the Colosseum and St Clement's; this derelict church is situated at the place where the woman who became pope died. She was heavy with child, and was questioned by an angel of God whether she would prefer to perish forever, or to face the world openly. Not wanting to be lost for eternity, she chose the embarrassment of public reproach.

The poet Petrarch, alone of Renaissance writers, gave her a hard time. He was appalled by the fact that a woman had sat on the papal throne. He claims that as a consequence 'in Brescia it rained blood for three days and nights. In France there appeared marvellous locusts which had six wings and very powerful teeth. They flew miraculously through the air, and all drowned in the British Sea. The golden bodies were rejected by the waves of the sea and corrupted the air, so that a great many people died.' This imagery is borrowed directly from the *Book of Revelations*.

Some time may have elapsed between whenever Pope Joan sat on St Peter's chair and the appearance of the first documentation of the story, but that does not necessarily mean that it is folklore or fiction. After all, the written references to the life of Christ do not appear until over a century after his death, but many people believe that Jesus was a historical figure.

The story naturally became embellished with intricate detail – especially when Boccaccio and Petrarch got hold of it – but the basic premise that there was a woman pope who was discovered when she got pregnant was accepted without question for centuries. She appears widely in iconography. Pope Joan even appeared among the busts of the pontiffs in Siena Cathedral which were completed around 1400. However, her bust was removed in 1600 by order of Clement VIII.

John Huss was burnt as a heretic after the Council of Constance in 1415, but no one at the Council contradicted him when he mentioned 'Pope John, a woman of England called Agnes' several times in his defence.

In the sixteenth century, the writer Mario Equicola of Alvito argued that God had elevated Joan to the papal throne to demonstrate women's equality. Others detected God's hand too. They claimed that a male pope was miraculously turned into a woman, or that a male pope miraculously gave birth to a child.

Other explanations have been mooted over the centuries. One of the more banal was that Pope Joan was an hermaphrodite. An apocalyptic one was that she was the Whore of Babylon from the *Book of Revelations* and that her appearance in Rome heralded the Day of Judgement. The 1785 edition of *A Present for a Papist* is prefaced with a woodcut of Pope Joan delivering her child in a rather splendid tent, surrounded by her prelates. Under it is a verse that reads:

> *A woman pope (as history doth tell)*
> *In high procession once in labour fell,*
> *And was deliver'd of a bastard son;*
> *Whence Rome some call the Whore of Babylon.*

This theory can safely be discounted. Pope Joan, if she lived, is a long time dead and we have not yet heard the sound of the last trumpets.

The most famous version of the story is undoubtedly the nineteenth-century Greek classic by Emmanuel Royds which was translated into English by Lawrence

Durrell. In it, Joanna first reveals her saintly nature as a baby, refusing the teat on fast days.

Catholic criticism of the story became increasingly vocal after the Reformation, but it was a Protestant, David Bondel (1590–1655), who most effectively savaged it in a treatise published in Amsterdam in 1647 and again 1657. His basic argument was that there was no contemporary record of there being a female pope, and nowhere to fit a female pope in between the known popes whose coronations and deaths (or depositions) had been well documented since the second century. Against that, the Church has always been skilled in covering up papal embarrassments.

However easy it is to dismiss the idea of a female pope, no one has satisfactorily explained where the idea came from. One possible explanation is contained in a letter from Pope Leo IX to Michael Cerularis, the Patriarch of Constantinople, in 1054. In it Leo condemns the Eastern church by saying: 'By promoting eunuchs indiscriminately against the First Law of the Council of Nicaea, it once raised a woman on to the seat of the pontiff.' Leo was mistaken in one respect. The Council of Nicaea only banned the promotion of eunuchs who had castrated themselves, or invited the mutilation. At that time, those who had been castrated against their will were still eligible.

But it is true that there were early stories of there being a female Patriarch of Constantinople. According to the *Chronicon Salernitanum* of around 980: 'At that time [in the eighth century] a certain patriarch ruled over Constantinople, a good and just man but undoubtedly defiled by carnal love, so much so that he kept his niece in his house as though she were a eunuch, and wrapped her all around in beautiful apparel. This patriarch, when close to death, commended his nephew, as she seemed to be, to the favour of all. Upon his demise they all, being in complete ignorance, chose a woman as their bishop. She presided over them for almost a year and a half.'

It all ended in tears, of course. The devil appeared in a dream to a certain Prince Arichis and told him about it. He sent envoys to Constantinople who discovered what the devil said was true – 'then this abomination was put to an end'. In another version of the story, after her overthrow, she was imprisoned in a nunnery and a plague was unleashed on the city as punishment.

There might be a firm basis for this story too. Around that time there was a Patriarch called Nicetes, who was a eunuch. He was certainly unable to grow a beard – in the Eastern Church the clergy are forbidden to shave – so to the Greeks he looked like a woman.

The Middle Ages is full of stories of women who, for whatever reason, dressed up as men and confined themselves to abbeys and monasteries. St Eugenia rose to become abbot, until a woman, whose advances she had spurned, accused the saint of misconduct and her true sex was revealed.

St Marina was the daughter of a monk. He took her into his monastery disguised as a boy. When he died, she stayed on until an innkeeper's daughter accused him of fathering her baby. She quit rather than reveal her true sex, which was only discovered after her death.

Another tale is that of St Theodora. She was the wife of Gregory, Prefect of Alexandria. She took a lover, then, in contrition, fled in disguise to a monastery. Again, a woman accused her of being the father of her baby. But, rather than reveal herself, she quit the monastery and adopted the child. After bringing the child up – he grew up to become an abbot – she went back into the monastery, where her true sex was also discovered after her death.

Pelagius, a beautiful Greek dancing girl and voluptuary, repented her sinful life after hearing Nonnus, the Bishop of Edhessa, preach. She dressed herself in men's clothing and went to live in a cell on the Mount of Olives. There, she was known as 'Pelagius, monk and eunuch'. Again the truth was only discovered after her death.

A young German girl called Hildegund was dressed as a boy when she went on a pilgrimage to Jerusalem with her father. He died during the trip. Left to fend for herself, she joined a monastery. Her sex somehow remained undiscovered even though she had to strip to the waist to be scourged.

It is popularly believe that since the tenth century, after his election a pope has to undergo a sex test. This legend sprung up independently of that of Pope Joan. According to the Dominican, Robert d'Usez,writing in 1409, the new pope would have to sit in a seat 'where it is said, the Pope is proved to be a man'. Five years later, the French monk Gaudridus de Collone from the abbey of St Pierre-le-Vif and Sens mentioned that this practice started as a consequence of the female pope, but also said that 'the Romans derived the custom of checking the sex of the pope elect through a hole in a stone seat'. Early chroniclers say this was done to check not just that the Church had not illegally elected a female pope, but also that the pope had not been castrated. A eunuch is not allowed to sit on the papal throne.

The *Sedes Stercoraria*, the 'groping chair', was 'open below' and, according to custom: ''Tis the youngest

deacon's office to handle the genitals of His Holiness.'
Felix Haemerlein, writing in 1490, describes the scene:
'Up to the present day the seat is used at the election of
the pope. In order to prove his worthiness, his testicles
are felt by a junior cleric present as a testimony of his
male sex. When this is found to be so, the person who
feels then shouts out in a loud voice: "He has testicles."
And all the clerics present reply: "God be praised." Then
they proceed joyfully to the consecration of the pope-
elect.'

Haemerlein asserts that this procedure was adopted
with the election of Benedict III (855–58) who, he says,
was Pope Joan's successor. Earlier accounts say that it was
first used during the consecration of Pope Pascal II in
1099, which is, coincidentally, around the date of the
first documented account of Pope Joan.

In his play *The Female Prelate*, first staged at the Theatre
Royal in 1680, Elkanah Settle presents a different version
of the procedure. As it would be totally out of order for
a cardinal or subdeacon to touch the genitals of His
Holiness, a reverend mother has to do the fondling.

Buchard and others say that actually two 'pierced'
seats were used. In fact, there are two still in existence.
Pius VII (1800–23) had them removed from St John's to
the Vatican museum in the late eighteenth century. One
is still there in the Museo Pio Clementino. The other was
taken to Paris when Napoleon looted the Vatican. Although many valuable works of art and the Vatican ar-
chives were eventually returned to Rome by the French,
the pierced chair remains in the Louvre.

A female pope appears in some versions of the tarot
pack as a counterpart to the male pope. But this woman
pope seems to have sprung from another source. In

1260, a woman named Guglielma of Bohemia – although in some versions she comes from England – arrived in Milan. She was wealthy and pious, and quickly gained a reputation for preaching. She died in 1281 and was buried in a Cistercian house in Chiaravalle. Soon a cult sprang up around her relics. Some of her followers were fanatics. They believed that Guglielma had been the embodiment of the Holy Ghost and she would return in 1300, kick the corrupt Pope Boniface VIII (1294–1303) off the papal throne and install a young woman from Milan called Maifreda di Pirovano as pope in his place.

With her disciples, Maifreda began to prepare for her pontificate. They planned a new college of cardinals which would consist largely, if not wholly, of women. Boniface and the Inquisition did not take too kindly to such talk and Maifreda and her Guglielmites were burnt at the stake. Some have claimed that Guglielma and Maifreda were the origin of the Pope Joan story. However, Pope Joan's story was recorded earlier, though it may well have inspired the Guglielmites. After all, if there had already been one woman pope, there would be nothing wrong with having another.

Maifreda is almost certainly the origin of the female pope in the tarot. A nun in the Umiliata Order at Biassono, she was a relative – probably the cousin – of Matteo Visconti. The Visconti family were responsible for commissioning several decks of tarot cards. One of them, attributed to the artist Boniface Bembo, is thought to be the first deck to show a female pope. The brown habit she is wearing belongs to the Umiliata Order.

For almost two hundred years, most tarot packs featured 'La Papessa'. Later, male and female popes were replaced with popes seated and standing, or popes bearded and clean-shaven. In some packs, the female pope is transmogrified into the High Priestess.

In the early nineteenth century, a card game called Pope Joan became popular. It was derived from the French game Yellow Dwarf, and slowly developed into the British game Newmarket. No one has been able to fathom the significance of the name.

6

The papal pornocracy

Pope Stephen VI (896–97) came perilously close to necrophilia when he had the body of his predecessor Formosus (891–96) dug up, dressed in papal vestments, set on a throne and tried for perjury and coveting the papacy.

The first of a new series of women pope-makers was responsible for this outrage. Her name was Agiltruda, Duchess of Spoleto. She was reputed to be very beautiful with blue eyes, long blonde hair and an impressive figure. She led an army which seized Rome in 894. The Holy Roman Emperor Arnulf took exception to this and sent out an army, with Pope Formosus at its head, to drive her back to Spoleto.

After Formosus took the city he died, probably of a heart attack – although some say he was poisoned by Agiltruda. He was buried with full papal ceremony in Rome and replaced by Boniface VI (896).

Boniface was hardly an ideal candidate for Pope as he had been defrocked twice for immorality. After the second time he was not reinstated, but he was nevertheless elected thanks to popular support – the Romans rioted in his favour. He lasted just fifteen days and was, almost certainly, a victim of Agiltruda's poison. She seized Rome again and installed Stephen VI as pope. He was, as everybody knew, raving mad, but this served her purposes well. It was at her suggestion that he had Formosus's rotting corpse exhumed and put on trial.

Agiltruda attended the infamous Cadaver Synod and enjoyed watching her arch-enemy Formosus being humiliated, even though he was some time dead. She brought with her a six-year-old girl called Marozia, who caught the eye of a thirty-six-year-old Cardinal named Sergius.

An eighteen-year-old deacon stood alongside the corpse and answered for Formosus. Sadly, he was no Perry Mason and Formosus was found guilty of the charges against him. He was stripped of his vestments again and had the three fingers of the right hand used to make the papal benediction lopped off. The body was then dragged through the streets and thrown in the Tiber.

The fingers were given to Agiltruda by Cardinal Sergius. As he handed over the grisly trophies, his eyes met those of the child Marozia. Despite the thirty-year age difference, a bond was formed in that moment that would shape the papacy for the next century.

At the very moment when Pope Stephen, Agiltruda, Marozia and Cardinal Sergius emerged from the Lateran Palace after the Cadaver Synod, there was a tremendous roar as the Basilica of St John, abandoned long before as dangerously unsafe, collapsed. The people of Rome saw this as a sign and the Cadaver Synod, which had seemed like a bit of harmless fun at the time, backfired badly. Rumours began circulating that the corpse had performed miracles. Soon there was an uprising against Pope Stephen. He was stripped of his papal insignia, deposed and slung in prison where he was strangled.

Agiltruda, angered by this, seized Rome yet again and imposed Pope Romanus (897) on the Church. After four months, she grew tired of him and installed Pope Theodore II (897) instead. He died an early death in mysterious circumstances. And so it went on. By 904, when Pope Leo V (903–04) and the anti-pope Christopher (also 903–04) who had overthrown him were murdered there had been eight popes in as many years. The changeovers were so frequent that the servants in the Lateran were making a good living by selling the trappings of the papal apartments each time one popped off.

Not surprisingly with a beginning like this, the papacy during the tenth century became a synonym for shameless abuse and corruption. The period became known as the papal pornocracy – because the papacy was run by what were considered by much of Christendom as a couple of whores. These were a mother and daughter combination, Theodora and Marozia, who were the mistresses of the popes.

At that time, there was no emperor in Rome. The city was effectively run by Theophylact, consul, commander of the militia and financial director of the Holy See. He was also, more importantly, husband of the ambitious Theodora. She was said to be a 'shameless strumpet, who lived at that time in Rome, having two daughters,

Marozia and Theodora, neither of much better reputation than their mother'. The younger Theodora was probably the daughter of the man who became Pope John X (914–28). Marozia seems to have had more of the benefit of her mother's coaching. She had also seen Agiltruda in action at the Cadaver Synod and was ambitious for power.

Theodora had put the mild-mannered Benedict IV (900–903) on the papal throne and Leo V and the anti-pope Christopher were both Theodora's men. They were followed by Sergius III (904–11), who was not a man to mess around with. He was the cardinal who had played a leading part in Stephen VI's Cadaver Synod. When the anti-pope Christopher threw Leo V in jail, Sergius marched on Rome and had Christopher thrown in jail too. He had himself consecrated pope and then, out of pity some say, had Leo and Christopher strangled. But Theodora knew just how to bring him to heel. She gave him her sexually precocious teenage daughter Marozia.

Marozia was just fifteen when she became the mistress of Sergius III. He was forty-five. He died four years later, leaving her with a son. The experience of being the Pope's lover had left a lasting impression on her. Three marriages and countless affairs could not extinguish her burning ambition for the papacy.

The teenage Marozia would often go to the Lateran Palace, as her father was the chief senator of Rome. When Sergius first slept with her she was still just a good-looking child. For the rest of his pontificate, he enjoyed the exquisite pleasure of watching his underaged love blossom into a woman of breathtaking beauty. For her part, in the Pope's arms, Marozia enjoyed, not the romantic passion of youth, but the ecstasy of power. She has been judged by history as 'that most impudent whore' and stands charged with the defilement of the papacy. Her son by Sergius became Pope John XI (931–36).

Sergius did not come out of it too well. Commentators charged that throughout his papacy he continued committing 'infinite abominations amongst light women'. According to the historian Baronius, Sergius was not just into underage sex, but was 'the slave of every vice and the most wicked of men'. In office, Sergius rebuilt the Lateran Basilica, which had lain in ruins since the Cadaver Synod and, for good measure, he tried Pope Formosus all over again. Formosus did not get off this time either.

Theodora picked the next two popes – Anastasius III (911–13) and Lando I (913–14). Neither was a paragon of virtue and Lando, it is said, 'an anointed bachelor, consumed the greatest part of his life amongst lewd women, and was at last consumed, having reigned for seven months'. He had a bastard son called John with whom Theodora, Marozia's mother, had fallen in love some years before. She had used her influence with Sergius, who was pope at the time, to have him made Bishop of Bologna, then Archbishop of Ravenna. But Theodora hated having her lover so far away and, when Lando died, she arranged for John to be elected to succeed his father in the Lateran Palace, where she could be 'his nightly companion'. He became Pope John X (914–28).

Luitprand, Bishop of Cremona, relates that Marozia was not at all happy with this and an unhealthy rivalry built up between mother and daughter. Marozia's son was only six, a bit young for the papacy, even in those times.

In 914, Marozia was twenty-two and, it is said, at the height of her beauty and charm. She kept a small establishment on Isola Tiberina, a small island in the middle of the River Tiber. There she entertained young nobles and prelates. Most of them were bishops of the type who said Mass with their spurs on, had hunting daggers hanging from their belts and had their horses saddled and ready outside so they could take off for an afternoon's boar hunting or falconry, directly the service was finished. They lived in luxurious houses which were decorated in purple and velvet, dined off gold plate while musicians played and dancing girls performed, and slept in silk sheets in beds inlaid with gold and decorated with mementos of former loves. Marozia was perfectly at home in this world.

A prince from Lombardy, Alberic, arrived in the midst of this decadent scene. He was seen as a threat, so Pope John X and Theodora decided that Marozia should marry him to keep him under the family's control. This was a dangerous move. In Marozia's hands, Alberic turned from a threat into a real danger. Instead of siding with her mother and her mother's lover, Marozia persuaded her new husband to attack Rome. The coup failed, Alberic was killed and John X forced the young widow to view her husband's mutilated corpse. This, again, was unwise. Marozia, who was now mother to Alberic's son, Alberic II, was more than capable of taking her revenge.

When Theodora died in 928, Marozia had John X imprisoned and, in the hope of advancing her first bastard son to the papacy, gave orders that His Holiness, her stepfather, be smothered with a pillow.

'She was nevertheless deceived in her aim,' says Luitprand.

> *For immediately on his death Leo VI was elected, yet Marozia soon made away with him by poison, to make way for her bastard. However she was mistaken a second time, for on him being thus poisoned, Stephen VII was elected, who died not for many years after in the same manner and by the same hand in the year 930.*

Finally, Marozia had her wish when her bastard son took the papal throne as John XI in 931. He was supposed to have spent much of his papacy with 'beastly lewd women'. In the meantime, his mother had not been standing still. Her first marriage had produced the ambitious Alberic II; and she planned to marry a second time to Hugo of Provence, Alberic's brother. He had a wife, but Marozia's son Pope John XI arranged a divorce for his uncle. He also officiated at their wedding, even though the marriage was illegal in the eyes of the Church, Hugo being Marozia's brother-in-law.

At the wedding breakfast, Marozia's son Alberic II and her new husband Hugo traded insults. A few months later, Alberic led an armed mob against the Castel Sant'Angelo. Hugo managed to escape over the city walls, hidden in a basket and wearing only his nightshirt, but Alberic II caught his mother, Marozia, and his half-brother, Pope John XI, and threw them in jail.

Once Alberic II had proclaimed himself ruler of Rome, he released John XI. However, he was kept under house arrest in the Lateran Palace, where he was allowed to do little more than administer the sacraments. But Marozia remained imprisoned in the basement of the Castel Sant'Angelo, which had been the mausoleum of Emperor Hadrian and was still the tallest and strongest building in Rome. She stayed there for over fifty-four years.

Alberic need not have been so harsh. He had a bastard son himself, Octavian, who went on to become Pope John XII (955–64), the first pope to change his name. He was also said to have included among his many mistresses 'one of his father's concubines'.

Alberic ruled Rome for the next twenty-two years and appointed the next five popes, one of whom, Marinus II (942–46), was said to be 'begat of a common woman, son of a necromancer'.

Finally, after Alberic was dead, Pope John XV (985–96) took pity on Marozia. In 986, he lifted the sentence of excommunication and sent a tame bishop to exorcise any demons that still possessed the ninety-four-year-old woman. Then she was executed. The day before she died, she was visited in her cell by the six-year-old Otto III, the Holy Roman Emperor. She was the prisoner of the pope, not of the civil authorities, but he just wanted to see the woman who had been the lover of one pope, the mother of another, the aunt of one and the grandmother of yet another. Between them, she and her mother had created nine popes in eight years. Two had been strangled, one suffocated with a cushion, and four deposed and disposed of in circumstances that never came to light.

A young bishop followed Otto into Marozia's cell. 'Marozia, daughter of Theophylact, are you among the living?' the bishop asked what seemed to be a pile of rags lying on straw in the corner of the squalid dungeon. 'I, Bishop John Crescentius of Protus, command you in the name of Holy Mother Church to speak.'

Without stirring, Marozia, who was lying staring at the wall, whispered: 'I am living, my Lord Bishop, I am living.' Then after a long pause she said: 'For all my sins, forgiveness...forgiveness.'

The bishop then began to read from the warrant. 'Inasmuch as you, Marozia, did from the beginning and at the age of fifteen conspire against the rights of the See of Peter in the reign of Holy Father Pope Sergius, following the example of your Satanic mother, Theodora...'

She was accused of trying to take over the whole world with her son Pope John XI and that 'she dared, like Jezebel of old, yet again to take a third husband'. She was even held responsible for the sins of her grandson Pope John XII, even though she had languished in jail through his scandalous nine-year reign. He was, after all, the son of the man who had put her in prison.

'Your grandson, Pope John XII,' the charges read,

> *perjured himself, breaking his oath to the Great Emperor. He stole the treasury of the popes and fled to Rome's enemies, was deposed by the Holy Synod and replaced by Leo VIII. Then the apostate returned to Rome, evicted Leo VIII, cut off the nose and tongue and two fingers of the Cardinal-Deacon, flayed the skin off Bishop Otger, cut off the head off Notary Azzo, and beheaded sixty-three of Rome's clergy and nobility. During the night of 14 May 964, while having illicit and filthy relations with a Roman matron, he was surprised in the act of sin by the matron's angry husband who, in just wrath, smashed his skull with a hammer and thus liberated his evil soul into the grasp of Satan...*

Marozia must have been heartsick that she missed all the fun.

When the young bishop had finished reading the warrant, an executioner slipped into the cell placed a cushion over her face and suffocated the old woman 'for the well-being of Holy Mother Church and the peace of the Roman people'.

Even though she was dead, Marozia's influence over the papacy continued via John XII's brother Gregory. Benedict VIII (1012–24) and John XIX (1024–32) were both great-grandsons of Marozia, and Benedict IX (1032–48) was her great-great-grandson.

Luitprand of Cremona summed up the whole period of the pornocracy:

> A *certain shameless strumpet called Theodora...at one time was sole monarch of Rome and – shame upon us even to say the words! – exercised power in the most manly fashion. She had two daughters, Marozia and Theodora, and these damsels were not only her equals but could even surpass her in the exercises that Venus loves.*

Marozia and her mother were described by Cardinal Baronius as 'vainglorious Messalinas filled with fleshly lust and cunning in all forms of wickedness governed Rome and prostituted the Chair of St Peter for their minions and paramours'.

This is a little harsh. Theodora and Marozia were hardly alone in their corruption. The papacy's abominable record in the tenth century was certainly matched by other clerics. Bishop Segenfried of Le Mans was married to his wife Hildeberga for thirty-three years. He insisted that she be addressed by the title 'Episcopissa' and when he retired he handed his wealthy diocese over to his son Alberic.

Another Alberic, the Bishop of Marsico, also handed his mitre and staff over to his son. But after several years retirement, he grew bored. He decided what he needed was to take over the famous abbey of Monte Cassino. So he promised a princely sum to a brigand to bring him the eyes of the abbot.

7

Roman orgies

I n the sexual department, John XII (955–64) was not a lot better than his grandmother Marozia. He was sixteen when he took holy orders and his heart was just not in it. It was said that he invented sins that had not been known since the beginning of the world and whole monasteries spent days and nights praying for his death.

John was an insatiable bisexual and gathered about him the loosest young nobles of either sex. He was accused of running a brothel out of St Peter's. He used the papal treasury to pay off his gambling debts, and enjoyed pranks such as ordaining a ten-year-old boy as a bishop. He gambled with pilgrims' offerings. His lovers were given gold chalices from St Peter's. He kept a stud of 2000 horses which he fed on almonds and figs steeped in wine. The sacred palace of the Lateran was said to have been turned into a harem and 'incest gave a flavour to crime when simple profligacy palled upon his senses'.

Citizens of Rome complained that the female pilgrims who formerly crowded the holy places were deterred by 'his promiscuous and unbridled lust'. These hapless pilgrims were abducted by John because he 'liked to have a collection of women,' said the chronicler Benedict of Socrate.

Scaring off the pilgrims was bad for business – as was consecrating a bishop in a stable. But when a cardinal pointed this out, John XII had him castrated. The cardinal died soon after.

In the tenth century that sort of behaviour was no real problem, but John really let the family down by not being a very adept politician. He supported King Otto I of Saxony against Berengar, the ruler of northern Italy. Then after he had crowned Otto Holy Roman Emperor in St Peter's in Rome, he changed his mind and opened negotiations with Berengar. Otto got wind of this and wrote to John, saying: 'Everyone, clergy as well as laity, accuses you, Holiness, of homicide, perjury, sacrilege, incest with your relatives, including two of your sisters, and with having, like a pagan, invoked Jupiter, Venus and other demons.'

John dismissed the charges as 'gossip that is repeated by lascivious bishops'. Others pointed out that John was just a young man. He must be allowed to sow a few wild oats. After that he would settle down.

But Otto was not satisfied. He set John a challenge – either he send him two bishops who would swear that the charges were not true or two champions who would decide the matter in a trial by combat with two of his own men. John refused to rise to the challenge, so Otto returned to Rome and set up a tribunal of prelates and nobles from Germany, France and Italy in St Peter's to try him.

The list of things John XII was charged with is seemingly endless:

> ...*of committing incest with two sisters, of playing dice and invoking the devil to assist him to win, of creating boy bishops for money, of ravishing divers virgins, of converting the sacred palace into a seraglio or stews, of lying with his father's harlot, with a certain Queen Dowager and with a widow called Anna and his own niece, of putting out the eyes of his father confessor, of going hunting publicly, of going always armed, of setting houses on fire, of breaking windows in the night...*

He is also said to have had a compact with the devil and drunk Satan's health, committed incest with his mother, violated holy virgins – that is, nuns – and committed adultery, homicide, profanation and blasphemy. That's a pretty impressive list, even for a medieval pope.

When John was called to answer the charges, he sent back a note in schoolboy Latin excommunicating Otto and all those attending the court. A second summons prompted the reply: 'The Pope has gone hunting.'

John was tried in *absentia*, duly found guilty of incest, adultery and murder, and deposed. Otto required a respectable priest to be installed in John's place, but the synod could not find one. So they installed Leo VIII (963–65), who was a layman. However, the Romans did not like having a pope forced on them in this fashion. As the eighteenth-century writer Cypriano de Valera puts it 'those ill women with whom the late pope conversed' rose up and attacked Otto's army. Otto, in turn, retook the city in a bloody battle, but could not hold it. John XII was eventually recalled – 'restored to the papacy by the power of whores'. He excommunicated Leo VIII, then set about punishing the clergy who had supported Leo. One was flogged. Another had a hand cut off. A third had two fingers and his nose cut off and his tongue torn out. And so it would have continued had John XII not died suddenly on 14 May. He was caught in bed by the husband of one of his mistresses in 'the very act of adultery'. The enraged husband stabbed him. Other reports say the husband hit him on the back of the head with a hammer. John XII died soon after. He was just twenty-four.

The manner of the Pope's death caused much amusement in Rome. It was said that he was lucky to have died in bed, even if it was somebody else's. Benedict V (964) was elected in John's place, but Otto was determined to put his own man, Leo VIII, back on the papal throne. He besieged the city which resisted stoutly until plague broke out and food began to run low. Then, on 23 June, the gates of the city were opened and Benedict was flung out. Leo VIII tore up his vestments and sent him into exile.

That was one story. Another version says that Benedict V, after dishonouring a young girl, took off for Constantinople with the papal treasury, only to reappear in Rome after funds had run out. When he was slain by a jealous husband, his body with a hundred wounds in it was dragged through the streets before being tossed into a cesspit. The Church historian Gerbert, who became Pope Silvester II (999–1003), called Benedict 'the most iniquitous of all the monsters of ungodliness'.

Although the leaders of the Roman resistance swore allegiance to the Emperor Otto beside St Peter's grave and said they would never rebel again, when Leo VIII died and John XII's son John XIII (965–72) replaced him, they took up arms once more. This time Otto was merciless. The leading citizens were hanged or blinded.

Otto handed the Prefect over to John, who was rather kinder. He had the Prefect hung by the hair from the statue of Marcus Aurelius. Then he was stripped naked, placed backwards on an ass with a bell on its tail, and driven through the streets with a sack of feathers on his head and two others tied to his thighs. Finally, he was exiled to the Alps.

Like the other popes in his family before him, John XIII was condemned as an adulterer. It was said 'none would serve his turn but virgins and votaresses; the Lateran Palace he made his stews; he defiled his father's concubine and his own niece'.

Par for the course really. He also brought a bit of style back to the papacy. He lived like a prince, dining off gold plates and drinking from jewelled goblets while being entertained by beautiful dancing girls.

According to the writer Gregorovius the popes of this period 'slept on silken pillows and on beds artificially inlaid with gold, in the arms of their paramours, leaving their vassals, servants and slaves to look after the requirements of their court'. They also played dice, hunted, rode horses with gold bridles and travelled in luxurious coaches 'surrounded by swarms of parasites'.

John XIII was another pope said to have died at the hands of an enraged husband, caught in the act of adultery.

8

Craving celibacy

*T*he death of Pope John XIII in 972 and that of Otto I the following year did nothing to stop the rivalry between the Roman nationalists and the Holy Roman Emperors. John XIII's successor, the Emperor's man Benedict VI (973–74) was the illegitimate son of a monk. His mother was a Frank. Under his pontificate many French, English and Spanish ladies who came to Rome were seduced or raped there, and stayed on as courtesans.

Benedict, seen as the source of this depravity, was dragged to the Castel Sant'Angelo 'for his wickedness' and strangled. The powerful Roman family who had led the insurrection, the Crescenzi, installed Boniface VII (974; 984–85) in his place. He was described as 'a horrid monster' by Pope Silvester II and the synod in Rheims decried him as 'a man who in criminality surpassed all the rest of mankind'.

Boniface was driven from Rome by the Emperor's young heir Otto II, but escaped to Constantinople with the papal treasure, becoming anti-pope when he was replaced by Benedict VII (974–83). When Otto II died suddenly in 983, Boniface returned and had Benedict's successor John XIV (983–84) arrested. His eyes were plucked out and he died in prison, either of starvation or poisoning. The Romans then turned on Boniface. He was killed, stripped naked and displayed under the statue of Marcus Aurelius. Afterwards, his body was dragged through the streets and 'barbarously used by the mob'.

John XV (985–96), the son of a priest, was succeeded by a twenty-four-year-old German cousin of the Imperial family, Gregory V (996–99). The Crescenzi family drove him from Rome and put the papal tiara out for tender. A rich Greek stumped up a large sum of money for it and became the anti-pope John XVI (998–1001). He 'behaved himself so wickedly that he became generally abhorred by the clergy and people of Rome'.

Otto II's successor Otto III was just three when his father died. By the time he was seventeen he was determined to put a stop to these papal shenanigans. He marched on Rome with a large army and found John XVI hiding in the Campagna. John must have regretted handing over such a huge amount of money for the papacy. He had his nose, tongue and ears cut off. His eyes were gouged out. He was dragged back to Rome when he was thrown in a monastery cell to die.

Gregory V was reinstated, but the Crescenzi were still holding out in the Castel Sant'Angelo. It fell on 29 April 998. The head of the family was captured. His eyes were plucked out and his limbs were mutilated. Then he was dragged through the streets on the skin of a cow. Finally he was beheaded on the battlements and his corpse was displayed on a gallows on the Monte Mario alongside bodies of twelve other leading insurrectionists.

When Gregory died, Silvester II (999–1003) replaced him. Silvester, it is said, gave himself to the devil in return for the papacy. It was also said that he was an atheist and that he was proficient in magic. A native of France, he had travelled to Seville where he was instructed in the black arts by a Moor. He was said to have stolen a magic book from the Moor with the help of the Moor's daughter, with whom Silvester had made 'unlawful converse'.

Silvester was involved in something of a scandal in his youth when he was secretary to the young Archbishop of Rheims, who was the 'son of Lothar of divine memory and his concubine' the divine Waldrada. The Archbishop was known to be 'steeped in vice, natural and unnatural', but when he added treason to the list, the King of France directed a synod to try him. He was found guilty and condemned. The young Silvester was also censured for his involvement in the Archbishop's 'misconduct'.

Silvester certainly took a lax attitude to clerical chastity when he became pope. He may have been married. While he was Abbot of Bobbio, he wrote a letter to his patron Emperor Otto II which alludes to his wife and children. With legitimate marriage and promiscuous profligacy almost universal in the church at the time, he was presumably admitting to the lesser of two evils.

Pope Silvester II was murdered on 17 May 1003. His successor John XVIII (1003) was born Giovanni Fasanus – which means 'cock' in Italian. He was poisoned seven months after taking office. Sergius IV (1009–12) was nicknamed Bucca Porci – 'Pig's Snout'.

Benedict VIII (1012–24), it is said, was the son of

Gregory, the Bishop of Portua. He was a layman and became pope through the influence of his nephew Theophilactus, an advisor to Silvester II. Theophilactus was supposed to have inherited the book of Negromantick Art that Silvester stole from the Moor of Seville. According to Cardinal Beno, he used enchantments to get wives to leave their husbands and to follow him.

Benedict VIII became pope after assassinating his predecessor. The Archbishop of Narbonne accused him of 'simony, assassination and usury; of disbelieving the Eucharist and the immortality of the soul; of employing violence to obtain the secrets of the confessional; of living in concubinage with his two nieces and having children by them; and finally of using the money received from indulgences to pay for the Saracens' invasion of Sicily'. Bishop Beno accused him of 'many vile adulteries and murders', while Pope Victor III mentions 'rapes, murders and other unspeakable acts'. There was an attempt to take him to Lyon to face these charges before the general council, but Benedict stoutly resisted.

Benedict VIII was the first pope to be 'sat in the pierced chair' – that is, the chair with a hole in the seat so that a cardinal could check a candidate was a man before he was elevated to papacy.

With the election of John XIX (1024–32), the corrupt Tuscolani family took over Rome. Their estates overlooked the city from the heights of Tusculum. When John XIX died in suspicious circumstances in 1032, one of his relatives had papal robes made to fit his twelve-year-old son, Theophylact, and sat him on the pontiff's throne. He became Pope Benedict IX (1032–44; 1045; 1047–48) and achieved something of a record by serving three separate terms. As a child on the chair of St Peter, he 'grew up in unrestrained licence, and shocked the dull sensibilities of a gross and barbarous age by the scandals of his daily life'.

It was also said that the child-pope Benedict 'manifested a precocity for all kinds of wickedness'. The position, not unnaturally, seems to have gone to the child's head. He was bisexual, sodomized animals and ordered murders. He also dabbled in witchcraft and Satanism.

'A demon from hell in the disguise of a priest has occupied the chair of Peter,' wrote one observer.

St Peter Damian said: 'That wretch, from the beginning of his pontificate to the end of his life, feasted on immorality.'

It is also alleged that, 'in woods and remote places, he was accustomed to invoke evil spirits, and by necromancy to work women to his lust', that the young Pope lived in the Lateran Palace like a Turkish sultan and that, during his time in office, papacy reached the utmost depth of moral degradation. He 'abandoned himself to excessive immorality and the most shameful debauchery'. Meanwhile, his brothers ruled the city as if they owned it and the result was a crime wave that filled the streets with robbery and murder. The writer Gregorovius describes the situation: 'All lawful conditions had ceased... Only an uncertain glimmer, however, falls on these days when the Vicar of Christ was a pope more criminal than Emperor Elagabalus.'

Dante, too, thought that under Benedict the papacy was at its lowest ebb. But in his *Inferno*, many of the popes were consigned to hell. The cardinals were stripped naked in the Fourth Circle and prelates were forced to push huge boulders for all eternity.

In the Lateran Palace, Benedict hosted lavish homosexual orgies and by the time he was twenty-three his riotous conduct was so appalling that there was an attempt to strangle him at the altar during Mass on the feast of the Apostles. However, he seems to have been saved by an eclipse of the sun. The darkness threw everything into confusion and he managed to escape.

In 1044, a conspiracy to rid Rome of Benedict IX was more successful. But the anti-pope Silvester III (1045), who bribed his way into the succession, was hardly an improvement. His takeover bid was accompanied by ferocious fighting, interrupted by an earthquake. Sensual and corrupt, Silvester was accused of being closer to Satan than to Christ. Again it was said that he consorted with the devil in the woods and used spells to attract women to his bed. Silvester occupied the Lateran Palace for just two months before Benedict IX returned, finding books of magic that Silvester had left behind in his flight. Silvester escaped to the Sabine hills and made no further attempts to take the Holy See.

Just two months after his return, Benedict grew tired of being pope again. He planned to marry his beautiful cousin, the daughter of Girard de Saxo who had stipulated that Benedict lay down the papacy if he wanted the hand of his daughter. So Benedict sold the papacy to his godfather, John Gracian, for 1500 pounds plus Peter's Pence – the tribute from the Church in England – for life. Gracian became Gregory VI. He claimed that his election was a blow against simony – the selling of ecclesiastical offices. News of the purchase of the papacy had not yet leaked out.

However, Benedict's prospective bride turned him down. So Benedict 'abandoned himself to his most infamous pleasures'. He continued to live in the Lateran

Palace which he converted into a brothel – the best in Rome it was said.

When it was finally discovered that Gregory VI had bought the papacy, he was deposed. But no one knew quite what to do with him. He could not be tried on the grounds established long before by St Symmachus. Benedict also denied that he had sold the papacy to Gregory. He claimed that he was merely being reimbursed the bribe money Benedict's father had paid to the conclave of cardinals to secure him the papacy in the first place.

King Henry III of Germany installed the Bavarian Clement II (1046–47) in Gregory's place, but after disturbances in Rome, Clement returned to his home in Bamberg. Explaining his absence from the Holy See in a papal bull, he talked of 'a sweet spouse' from whom he could not bear to be parted. He died in Bamberg of poisoning. Some blamed the former Benedict IX who took over the papacy once more.

Benedict had not mended his ways. He was driven from Rome once and for all in 1048 and died in obscurity sometime after 1055. Some Church records, perhaps self-servingly, portrayed him as having died as a penitent in a monastery. But that seems unlikely given his track record.

Fortunately, Henry III had a good supply of popes. He installed Damasus II (1048), who died after less than a month in office, probably poisoned. Henry replaced him with Leo IX (1049–54).

9

Sex and violence

I n the eleventh century, there was a new attempt to clamp down on immorality. Distinguished theologians began discussing once more, in all solemnity, the appropriate penances for masturbation, impure thoughts, swallowing semen, drinking menstrual blood and kneading bread on a woman's naked buttocks.

Whipping was all the rage. Theologians recommended the kiss of the lash as the cure for almost any sin. The clergy indulged in a great deal of self-flagellation, while the sinful laity were whipped by the local priest. This often took place in private rooms in the church and could have led to some abuse. Some claimed that clerical whipping 'inflamed the passions it sought to suppress'.

Sodomy was particularly frowned on at this time. In the eleventh century. St Peter Damian wrote a long treatise called *The Book of Gomorrah* about homosexuality and the priesthood. He also came up with his own list of punishments. These, naturally, included a good deal of flogging.

'A cleric or monk who seduces youths or young boys or is found kissing or in any other impure situations is to be publicly flogged,' he wrote. 'And he is to lose his tonsure. When his hair has been shaved off, his face is to be besmeared and he is to be bound in iron chains. For six months, he will languish in prison.' He was allowed to eat only barley bread, for 'whoever acts like a mule...should feed on the grain of mules'.

According to the reports of Byzantine ambassadors, every priest about to be consecrated a bishop in the Catholic Church at that time was asked four questions: 'Have you sodomized a boy? Have you fornicated with a nun? Have you sodomized any four-legged animal? And have you committed adultery?' It is not clear which questions you were supposed to answer yes to and which no. After all, according to *The Book of Gomorrah* venality, lechery, bestiality and murder were common among prelates.

Damian tried to persuade Leo IX (1049–54) to expel sodomites from the clergy, but Leo refused. As his first act as pope was to fulminate against heterosexual unchastity among priests, if he got rid of the gays, perhaps he feared he would have had no one left.

St Peter Damian also tried to impose celibacy on the clergy of Milan, with little effect. He railed against their wives:

I address myself to you, you darlings of the priests, you tit-bits of the devil, poisons of the minds, daggers of souls, aconite of drinkers, bane of eaters, stuff of sin, occasion of destruction. To you I turn, I say, you gynecaea [whores] of the ancient enemy, you hoopoes, vampires, bats, leeches, wolves. Come and hear me, you whores, you wallowing beds for fat swine, you bedrooms of

unclean spirits, you nymphs, you sirens, you harpies, you
Dianas, you wicked tigresses, you furious vipers...

But the priests just could not see that having sex with
their wives was, technically, adultery. What's more,
Damian was embarrassed to discover that the clergy in
Piedmont, who excelled in every other way, were all
married. Nevertheless, he continued his crusade with
renewed fervour. To make his point, he had some married priests castrated.

Leo's successor, Victor II (1055–57) had another
crack at anathematizing clerical unchastity. Several bishops were deposed, but there is no evidence that this
helped stamp out sex.

Nicholas II (1058–61) begged his bishops to take
some sort of lead in the area of sexual morality. They said
they were sorry, but they just were not up to the challenge of celibacy. Clerical marriage was so common at
that time that it was no longer punished by canon law.
The bishops could not be bothered to issue a reprimand,
provided priests generally behaved themselves and did
not go marrying a second or third time. But this did not
please the Pope, who insisted that it was more sinful to
marry than to keep a mistress.

Alexander II (1061–73) took a more practical ap-
proach. He gave up the struggle against sexual sin almost
completely. When a priest in Orange was caught having
sex with his father in 1064, Alexander did not sack him.
He did not even deprive him of the holy communion.
After all, the man had not married. Similarly, in 1066, he
pardoned a priest from Padua who had committed incest with his mother.

Gregory VII (1073–85), it is said, 'attained the papacy

86

by conjuration'. He was a midget and demanded that all princes kiss his feet. He also employed a skilled school of forgers to generate seemingly ancient documents enshrining powers that he wanted for the papacy. He was the first Pope to excommunicate an emperor, Henry IV, and it is said that he 'poisoned six bishops and deposed his master Alexander'.

Despite his own shortcomings, Gregory was determined to stamp out moral abuses in the Church. To that end, he tried to enforce his predecessors' ban on clerical marriage and concubinage. His reasoning was simple: 'The Church cannot escape from the clutches of the laity unless priests first escape from the clutches of their wives.'

At the first council of bishops in Rome in 1074, Gregory deposed all married priests. He did this in council with the Countess Mathilda, who was said to be his mistress, sitting by his side.

Gregory's attempt to impose clerical celibacy met with fierce resistance, especially in Germany and France. Gregory was accused of being an atheist and a hypocrite. It was common knowledge that he 'had commerce with the Countess Mathilda' who 'was greatly beloved by the pope'. One critic's exasperation at Gregory's edict was summed in the words: 'This pope, as filthy an adulterer and fornicator as he was, forbad chaste matrimony to the priests.' Much of the trouble was stirred up by Mathilda's husband, Godfrey the Hunchback, who had lived for years in exile with her enemies in Germany. The tension did not calm down when Godfrey was mysteriously murdered in 1076.

The Archbishop of Mainz and the German bishops agreed that Gregory had forfeited all right to the papacy.

The Patriarch of Constantinople gleefully joined in, saying: 'In the Western churches, there is a vast number of children, but no one knows who the fathers are.' But still the Pope's campaign against 'fornication' continued. Sinful priests, Gregory maintained, were no longer priests. 'Would the Pope say a sinful man is no longer a man?' critics replied.

The effect of Gregory's legislation was to make 'virtual prostitutes of the thousands of innocent wives of bewildered and angry little clergymen'. Husbands and wives were separated in large numbers. Many abandoned women committed suicide.

Gregory had more trouble in Rome itself. There were sixty married laymen called the mansinarrii, who guarded St Peter's Basilica. They would dress up in cardinals' robes, pretend to say Mass for the pilgrims who flocked to Rome, and collect the rich offerings and valuables the pilgrims had brought with them. This provided them with a sumptuous and often riotous living. As well as their wives, they kept mistresses. They would even hold orgies on the steps of the Basilica with local streetwalkers. Gregory, outraged by this behaviour, dismissed them all. They quickly joined the swelling ranks of his enemies.

On Christmas Eve 1075, while Gregory was performing midnight Mass, a group of armed soldiers burst into the crypt of St Maria Maggiore. They grabbed him by the hair and dragged him, wounded, from the altar. He was locked up in the fortified tower belonging to the nobleman Cencius de Praefecto, where Cencius and his sisters mocked and tortured him. The city was in uproar, but next day a mob found out where Gregory had been taken and stormed the Cencius tower. The Pope was released and returned to finish off the Mass he had started.

Nevertheless, the crisis continued. The German clergy wanted to know where they were going to find angels to replace the married men who had been driven out of the priesthood. In 1076, a group of Italian bishops, led by the Bishop of Pavia, excommunicated the Pope for separating husbands and wives and, consequently, favouring licentiousness in the clergy over honourable marriage. And the Council of Brixen in 1080 condemned Gregory for 'sowing divorce among legitimate spouses'.

Eventually, Gregory relented in his campaign against 'fornication'. Had he carried out his threat of sacking all sexually incontinent priests, he would have wiped out the Catholic Church.

Gregory VII also thought that it was not a good thing for people to read the bible. It might provoke thought, and thinking led to heresy.

Gregory's strictures brought him into conflict with the Holy Roman Emperor, Henry IV. Henry put together a synod of twenty-six German bishops to depose Gregory, one of the charges being, tellingly, his 'scandalous association with women', particularly the Countess Mathilda. Gregory turned out to be the more powerful. He excommunicated Henry and declared him deposed as Emperor. Henry, robbed of much of his support, rode south from Germany to beg forgiveness. Gregory, wary of Henry's intentions, sought refuge with Countess Mathilda in Tuscany. When Henry turned up, truly penitent, Gregory left him waiting for three cold January days, wearing only a hair shirt, outside the triple walls of the Countess's fortress home. Gregory, who regularly scourged himself, took great pleasure in watching Henry suffering in the cold outside. It was only when Countess Mathilda convinced the Pope that Henry would die if he was left outside the walls a moment longer that Gregory deigned to see him. The young, good-looking Henry, in his rags, towered over the tiny, tiaraed dwarf Gregory. Nevertheless Gregory forced Henry to give up the Imperial crown in return for absolution.

Henry was not penitent long, though. He was still king of Germany, after all. In 1084, he took Rome and installed his own anti-pope, Clement III (1084–1100). Gregory, holding out in the Castel Sant'Angelo, was rescued by an alliance of Normans, Saracens from Sicily and bands of wild Calabrian peasants. Henry withdrew.

But for Gregory, the cure was worse than the disease. Once his supporters had re-installed him in the Lateran Palace, they set about looting, pillaging and, especially, raping. The Romans blamed Gregory for this. He never recovered and died of shame the following year in Salerno.

Gregory's successor Victor III (1086–87), it was said, 'obtained the papacy by help of Mathilda, his mistress'. This is the same Countess Mathilda who had been 'Gregory VII's concubine'. After his election and before his consecration, he was forced to flee from Rome because of rioting by Gregory's outraged followers. His successor Urban II (1088–99), it was said, rose to the papacy 'by the like policy' – that is, via Mathilda's bed.

Nevertheless, once on the papal throne, he renewed Gregory's legislation banning clerical marriages; but he could not ban sin. Under Urban, the French King William mounted a crusade. On his shield, instead of the standard crusaders' cross, he had a painting of his mistress in the nude. The crusade was a disaster, but William comforted himself by taking a holiday in Antioch with fellow crusader Norman Tancred, where he drafted plans for a nunnery where the nuns would be the finest prostitutes in the duchy.

The matter of clerical celibacy was settled at the Council of Piacenza in 1095. Four hundred clerics and 30,000 laymen passed a resolution finally outlawing the marriage of priests. And to show they meant business, they sold the priests' wives into slavery. That was not the only way the new ruling could be used to make money for the Church. Soon the Pope introduced the infamous *cullagium*. This was a sex tax. It allowed a clergyman to keep a concubine as long as he paid a regular annual fee.

Urban had particular problems making his rule of clerical celibacy stick in England. Since the beginning of the Church there, English clerics made it clear that they did 'not wish to remain single'.

'Priests know full well that they have no right to marry,' ran a tenth-century statute, 'but some are guilty of worse practice in having two or more wives, and others, though they forsake their former wife, afterwards take other wives while the first is still alive, a thing no Christian man ought to do, let alone a priest.'

The Miller in Chaucer's *The Canterbury Tales* says his wife is the daughter of a priest. And one priest justified raping one of his parishioners by saying: 'He must needs have his pleasure of her.'

The next pope, Paschal (1099–1118), a monk since boyhood, was even tougher on Henry IV than Gregory VII had been. He renewed Gregory VII's excommunication and encouraged Henry's son to rise up against him. His hatred of Henry did not end when Henry died – 'so great was his hellish rage against the dead carcass of Henry, that he dug it up and cast it out of the church'.

Callistus II (1119–24) was more straightforward. He decreed that it was adultery for bishops to abandon their See to marry. At the first General Council of the West, known as the First Lateran, a thousand prelates reinforced the Council of Piacenza and decreed that clerical marriages were invalid. They were to be broken up and the spouses forced to do penance.

A little poem was made up about Callistus and his efforts to rid clerics of their wives:

> *The clergy now thee, good Callistus, hate;*
> *For heretofore each one might have his mate.*
> *But since thou mounted hast the papal throne,*
> *They must keep punks or learn to lie alone.*

Many kept 'punks' – catamites – rather than learn to lie alone.

Callistus's successor, Honorius II (1124–30), was equally tough on sex and the clergy, but to rather less effect. In September 1126, he sent the Cardinal John of Crema as papal legate to England to denounce the concubines of priests. The Pope instructed him to declare that it was a horrible sacrilege on the body of Christ that the Mass should be performed by a man who had just left the bed of a harlot.

The Cardinal assembled a great council in London and, against much opposition, passed a canon threatening the demotion of all clergy who would not give up wives or courtesans. Then he celebrated a solemn Mass and the assembly dispersed.

But the English clergy knew full well what their Italian

brethren were like. They kept a careful watch on the Cardinal's lodgings. That night, a muffled figure was seen creeping out of a back door. They followed it down the streets to the house of a well-known prostitute. The figure knocked and went in. After ten minutes or so, a couple of English clergymen burst in to the house to find the Cardinal *nudatus usque ad unguem* – naked to his fingernails – with a 'fayre ladye' in a similar state of undress. After raising a toast to the Cardinal's appropriately scarlet face, they left him to get on about his business.

The events of that night 'brought no small scandal on the church'. But it was the end of John of Crema's campaign against the wives and concubines of the English clergy. He was packed off back to Rome with instructions to tell the Pope to put his own house in order first. It was well known that another member of the Sacred College of Cardinals, Cardinal Pierleoni, slept with his own sister and had several children by her. Unlike Cardinal Crema, Pierleoni never travelled anywhere in his role as papal legate without a concubine. A monk named Arnolfo, who denounced him, was found murdered. Cardinal Pierleoni went on to become Pope Anacletus II (1130–38).

After the death of Honorius II, the college of cardinals split and elected two popes – Innocent II (1130–43) and Anacletus II. Followers of Anacletus said that Innocent had Jewish blood in his veins, while Innocent's followers pointed out that, as well as committing incest with his sister and other relatives, and keeping a prostitute as his mistress, Anacletus had a terrible habit of raping nuns. But Rome rallied to Anacletus and Innocent fled to France. Better a fornicator than a Jew. On Anacletus's death, however, Innocent II resumed the papacy.

Celestine II (1143–44) was by all accounts an honest-to-God brutal sadist. He had a certain Count Jordan condemned to a horrible death, strapped naked to a scalding iron chair while a red-hot crown was nailed to his head. Celestine did have his nicer side, though. He was a life-long admirer of the philosopher and theologian Peter Abelard, whose sexual misdemeanour is the stuff of literature. Alexander III (1159–81) was another fan of Abelard's and Celestine III (1191–98) was a student of the unfortunate Abelard in his youth. As a subdeacon, he defended Abelard at the Council of Sens where Abelard was condemned by Pope Innocent II (1130–43).

Around the time Abelard was teaching the future Pope Celestine III, he had another more comely student, the fair Heloise. She was the precocious niece of a canon and was just fourteen when she was sent to study under Abelard. He was in his mid-thirties and a clergyman. He was immediately impressed with her literary talents. In his book *The History of My Misfortunes*, he said that she was also very beautiful.

'I weighed up all the qualities that usually incite lovers and decided that she was the one for me,' he wrote. He also knew that he was a good-looking man and that he could have any woman 'I deigned to favour with my love'. Heloise, he thought, was a cherry ripe for plucking.

To facilitate his seduction, he arranged with Heloise's uncle that he become her private tutor and move into the family's house. The uncle gave him enough money to quit school teaching and placed the fair Heloise completely under his control. He was even to punish her if he found her remiss. Abelard said simply: 'I would have been no more astounded than if he had given a tender lamb to a ravenous wolf.' But then Abelard was known as a good man and had a reputation for chastity.

As Abelard had predicted, the seduction was easy: 'Under the pretext of work we made ourselves free for love and the pursuit of her studies provided the privacy we required.' The lessons soon fell by the wayside. Rather than reading, they gazed into each other's eyes. Abelard began neglecting his other work, but no one suspected that it was for the love of Heloise. After all, everyone knew he was a celibate.

When Heloise became pregnant, Abelard disguised her as a nun and took her off to his family in Brittany where she gave birth to their son, Astralabe. They married secretly, to preserve his position as a clergyman, and returned to Paris where they explained the situation to Heloise's uncle. The uncle was not satisfied with a secret wedding. To allay his disgrace, he had to let it be known publicly that his niece was married. This would have ruined Abelard's career as a clergyman and stopped him teaching, so both Heloise and her lover denied they were married. Her uncle grew angry and Abelard sent Heloise to the convent at Argenteuil for her protection.

With Heloise out of the way, Abelard was more vulnerable. Heloise's uncle and the rest of the family conspired against him. They bribed a servant at Abelard's lodgings to let them in one night. They grabbed Abelard while he slept and 'cut off the organs by which I had committed the deed which they deplored'. They did not get off scot-free, though. The servant and another of the attackers were captured and, likewise, castrated.

The next morning, the whole city of Paris turned out

to express sympathy, but Abelard found this and the embarrassment harder to bear than the pain.

Heloise took her vows as a nun and Abelard became a monk. They continued their studies, separately. Abelard actually became rather proud of his enforced chastity. But Heloise continued to burn with passion for him. He wrote letters of comfort to her. In her letters back, she could not help writing of the sexual pleasure they had enjoyed. Even during Mass, she confessed, she could not help having lewd visions about their time together. Later, they published a book of their letters and theological speculations, a masterpiece of the literature of love.

The celebrated affair of Abelard and Heloise was not the only outbreak of clerical unchastity at the time. Pope Innocent II was having trouble in Spain too. Because of the Moorish invasion, the Spanish clergy were given an easy time, left to get on with their lives with their wives. Innocent wanted something done about it. An example had to be made.

After being openly criticized by his archbishop seven times for immorality, the Abbot of the Santo Pelayo de Antealteria was finally brought to trial. Reliable witnesses said that he had seventy concubines. He was found guilty and sacked, but the Church had to give him a huge pension to support his mistresses and his numerous offspring.

There were more problems in France, too. Around that time, Robert Arbissel, who ran a convent of 4000 nuns, was roundly criticized. He declared himself to be a sinner and one of his penances was 'frequently to sleep amongst and with the women' to mortify his flesh. And the punishments he imposed on the nuns usually involved them stripping naked.

Despite the huge efforts a number of popes had made to enforce clerical celibacy, things carried on in much the same vein. Hadrian IV (1154–59), formerly Nicholas Breakspear and the only English pope, was the son of a monk called Robert from St Albans.

Pope Alexander III, another of Abelard's followers, found himself overwhelmed by the number of clergymen who kept concubines now that they could no longer marry. He begged his priests at least to abstain from sex for three days and nights before touching the Host. He even planned to permit clerical marriage again. The Curia backed him, but one man stayed his hand – his chancellor, the ascetic monk Alberto de Morra who went on to become Pope Gregory VIII (1187). He was such a spoil-sport that during his one year in office he banned extravagant clothes and gambling.

Like other popes, Alexander III had particular problems with the clergy in England. Determined to have someone celibate in the See of Canterbury, he appointed the monk Clarembald, only to discover that he had seventeen illegitimate children in one village alone.

At that time, the Bishop of Lincoln was concerned about the debauchery of nuns in England. So he developed a novel test to see if they were living up to their vows of chastity. He would go through the convents fondling the nuns' breasts to see how they would react.

Pope Alexander was all too well aware of the clergy's ability to get around the rules. 'The pope deprived the clergy of sons and the devil sent them nephews,' he said.

Celestine III (1191–98) was even looser than Alexander. He allowed a form of divorce, saying that a marriage between Christians could be dissolved, even if it had been consummated, if one of the parties became a heretic. This created a lot of heretics. For suggesting such a thing, Celestine was branded a heretic himself by Pope Hadrian VI (1522–23). Celestine probably would not have cared. He certainly did not complain about the Holy Roman Emperor Henry VI's habit of having nuns stripped and smeared with honey, then decorated with feathers and sent on horseback through the jeering ranks of his soldiers. His successor, Pope Innocent III (1198–1216) was into persecution and torture in a big way.

In the eleventh century, a group calling themselves the Cathars had grown up. Cathars were monks who believed that God and the devil struggled to rule the world. They mortified the flesh, practised savage flagellation and were vegetarians on the grounds that animals were produced by sexual intercourse and were therefore sinful. They did eat fish, though, in the mistaken belief that fish did not copulate. The Cathars discouraged marriage on the same grounds. However, they did practise sodomy. Apparently, it was permitted as it did not risk what they saw as the sin of procreation.

In 1208, Innocent III denounced the Cathars as Satanists and sent a crusade against them. The methods used got results. Cathars were forced to confess to sodomy, for example, by being lowered naked on to a red-hot spike. This method of torture was called the *Chambre Chauffee* and it was the approved method of interrogation of suspected sodomites until 1816.

Innocent also persecuted the Albigensians in the Languedoc, who were fiercely anti-sex. They said that marriage was a state of sin, that sex in marriage was no better than incest, the forbidden fruit of the Garden of Eden was sexual pleasure and that a pregnant woman had the devil inside her. This did not sit well with priests who heard matins in bed with their mistresses.

Innocent III also fell out with England's King John. John married his cousin Isabel of Gloucester without even asking for a dispensation, then abandoned her and married the young and beautiful Isabel of Angoulême. When Innocent expressed his displeasure, John made amends by building a Cistercian abbey, albeit with stolen money, and sending a thousand men to the Crusades. The pope found he could approve the second marriage, but when John made his own man Archbishop of Canterbury, Innocent put the whole of England under an interdiction. John responded by taxing the clergy. His favourite tax was the so-called 'sin tax'. His men would seize the clergy's wives and concubines – then known as *focarie*, or hearthmates – and forced the priests to buy them back at exorbitant prices. A priest had to pay as much as £2 a year to keep a mistress.

During his prolonged battle with the Pope, King John became more of a tyrant at home, extorting money from the Jews and sleeping with any woman who took his fancy. This caused growing internal unrest and, finding himself fighting on two fronts, John made it up with the Pope. But it was too late. The Barons rebelled and forced King John into signing the *Magna Carta*, which Pope Innocent III condemned as 'contrary to moral law'.

Innocent was not really interested in moral law. He favoured gold and jewels. He had a special tiara made from white peacock feathers, covered in jewels and topped by a sapphire. He also insisted on having his feet kissed by one and all and aspired to be ruler of the world. In May 1204, he oversaw the sacking of Constantinople during the Fourth Crusade. The cathedral of Santa

Sophia was desecrated. Relics were stolen and nuns were raped.

Innocent III also oversaw the Fourth Lateran Council, which again tried to stamp out clerical marriage. The problem was that, when the bounds of marriage were taken away, priests became totally promiscuous. As Bernard of Clairvaux said: 'Take from the Church an honourable marriage and an immaculate marriage bed and do you not fill it with concubinage, incest, homosexuality and every kind of uncleanness?' But that was not the point. Married priests have divided loyalties. They are loyal to their families as well as to the Church. Whereas unmarried priests – be they fornicators, adulterers and perverts on a monumental scale – are loyal only to the church.

Pope Gregory IX (1227–41) was another Pope who took a great deal of interest in heretics. In 1232 and 1233, he issued two papal bulls against a sect in the remote town of Steding in north Germany. He seemed to be fascinated by the Stedingers and wrote, in detail, about their practices. According to Gregory, new converts to the sect had to kiss all those present on the posterior and on the mouth, drawing the tongue and spittle into their own mouths. The novice would then kiss a corpse and all traces of his Catholic faith would disappear. After a celebration dinner, all those present would kiss a cat 'under the tail' then 'each man took the first woman who came to hand and had carnal intercourse with her'. Later, a man who was smooth on the top half and had very hairy legs turned up. Gregory charges that the Stedingers were worshipping Satan.

It was Gregory who founded the Inquisition in 1231. One of his chief lieutenants was an ascetic priest called

Conrad. One day, while watching a Cistercian being burnt for heresy, Conrad conceived the idea that you could only come to salvation through pain.

One of Conrad's most famous converts was Elizabeth, widow of the Margrave of Thuringia. When she was just eighteen, he persuaded her to abandon her three babies and follow him. To make her more spiritual, he would get her to strip and beat her until her young body was covered in blood. 'If I fear a man like this,' she told her confessor, 'what must God be like?'

Conrad was chosen personally by Gregory to investigate a group of German heretics called the Luciferians. In Strasbourg alone, he burnt more than eighty men, women and children in order to save their immortal souls.

Gregory IX's paranoia about 'heretics' left the Church in disarray. When he died, the division was such that picking a successor proved impossible, so the governor of Rome, Senator Matteo Rosso Orsini, devised the 'conclave' system to speed up the cardinals' deliberations.

He rounded them up and had them roughed up by his own men, as a preliminary intimidation. Then he tied them up and publicly beat and abused them to instil a proper sense of shame. After that they were hurled bodily into the main hall of the Septizodium, a huge building on the Via Appia. The windows were boarded up and the doors were locked. They were to stay there until a pope was chosen.

Inside there were a few broken-down beds with insufficient bed linen, chairs and benches. No doctors were allowed in. Only the simplest food was provided. There was a little cold water for drinking, but no water for washing. They could not change their clothes and the latrines were not to be emptied until a decision was made.

The heat in the summertime in Rome can be oppressive. The air became fetid. One dying cardinal was put in a coffin while still alive and a funeral service said over him. On the roof of the Septizodium, there were armed guards who were forbidden to move from their posts. They used the gutters as a lavatory. When a thunderstorm broke, the sudden downpour sloshed excrement, urine and other rubbish down over the assembled cardinals.

When they picked a new pope, the candidate was unacceptable to Senator Orsini. He threatened to dig up Gregory IX and put his decaying corpse in the hall with them to help them come to a decision more quickly.

Eventually, after fifty-five days in one room, the cardinals elected Godfrey, who chose to reign as Celestine IV (1241). Unfortunately, the conclave had proved so harrowing for him that he died two weeks later without actually being consecrated.

By this time the cardinals had fled and tried to pick a successor by post. When this did not work, Emperor Frederick of Germany tried to round them up again, but they escaped to Rome. Frederick managed to starve them of funds and, eventually after a year and a half, they picked Innocent IV (1243–54).

Innocent IV was a man of liberal leanings. When he was forced to leave Rome after a dispute with Frederick II, he sought safety in England. But the peers of the realm refused to have him there, claiming that green and sweet-smelling England could not bear the smell of the papal court there. Instead he took refuge in Lyons, where he lived for eight years. When he left to go back to Rome, having made it up with Frederick, a cardinal made a speech extolling the benefits to Lyons of Pope

Innocent's protracted stay in the city. 'Friends, since our arrival we have done much for your city,' the cardinal said. 'When we came we found three or four brothels. We leave behind but one. But it extends without interruption from the eastern to the western gate.'

However, Innocent IV did give the Inquisition permission to use torture to obtain confessions. Soon old women were being burnt at the stake after admitting, under torture, that they had had sex with Satan. In 1275, the inquisitor Hugues de Baniols heard the confession of a sixty-year-old woman, Angele de la Barthe, in Toulouse. She was accused of having sexual intercourse with the devil. The resulting child, she said, was a demon who ate only the flesh of dead babies and she murdered children and dug up fresh corpses to feed it.

The tortures used to obtain such confessions were so barbaric that it is hard to imagine that inquisitors – and the popes that drew up the rules – did not get some perverted sadistic kicks out of them. The details of just what an inquisition could and couldn't do were spelt out in *The Black Book*, or *Book of Death*, which was on display in the Casa Santa in Rome until the mid-nineteenth century. It did not mince words:

> *Either the person confesses and he is proved guilty from his own confession, or he does not confess and is equally guilty on the evidence of witnesses. If a person confesses the whole of what he is accused of, he is unquestionably guilty of the whole; but if he confesses only a part, he ought still to be regarded as guilty of the whole, since what he had confessed proves him to be capable of guilt as to the other points of accusation... Bodily torture has ever been found the most salutary and efficient means of leading to spiritual repentance. Therefore, the choice of the most befitting*

103

mode of torture is left to the Judge of the Inquisition, who deter-
mines according to the age, the sex and the constitution of the
party... If, notwithstanding all the means employed, the unfor-
tunate wretch still denies his guilt, he is to be considered a victim
of the devil; and, as such deserves no compassion from the ser-
vants of God, nor the pity and indulgence of Holy Mother
Church: he is the son of perdition. Let him perish among the
damned.

The dice were certainly loaded in favour of the Inquisition. There is no record of an acquittal, which is hardly
surprising as the accused was not told what he was
charged with and was forbidden to ask. No defence
council was permitted and no defence witnesses could
be called. Witnesses for the prosecution were always under the threat of being charged themselves and their
identities were withheld from the prisoner. Parents were
ordered to betray their children and children their parents. Not to do so was a sin against the Holy Office.
However, boys under fourteen and girls under twelve
were exempted from torture. And there was, of course,
no appeal. What court could be higher than one sitting
in the name of the pope?

According to *The Black Book*, inquisitors were not supposed to mutilate or kill their victims in the course of
their investigations – that came later. But arms and legs
were often broken and even the loss of a few fingers or
toes was not enough to stop the proceedings.

Usually, the victim was stripped naked and tied to a
trestle. They were then told: 'Tell the truth for the love
of God, as the inquisitors do not wish to see you suffer.'
Cords were tied around the arms and thighs. Others
passed over the shoulder and were connected to a belt

around the waist. The cords were tightened and the inquisitor would ask the victim to 'tell the truth'. If the victim asked what he had been charged with, or what the inquisitors wanted him to say, he was told again to 'tell the truth'.

The cords would be tightened again. Each time the hapless victim would be told to 'tell the truth'. If no confession were forthcoming, a rod would be pushed under the cord and twisted, tightening the cords further.

In particularly stubborn cases, the strappado was used. The victim's hands were tied behind him and secured to a pulley. He was winched up to the ceiling, then dropped – to be stopped just short of the floor with an agonizing jerk.

Another favourite was the water torture. A piece of linen was stuffed down the throat and water was poured on it. Up to two gallons was poured into the victim this way. Many simply drowned or suffocated.

According to papal decree, torture could only be used once. But as victims were chained alone in filthy cells and left to wallow in their own excrement between times, it was argued that several sessions in the hands of the inquisitors was one part of one torture.

The Dominicans were particularly harsh, because in their order they willingly inflicted pain on themselves. The screams of their victims were music to their ears – it meant that one soul was coming closer to God.

Despite his use of the Inquisition and his sadistic attack on 'heretics', Innocent IV did not say a word against his protector, the Holy Roman Emperor Frederick II, who had a harem of Moslem mistresses guarded by black eunuchs.

Innocent IV's successor Alexander IV (1254–61) was

no sadist. He tried to ban clerical scourging, but people had learned to enjoy it. Even Louis, King of France, let himself be whipped and handled roughly by his confessors. Alexander also planned to abandon priestly celibacy, believing that it led to vice. He was a man who relished a risqué story. He once told the Franciscan monk Salimbene de Adam an off-colour tale about a priest who heard the confession of a woman he fancied. Instead of giving the woman absolution, the priest tried to chat her up. When that did not work, he tried to rape her behind the altar. To fend him off, the woman told him that it was neither the time nor the place for 'the work of Venus'. So, disingenuously, she suggested a time when that they could get together in more amorous surroundings. The priest was happy with this, but the woman was determined to get her own back. So when she got home, she made a pie filled with her own excrement and sent it to the priest with a bottle of wine. The priest was very impressed by the pie. He thought it was so good that he did not eat it himself. He sent it to the bishop.

When the bishop cut it open and discovered what was inside, he was not at all amused. He had the priest brought before him and asked what he, the bishop, had done to deserve such an insult. The priest protested his innocence and told the bishop that he had not made the pie himself, but a woman parishioner had given it to him. So the bishop sent for the woman. She confessed that she had sent the pie to the priest, but explained that the priest had tried to seduce her during confession. The bishop praised the woman and punished the priest.

Alexander IV thought this story was very funny indeed. As far as he could see the woman had made just one mistake. She should have filled the bottle with her own pee instead of sending wine.

The Pope's confidant, Salimbene, recorded the state of the Church under Alexander IV:

> *I have seen priests keeping taverns... and their whole house full of bastard children, and spending their nights in sin and celebrating Mass next... One day, when a Franciscan friar had to celebrate Mass in a certain priest's church on a feast day, he had no stole but the girdle of the priest's concubine, with a bunch of keys attached; and when the friar, who I know well, turned around to say,* Dominus Vobiscum, *the people heard the jangling of the keys.*

No wonder Alexander IV had to issue a papal bull bemoaning the fact that – at a time when bishops kept harems and every nun had her lover – the clergy were not reforming their congregations, but corrupting them.

Indeed, in France, convents were known as 'palaces of pleasure'. Nuns in Poitiers and Lys were famous for their gallantries with the Franciscan friars of the city, while the nuns of Montmartre gave themselves over to prostitution and poisoned a Mother Superior who tried to reform them. Brothels returned the compliment. Madames were called abbesses and whore-houses abbeys. In his flowery medieval way, Charles VI of France writes of going to 'hear the supplication which has been made us on the part of the daughters-of-joy of the brothel of Toulouse called the Great Abbey'.

In Germany, there was a new form of temple prostitution. Prostitutes would hang out in the cathedrals and ply for trade. These 'cathedral girls' were banned from

Strasbourg Cathedral only in 1521. The Bishop of Strasbourg also ran a brothel and the Dean of Würzburg
Cathedral was entitled by law to receive from each village
in the diocese one horse, one dinner and one girl each
year.

A more direct form of temple prostitution was reintro-
duced to Rome in the thirteenth century. All the local
whores were rounded up and put to work in the underground chapel at St Mary's church, surrounded by some
of the most sacred objects in Christendom. Urban IV
(1261–64) wrote a letter condemning this sacrilegious
debauchery, to little effect.

The Pope's secretary, Bishop Dietrich of Niems, had
to inform His Holiness of the goings-on in Norway and
Iceland.

> *When the bishops go twice a year to pay visits to their curates,
> they have to take their mistresses with them. The women will not
> let them make the trip without them, because the bishops are
> magnificently received by the curates and their own concubines
> and the bishop's mistresses fear that they will find the concubines
> of the priests more beautiful than they are and become amorous
> of them.*

As the Catholic Church grew more powerful, some
priests even assumed the lord of the manor's feudal *jus
primae noctis*. They insisted on sleeping with the bride on
her wedding night, before the husband enjoyed his conjugal rights.

In his letters to the Pope, Bishop Dietrich of Niems
goes into great detail when describing the debauchery
of his nuns. According to him, they were prey to the lust
of bishops, monks and lay brothers. The children 'born

out of this libertinage' were placed in convents, thus providing a new generation of loose nuns.

'If any secular woman were guilty of the foul deeds that these nuns commit,' he wrote, 'they would be condemned, according to the law, to the extreme penalty.'

These practices continued into the fourteenth century when, according to Cardinal Pierre d'Ailly, priests were 'not ashamed to have concubines and publicly acknowledged them'. D'Ailly also wrote of convents being places of debauchery and 'assemblages of prostitutes'.

Shocking though these things may be to twentieth-century ears, they would have come as no surprise to Urban IV himself. He had been 'familiar' with a woman named Eva before he became pope. And his successor Clement IV (1265–68) had been married and had two daughters – some say three – before he took holy orders.

The first conclave of 1241–43 – when the cardinals had been locked in the Septizodium – had not taught them a thing. With the death of Clement IV, they became deadlocked again. This time they were locked in the Archbishop's palace in Viterbo and told they would stay there until they had picked a new pope. Sheets were hung from beams to make cubicles and the cardinals were given only bread and wine. When they failed to produce a pope speedily, water was substituted for the wine. When that failed too, the roof of the palace was removed so that the cardinals would be exposed to the heat of the day and the cold of the night.

The cardinals retaliated by excommunicating the people of Viterbo and banning all religious ceremonies there. The response of the authorities was straightforward: 'We may live without religious worship, but you will certainly die of hunger, disease and hardship. Choose a pope!'

Eventually, after three years' deliberation, they picked Gregory X (1271–76). He was little more than a rough crusader and was in Palestine at the time of his election. It was another seven months before he could get back for his consecration in St Peter's.

Gregory X had been archdeacon of Liège before he became Pope. In 1274, he had to depose his former boss, the Bishop of Liège, at the Council of Lyons 'for deflowering virgins and other mighty deeds'. The bishop had seventy concubines, some of whom were nuns, and sixty-five illegitimate children. 'His lust was promiscuous,' it was said. 'He kept as his concubine a Benedictine Abbess. He had boasted in a public banquet that in twenty-two months he had fourteen children born. This was not the worst – there was foul incest, and with nuns.'

Gregory was no prude. At first, he had tried to reason with the bishop. He wrote to him asking only his repentance. When that failed, the Pope had no alternative but to sack him. The defrocked Bishop of Liège was eventually murdered by a Flemish knight who was outraged at what the former bishop had done to his daughter.

The corruption in the Church ran from the bottom to the top. St Bonaventure, a close friend of Innocent V (1276), compared Rome to the harlot of the Apocalypse, drunk with wine of her whoredom. In Rome, Bonaventure said, there was nothing but lust and simony, even in the highest ranks of the Church. It was quite simple, he explained. Rome corrupts the prelates. The prelates corrupt the clergy. And the clergy corrupt the people.

Pope John XXI (1276–77) was criticized by his contemporaries for 'moral instability' and Martin IV

110

(1281–85), it is said, 'took to his embraces his predecessor's concubine'. His predecessor was Nicholas III (1277–80). Martin IV had another strange preoccupation. According to Cypriano de Valera, he 'removed from his palace all pictures of bears, lest his sweet-heart seeing them might bring forth one of those beasts'.

The conclave following the death of Pope Nicolas IV (1288–92) made a terrible mistake. After over two years of stalemate, they elected a genuinely good man – a hermit called Peter of Morone who lived in a cave a thousand feet up in the Apennines near Abruzzi. He was crowned Celestine V (1294), but he could not stand the licentious ways of Rome and moved to Naples.

The cardinals soon began to realize their mistake when Celestine began giving away the wealth of the Church – to the poor, of all people! He had no flair for corruption or simony at all. And the princes of the Church were worried that they would soon be bankrupt. Cardinal Benedict Gaetani, the papal notary, saw his chance. To gain Celestine's confidence, he built the old hermit a humble wooden shack inside the huge rooms of the Castello Nuovo, the five-towered castle that over-looks the Bay of Naples. There, Gaetani prevailed upon Celestine to abdicate.

Just fifteen weeks after his consecration, Celestine called his cardinals together, begged them to banish their mistresses to nunneries and to live in poverty like Jesus. Then, as an example to them all, Celestine put aside his papal gown, resumed his hermit's rags, re-signed and rode off, like Jesus, on a donkey.

Having engineered this coup, Gaetani had himself elected pope by the grateful cardinals and was crowned Boniface VIII (1294–1303). Just to be on the safe side, his first act as Pope was to have Celestine locked up in the Fumone castle, where he died of starvation and neglect a few months later.

But if one pope could be removed from office, so could another. The Gaetani family had long been rivals of the Colonnas, who formed an alliance with Boniface's arch-enemy Philip the Fair of France. They charged Boniface with gross sexual misconduct, as well as 'heresy, tyranny, unchastity and intercourse with the Devil'. Apparently he wore a ring on his left index finger in which an evil spirit lived. The spirit talked with him and came out at night to sleep with him. Dante consigned Boniface to the lowest reaches of hell.

Boniface's sexual proclivities were well known before he was elected pope. A libertine, he once kept a married woman and her daughter as his mistresses. There was no secret about his sexual adventures after election, either. They were widely published by Pandulphus Colenucius in his *History of Naples*.

Nevertheless, in the summer of 1303, Philip the Fair called a parliament in Paris to try Boniface. The charges included not believing in life after death, wizardry, dealing with the devil, declaring that the sins of the flesh were not sins and, with others, murdering Pope Celestine – along with heresy, simony and rapacity. An attempt to seize Boniface and bring him to trial failed. Nevertheless, the proceedings went ahead without him.

A young shoemaker called Lello from the diocese of Spoleto testified that he was in Perugia selling shoes shortly after the death of Pope Nicolas IV in 1292. Boniface – then Cardinal Benedict Gaetani – was staying in the town at the time and one of his entourage summoned the shoemaker. The Cardinal, he said, wanted a pair of shoes. So Lello, who was in his mid-teens, went to the house where Boniface was staying and fitted him up with some shoes. Then, the shoemaker said, Boniface started kissing him and coaxing him.

'I want you to do what I want,' the Cardinal was supposed to have said. 'I want to lie with you and I will do a lot for you.'

But Lello was not that sort of a chap.

'Lord, you ought not to do this, because it is a great sin,' he told the future pope. 'Today is Saturday, the fast of the Virgin Mary.'

But Boniface, in his ecclesiastical role, reassured the young man.

'It is no more sin than to rub your hands together,' he said, clutching him. 'And as for the Virgin Mary for whom you fast, she is not more a virgin than my mother who had many children.'

Lello, realizing that his virtue was in imminent danger, started to scream. Master Pietro of Acquasparta, who was outside, came rushing in. Boniface let go and Lello escaped. He ran from the house, without even getting paid for the shoes.

When still a cardinal, Boniface made similar remarks to a French doctor. The court was told that Boniface had told the doctor that there was no life but this one and that sodomy was only a moderate sin, rather like 'rubbing one hand against the other'.

Boniface was particularly familiar with the family of Giacomo de Pisis, who had been his gay lover. A monk of the San Gregio monastery in Rome said that he had seen Boniface holding Giacomo's son Giacanello between the thighs and that it was well known that he had abused the son as he had abused his father before him. Another member of the de Pisis family said that he had seen the Pope in bed with Giacomo's wife, Lady Cola. The two of them used to play dice together. Boniface also slept with Giacomo's daughter Gartamicia.

Giacomo de Pisis did not seem to mind his whole family being used this way, but he was jealous of the Pope's other lovers. There was once a falling out between Giacomo and another of Boniface's boyfriends, Guglielmo de Santa Floria.

'You are Pope Boniface's whore,' Giacomo had screamed.

'No, you are his whore,' replied Guglielmo.

'You were his whore before I was, because at the time when he was still a cardinal I found you in his chamber doing the business with him,' Giacomo said.

'If I was his early whore, you are his only whore,' Guglielmo riposted, 'because everything that you possess he gave you because you are his whore.'

A knight from Lucca said that, in about 1300, Boniface had told a knight from Bologna that there was no other life but this one and that it was no sin for a man to do what pleased him, particularly if that involved lying with a woman. Again the knight reported that Boniface had said to lie with a woman or a boy was no more of a sin than to rub one hand against the other. This exchange, the knight said, had occurred in a bedroom at the Lateran Palace in front of the Luccan, Florentine and Bolognese ambassadors. The knight told the court that he took Boniface's pronouncement to mean that 'everybody ought to try and enjoy himself'.

Boniface was also charged with eating meat during Lent. But he was not criticized for his love of wine, silk, pearls and gold. He was also supposed to have said that the Eucharist was 'just flour and water'.

Boniface did not attend the trial and could not be brought to book. But he eventually went mad and committed suicide. This was not good enough for Philip, though. He got Pope Clement V (1305–14) to dig up Boniface's body and have him burnt as a heretic.

10

Adultery in Avignon

Clement V (1305–14) was very much Philip of France's man. He would do just about anything that Philip told him. He was the first of the popes to leave Italy and, for the next century, the Holy See was run from Avignon in France.

Clement was most famous for suppressing the Knights Templar, who had been formed around 1119 to protect pilgrims bound for Jerusalem during the Crusades. Suppressing them was Philip's idea. He was jealous of their wealth and aimed to seize their lands in France. He threatened Clement with re-opening the embarrassing proceedings against Boniface VIII if he did not comply.

The Templars were arrested in 1307 and Clement charged them with heretical ideas, blasphemous rites and immoral practices. As their confessions were wrung out of them by torture, they tend to reflect more the warped preconceptions of the inquisitors – and Clement, who laid the charges – than what had actually happened.

It was said that, to join the order, a novice would have to kiss the enroller on the mouth, the anus and the *virga virilis*. Members were told that they had permission to commit sodomy among themselves. This testimony was given by a man who said he had left the Templars when he fell in love with a woman.

Some Templars said that there had been a misunderstanding. Members were only told that if there was a shortage of sleeping accommodation they would be allowed to sleep two or three to a bed. Others said that they were told that if one of the brothers felt 'moved by natural heat' at the initiation ceremony they might 'call any one of the brethren to their relief and that they ought to relieve their brethren when appealed to under the same circumstances'.

One knight denied the charges of sodomy among the Templars 'because they could have every handsome and elegant woman they liked and that they did have them frequently when they were rich and powerful enough to afford it'.

'On this account,' he admitted, 'other brothers of the order were removed from their houses.'

Other witnesses claimed that Templars deflowered virgins and if a child were born of such a union 'they roasted it and made unguent of its fat and anointed their idol'. Their idol was the figure of Baphomet, which had a goat's head, female breasts and an erect penis.

No matter how unlikely and contradictory this testimony may seem, Clement had the leaders of the Templars burnt at the stake and Philip made off with the order's wealth.

Clement V himself was not without his critics. He was described as 'a public fornicator and kept for his leman'

– or lover – 'the Countess Perigord, a most beautiful lady and daughter of Earl Foix'. Those who sought the Pope's blessing had to lay their petitions on the Countess Perigord's 'silky white bosom'.

It was said that Clement was 'a whore-monger and a patron of whores [who] removed the Papal See to Avignon that he might perpetrate his wickedness with greater privacy'. At Avignon, it was true that the 'Ladies of the Pope's Household' began to play a more important role in papal affairs.

Clement's papal palace in Avignon cost £25,000 a year to run and he spent £3000 a year on food and wine. For those times, this was a vast expenditure. He raised the money to cover his outgoings by taxing the clergy. When a priest was given a living, he had to pay his first year's salary to Clement.

He stopped the ancient custom of allowing the people to loot the property of a dead bishop. The Holy See must substitute itself for the people, he said. So the property of a dead bishop reverted to the Pope.

He also greatly expanded the sin of incest. Couples could not marry if they were related within four degrees – that meant it was incestuous to marry your great-great-grandmother or your third cousin. By expanding incest this way, more people would have to ask, and pay, for dispensations from the Pope if they wanted to wed. The discovery of such a degree of relations in a marriage meant that a couple could divorce, provided they applied to, and paid, the Pope.

There was some opposition to this. In Novara, Dulcinus and Margaret developed a creed which, according to the papal historian Platina, 'allowed men and women to live together and exercise all acts of uncleanness'.

118

Clement immediately declared this a heresy and sent an army to the Alps where the group was hiding. Dulcinus and Margaret were caught and torn to pieces, the bones burnt and scattered to the air.

A dedicated nepotist, Clement made five of his family cardinals. He died at the hands of a monk in Florence, who slipped poison into his chalice at Mass.

John XXII (1316–34) succeeded Clement. Emperor Louis IV deposed him in 1328, but John continued his papacy in Avignon undeterred.

John was one of the Avignon popes who excommunicated fellow clergymen for not paying their taxes. He also had a good line in absolution, for a price, and did an especially brisk trade in incest and sodomy. He was obviously pretty good at absolving himself from sin too, as he created one of his own sons a cardinal.

John also had the brilliant idea of extending the *culla-gium*, or annual sex tax that clergymen had to pay if they wanted to keep a concubine. He made celibate clergymen pay it too, just in case they got lucky and took up with a woman before the year was out.

It was around this time that the laity in Spain demanded that their priests took a female consort before they arrived at a new parish.

When Louis deposed John XXII in 1328, Nicholas V (1328–33) was waiting in the wings. Wed as a youth, he left his wife, Giovanna Mattei, and their children after five years of marriage, to join the Franciscans. His supporters represented him as a saintly ascetic; but his critics characterized him as a hypocrite of doubtful reputation. He was 'famous for the love of liquor'. Although Nicholas V had committed the sin of matrimony, the Emperor Louis sorted that out by paying Giovanna

119

Mattei off. Nicholas V sat in Pisa while John XXII sat in Avignon.

As anti-pope, Nicholas did not have much of a following, so he spent his time amassing wealth by pillaging churches. His standing was hardly enhanced when in 1329, in a bizarre ceremony in the cathedral at Pisa, he put on trial a straw puppet dressed in papal robes, which was said to be John XXII. The straw doll was found guilty, degraded and handed over to the secular authorities for punishment.

When Louis abandoned him, Nicholas left Pisa and tried to patch it up with John XXII. John had promised to treat him like a kind father if he repented, but behind his back, he cursed him. 'May his children be orphans and his wife be a widow,' John said.

However, when Nicholas turned up in Avignon, John did not kill him – well, not straight away. He locked him up in the papal palace, where he died four years later.

This left John XXII to go his own sweet way unopposed. He loved good living and lavished money and high office on his relatives and friends. At a feast to celebrate the marriage of his great-niece, Jeanne de Trian, to Guichard de Poitiers, the guests went through 4012 loaves of bread, 8 oxen, 55 sheep, 8 pigs, 4 boars, a large quantity of different kinds of fish, 200 capons, 690 chickens, 580 partridges, 270 rabbits, 40 plovers, 37 ducks, 50 pigeons, 4 cranes, 2 pheasants, 2 peacocks, 292 small birds, 3 hundredweight of cheese, 3000 eggs, 2000 apples, pears and other fruit. They drank eleven barrels of wine.

Jacques Fournier, who later became John's successor Benedict XII (1334–42), started his career an inquisitor on the Cathar heresy. That meant, essentially, he had to pry into the sex lives of the clergy. In 1320, he began investigating the case of the priest Pierre Clergue, curate of the small village of Montaillou.

The widow of one Pierre Lizier told the Inquisition that, seven years before, Clergue had come to her mother's house during the harvest when she was about fourteen or fifteen. He had proposed sexual intercourse and she had agreed. He deflowered her in the hay in the barn. After that he would come to her mother's house regularly for sex. He did it during the day, so no one would suspect. Her mother found out, but let the arrangement continue. The following January, she married Pierre Lizier, with Curé Clergue presiding. However, this did not curb the priest's amorous antics.

'Over the next four years, the Curé continued to know me carnally with the knowledge and consent of my husband,' she told the future pope. Her husband would even warn her against the attentions of men other than the priest and the affair continued right up to Monsieur Lizier's death.

When the future pope asked whether she thought that having intercourse with a priest displeased God, she replied that she did not think that it was a sin because they both enjoyed it so much.

But Curé Clergue had not stopped at having just one lover. He had a dozen, each of whom he told that he loved more than any other woman in the world. One was a young widow named Beatrice de Planissoles. She told the future pope that the Curé had sent a pupil to her who asked her whether she would sleep with the priest. When she agreed, the boy led her to the local church, St Peter's, where the Curé had made up a bed.

'How can we do such a thing in St Peter's church?' she asked.

'Pity for St Peter,' he replied.

Then they got into bed and made love. At dawn, he escorted her home.

But if breaking the priestly vows of celibacy and desecrating a church were not bad enough, in the eyes of the future pope these sins paled into insignificance beside the real sin – they used some sort of primitive contraceptive device.

When Beatrice had protested that becoming pregnant would be her undoing, Clergue produced some herbs. These were usually used for preventing milk curdling, but he said they would stop her becoming pregnant. He put a bag of these herbs on a cord that hung down between her breasts. When he made love to her for a second time, he would push them up her vagina. When they had finished making love, he would take the bag away, so that she could not make love to any other man without fear of pregnancy. He was particularly jealous because one of Beatrice's other lovers was Clergue's cousin Raymond.

Clergue also said that Beatrice did not have to confess her sins to any other priest. He convinced young Beatrice that God already knew what she was up to and doubtless absolved her.

The future Pope Benedict sent Beatrice to jail for fifteen months for her part in the affair. The priest, Pierre Clergue, turned spy for the Inquisition in order to escape punishment, but he eventually died in jail anyway for other misdemeanours.

Hearing such revelations must have really tested the strength of the future pope's resolve to ignore the temptations of the flesh.

Another priest confessed to the future Benedict XII's Inquisition that after he had gone with a common whore, his face swelled up and he was convinced that he had got leprosy from this unholy communion. Back then in Toulouse, lepers were burnt. Out of fear, he swore he would never have sex with a woman again and instead started abusing the boys in his charge. One complained that the priest had come to his bed every night. When he thought he was asleep, the priest would put himself between the boy's thighs 'as though he was having his way with a woman'. The priest was arrested, destined perhaps for the *Chambre Chauffee*. The future Pope Benedict XII wrote all these cases up and compiled them in loving detail in his *Inquisition Register*.

In office, Benedict XII attracted a lot of criticism. He was accused of being 'a Nero, death to the laity, a viper to the clergy, a liar and a drunkard'. The Renaissance poet Petrarch described him as an unfit and drunken helmsman of the Church. This could have been for personal reasons. Petrarch had a very beautiful sister whom Benedict fancied 'like an old lecher'. Benedict offered Petrarch a cardinal's hat if he could have his sister. The poet stoutly refused. But Benedict 'bought her for a great sum of money from her other brother, Gerhard, for his pastime, whereby it appears, though the popes abhorred lawful wives, they loved unlawful whores'.

Other contemporaries describe Benedict as weak and dissolute. Petrarch says he was laughed at and scorned by his licentious court. He described the scene at Avignon as 'the shame of mankind, a sink of vice, a sewer where is gathered all the filth of the world. There God is held in contempt, money alone is worshipped and the laws of God and man are trampled under foot.

Everything there breathes is a lie: the air, the earth, the houses and above all the bedrooms.'

Petrarch describes the Avignon period as 'the Babylonian Captivity of the Papacy' and paints a picture of extreme corruption and wild debauchery. Avignon was, he says, 'the fortress of anguish, the dwelling-place of wrath, the sink of vice, the sewer of the world, the school of error, the temple of heresy, once Rome, now the false and guilt-ridden Babylon, the forge of lies, the horrible prison, the hall of dung'.

And the poet Alvaro Pelago complained: 'Wolves have become the masters of the Church.'

Matters only got worse. The next Avignon pope, Clement VI (1342–52) said: 'Before me, no one had any idea how to be pope.' His formula was simple. Enjoy the wealth and position the pontificate conferred and be easygoing with those in power. 'If the King of England wants his ass made a bishop,' he quipped, 'he only has to ask.'

Soon afterwards a donkey turned up at a consistory with a sign round its neck which read: 'Please make me a bishop too.' Clement thought this was very funny. He was also amused when a gift turned up with a note saying: 'From the Devil to his brother Clement'.

Clement VI loved to spend money and gave even the greediest petitioner more than he dared ask for. Blessed with the easygoing manners of a *grand seigneur*, he was generous to one and all and showered money, gifts and high office on family and friends. Cardinals clocked up hundreds of rich livings. They surrounded themselves with beautiful 'ladies in waiting' or, if they were so inclined, handsome page boys. Bacchus and Venus, it was said, were more honoured in Avignon than Jesus.

Clement's gorgeous retinue was said to be more like that of a secular prince. He was a great admirer of beauty, especially in women. And his luxurious court was 'home to wine, women, song and priests who cavorted as if their glory consisted not in Christ but in feasting and unchastity', Petrarch said. He jibed that the Pope's horses were shod with gold. In fact, only their bits were golden.

Even the *Catholic Encyclopaedia* admits that Clement was 'a lover of good cheer, of well-appointed banquets, to which ladies were freely admitted'. But it was not just to the dining room that they were admitted. Clement had entered religious orders at the age of ten and was 'much given to women'.

'While he was an archbishop, he did not keep away from women but lived in the manner of young nobles,' wrote a Florentine historian, 'nor did he as Pope try to control himself. Noble ladies had the same access to his chamber as prelates, and among others the Countess of Turenne was so intimate with him that in large part he distributed his favours through her.'

Petrarch describes Clement VI as 'an ecclesiastical Dionysus with his obscene and infamous artifices'. And he says that Avignon in Clement's time was 'swept along in a flood of the most obscene pleasure, an incredible storm of debauch, the most horrid and unprecedented shipwreck of chastity'.

Indeed, prostitutes were so plentiful that Clement started taxing them. The historian Joseph McCabe even unearthed a deed of sale, showing papal officials buying 'a fine new respectable brothel' from a doctor's widow. The deed notes piously that the purchase is being made 'in the name of Our Lord Jesus Christ'.

Clement VI began a period of unbridled papal luxury. He bought in forty different types of gold cloth from Syria, silk from Tuscany and fine linen from Rheims, Paris or Flanders. Fur was considered a luxury and was restricted to knights, pages, squires, gentlemen of the bedchamber and the ladies of the court. Nevertheless Clement VI used up 1080 ermine pelts – 68 for a hood, 430 for a cape, 310 for a mantle, 150 for two more hoods, 64 for yet another hood, 30 for a hat, 80 for a large hood and 88 for birettas or papal capes.

An eyewitness account of a reception given by Cardinal Annibale for Clement VI on the outskirts of Avignon in 1343 gives some idea of the scale of the entertainment.

The pope was led into a room hung from floor to ceiling with tapestries of great richness. The ground was covered with a velvet carpet. The state bed was hung with the finest crimson velvet, lined with white ermine, and covered with cloths of gold and of silk. Four knights and twelve squires of the pope's household waited at table; the knights received from the host a rich belt of silver and a purse worth 25 gold florins; and the squires, a belt and a purse to the value of 12 florins. Fifty squires from Cardinal Annibale's suite assisted the papal knights and squires. The meal consisted of nine courses, each having three dishes, that is a total of twenty-seven dishes. We saw brought in, among other things, a sort of castle containing a huge stag, a boar, kids, hares and rabbits. At the end of the fourth course, the cardinal presented the pope with a white charger, worth 400 florins, and two rings, valued at 150 florins, one set with an enormous sapphire and the other with an equally enormous topaz; and last of all, a nappo worth 100 florins. Each of the sixteen cardinals received a ring set with fine stones, and so did the twenty prelates and the noble laymen. The twelve young clerks of the papal household were each given a belt and a purse worth 25 gold florins; and the twenty-four sergeants at arms, a belt worth three florins. After the fifth course, they brought in a fountain surrounded by a tree and a pillar, flowing with five kinds of wine. The margins of the fountain were decked with peacocks, pheasants, partridges, cranes and other birds. In the interval between the seventh and eighth courses, there was a tournament, which took place in the banqueting hall itself. A concert brought the main part of the feast to a close. At dessert, two trees were brought in; one seemed made of silver, and bore apples, pears, figs, peaches and grapes of gold; the other was laurel, and was decorated with crystallized fruits of many colours.

The wines came from Provence, La Rochelle, Beaune, St Pourçain and the Rhine. After dessert, the master cook danced, together with his thirty assistants. When the pope had retired to his apartments, wines and spices were set before us.

The day ended with singing, dancing, tournaments and a risqué farce which, apparently, the Pope and cardinals found highly diverting. According to Petrarch, an orgy inevitably followed.

Clement bought the town of Avignon for 80,000 gold sovereigns and built a new palace, the Palais Neuf, there. It was said to be the finest and strongest palace in the world, decorated with the best tapestries and silks. The frescos depicting nymphs and satyrs at play which adorned his bedroom can still be seen.

Much of the palace was given over to the Inquisition. Clement was extremely squeamish about what went on there and seldom visited the Salle de Torture. His own favourite room was a small room in the tower, which was furnished with a double divan. It was there he would pass blissful hours with his noble head resting in the lap of the incomparable Cecile, Countess of Turenne.

She was not, however, the only one he entertained there. Clement disported himself naked with his many mistresses between sheets lined with ermine, while victims of the Inquisition, also naked, were tortured to death in the dungeons below him for crimes as trivial as eating meat during Lent.

Every evening, after vespers, Clement VI would hold an audience for women only. But one of his critics stood outside the palace doors and counted the women as they went in and counted them again as they came out. He soon discovered that fewer came out than went in, and drew the obvious conclusion.

Soon the rumour spread that the Pope was entertaining women at night. The gossip reached the ears of the Pope's confessor, who warned Clement that he must give up this practice and live chastely. But Clement replied that he had got accustomed to sleeping with women when he was younger and only continued now on the advice of his doctors.

This answer did not satisfy the cardinals and the papal court began to turn against him. But Clement turned up to an audience one day clutching a little black book. In it, he had written down the names of his predecessors on the papal throne and demonstrated that those who had been lustful and unchaste had ruled the Church better than those who had been sexually continent. He was certainly not discreet with his amorous activities or 'sessions of plenary indulgence' as he called them. But he was generous enough to legitimize his offspring.

Accounts differ on how he reacted when the black death made its appearance at Avignon in 1348. Sixty-two thousand people died between 25 January and 27 April; 1312 in just one day. More than 7000 houses were shut up. All 166 inhabitants were found dead when a Carmelite monastery was broken into.

The first symptom was spitting blood and the victim frequently died within three days. 'Men are infected by touching the sick, but it was not necessary even to touch them,' wrote Boccaccio. 'The danger is the same if one were within range of their words or only cast one's eye upon them.'

Another contemporary wrote: 'The people died without servants and were buried without priests. The father visited not his son, nor the son his father. Charity was dead and hope cast down.'

Some say Clement showed great courage and defended the Jews when they were blamed for the contagion. Others say that he shut himself up in the Palais Neuf and surrounded himself with large fires. If so, this saved him, but three-quarters of the population of Avignon died.

In 1350, he declared an amnesty on sin for all Christians making the pilgrimage to Rome. He may have had an ulterior motive for this as he had so many sins of his own. Everyone agrees that the charges brought by contemporaries about his sexual immorality cannot be explained away. Petrarch particularly attributed the most lascivious remarks to the Pope which leave no doubt about Clement's illicit love affairs and amount to an overwhelming indictment of the morals of Clement VI. 'I speak of things seen, not merely heard,' Petrarch said.

Clement's dissolute lifestyle and the 'whores of the New Babylon' in Avignon were also seen as a possible cause of the plague. By 'permitting the fornication of his priests and giving the possessions of the church to the rich', Clement had attracted divine retribution it was said. The day he died, a lightning bolt hit the Basilica of St Peter's, melting the bells. This was seen as a message from God.

News of Clement's death was greeted with celebration. Everyone was convinced that he was directly on the way to hell. For nine successive days, fifty priests said Mass for the repose of his soul, but it was generally agreed that not even that was enough.

The only way to return to the path of righteousness, it seemed to many, was to return the Holy See to Rome. In 1367, Urban V (1362–70) tried to do just that. As he set off, the crowds, cried out: 'Evil Pope...impious Father, where are you taking your children?' He found Rome in ruins. The Lateran Palace was full of bats and owls. Three years later he returned to Avignon.

In 1377, the nun Catherine of Siena came to beg Gregory XI (1370–78) once again to leave Avignon and return to Rome. Avignon, she thought, was a sink of corruption. 'The stink of the Curia, Holiness, has long reached my city,' she said. 'At the Papal Court, which ought to have been a paradise of virtue, my nostrils were assailed by the odours of Hell.'

The Pope was impressed by her religious ecstasy during communion, but the cardinals feared that, under her influence, they might be forced to close down their salons, where handsome young men, the sons of princes and dukes, came to seek preferment. During Mass, the prelates began pinching or pricking her to see if her trance was genuine. One woman stabbed a needle through Catherine's foot and she had trouble walking for days. But nothing could shake Gregory's favourable impression.

He did as she requested. He upped sticks and started to make his way back to Italy, leaving behind six cardinals who were unwilling to give up their luxurious homes, the good Burgundy wine and the enchanting Provençal women.

When Gregory left his palace at Avignon, his mother tore open her robe to show him the breasts that had suckled him and begged him not to go back to Rome. She was convinced that he would be killed there. He nearly was. Italy was the scene of a bloodbath at the time, courtesy of the soldier Robert of Geneva, who would become Pope Clement VII (1378–94). Gregory retired to Anagni, where he died of exhaustion. He had been back in Italy for less than a year.

This created a new problem. With the Holy See more or less back in Rome, the Romans wanted a Roman pope; but the college of cardinals was now packed with Frenchmen. The best the conclave could come up with was a Neapolitan, Bartolomeo Prignano, Archbishop of Bari. He was an Italian, at least. To hold off the Roman mob until he could reach the city, the cardinals dressed the senile eighty-year-old Roman Cardinal Tibaldeschi in the pontifical robes and presented him to the crowds. Bartolomeo Prignano, who became Urban VI (1378–89), was a bad-tempered drunk. At his coronation feast, he drank eight times as much as any member of the Sacred College, according to the Cardinal of Brittany, abused Cardinal Orsini and had to be restrained from physically assaulting the Cardinal of Limoges. So the cardinals tried to depose him.

The rebellious College was backed by the excommunicated King Charles of Naples, who besieged Urban VI in his castle at Nocera. Rescued by the Genoese, Urban took five rebel cardinals prisoner and had them tortured to death while he tottered about drunkenly, praying.

Born a pauper in the back alleys of Naples, Urban was particularly dismissive of the effete French cardinals. To escape his wrath, they slipped off to Anagni where they declared that Urban VI was not pope. They said they had only elected him because they were afraid of the Roman mob, and elected another pope – Robert of Geneva, who was well known for his ability to decapitate a man with a pike. In 1375, he had led 6000 cavalry and 4000 infantry to subdue Bologna and Florence. His brutality was infamous. In Cesena alone, he had massacred 4500 people. Robert became Clement VII (1378–94). Now there were two popes. This was the beginning of the Great Schism.

The anti-pope Clement VII returned to Avignon, where he fitted in nicely with his predecessors there. Clement was thirty-six when he became pope and 'much given to fleshly pleasure'. He liked to keep it in the family, though. It is said that he chose his favourites and mistress from among his own relatives. He surrounded himself with page boys, whose jackets, it was noted, shrunk from being knee length, as in the time of Clement VI, to mid-buttock 'or even worse'.

Clement VII knew that to hold on to the papacy he needed the backing of earthly princes. He blithely legitimized three of King James V of Scotland's bastards so that they could make a career for themselves in the Church. Clement also sucked up to Charles VI of France who offered to escort him to Rome, but the expedition was postponed when King Ladislas of Sicily backed Urban VI's claim. When Charles VI was injured in a campaign against the Duke of Brittany he temporarily lost his mind and had to be locked up. His sanity partially returned and he returned to the pleasures of his licentious court, but it became clear that his mental problems were cyclical and he and the Queen, Isabeau of Bavaria, could no longer stay together. If he were to turn nasty and murder her while he was no longer in control of his faculties, it could result in war with Germany. A young girl named Odette de Champdivers was found. She was given two manors at Créteil and Bagnolet in exchange for keeping the King company. She discharged her offices faithfully and became known as 'the little Queen'. She also bore the King a daughter, Marguerite. Meanwhile, Queen Isabeau consoled herself secretly with Duke Louis of Orleans.

In October 1389, Urban VI died. He had appointed twenty-six new cardinals who elected one of their number Boniface IX (1389–1404). The new Pope was a murderer who used simony to fill the depleted papal coffers. He also charged for indulgences, the canonization of saints and the authentication of recently discovered religious relics, such as Christ's foreskin which was doing the rounds at the time. It is said that he charged one ducat for every document he signed as Pope – with the exception of the excommunication of his rival, the Avignon anti-pope Clement VII. Much of the money went to his brothers, his 'nephews' and his mother.

Clement's successor in Avignon was Benedict XIII (1394–1417). In 1396, he gave a dispensation for the twenty-nine-year-old Richard II of England to marry Isabella, the seven-year-old daughter of the King of France. At the wedding feast, the tiny bride was carried in on a silken litter. There is a touching account of their last parting in 1399. The King smothered his by then ten-year-old bride with more than forty kisses. Richard was killed, probably murdered, that same year. At fifteen, Isabella turned to the Pope in Rome, Innocent VII (1404–06) for a dispensation to marry Charles d'Orleans. The bridegroom, a count, was just thirteen. Meanwhile the Duke Louis of Orleans applied to Benedict in Avignon because he wanted a dispensation for his daughter to marry the Dauphin. She was just four months old. The granting of papal dispensations provided both Innocent and Benedict with political influence.

In Rome, Innocent was replaced by Gregory XII (1406–15), well known for his large number of 'nephews'. He was elected on the promise that he would heal the schism, but once in office he changed his mind. All but three of his cardinals defected and met with some of Benedict's Avignon cardinals at a council in Pisa in 1409.

The council issued a decree condemning both Benedict XIII in Avignon and Gregory XII in Rome. They elected yet another pope, Alexander V (1406–10). He was a famous glutton who spent half the day eating. There were four hundred liveried servants in the palace, all female. He was generous with the distribution of livings and rode through the streets of Pisa in full papal robes, humbly, on the back of a white donkey.

If having two popes was not confusing enough, now there were three, and wits proposed a new creed: 'I believe in the three holy Catholic Churches.' The three popes, naturally, excommunicated one another. They had their own papal courts, appointed their own cardinals and clergy, issued their own bulls and sold their own indulgences. Each claimed that the other two popes was false and hired spies, assassins and mercenaries to cheat, bribe, betray and kill to try to bring the other two down.

11

Incontinence in Constance

Anti-pope John XXIII (1410–15) began his career as a common pirate and a soldier of fortune. As Baldassare Cossa, he was a Neapolitan of a noble but impoverished family from Ischia. He reversed his family's fortunes by taking to the high seas in the war between Louis II of Anjou and Ladislas of Sicily who was now king of Naples, doing well enough out of the war to buy himself a pardon from Ladislas.

Then, like all good crooks, he went on to study law. He was a student in Bologna, where he became renowned for his gluttony and lechery. After his graduation, the Roman Pope Boniface IX (1389–1404) appointed him papal treasurer. A grasping, ambitious man, he assisted the pope in numerous dubious money-making schemes, including selling papal offices to the highest bidder. Cossa then helped engineer the election of Alexander V, the Pisa pope. In return, Alexander made Cossa cardinal and sent him back to Bologna as papal legate.

Described as an 'unblushing libertine', Cardinal

Cossa kept a household at Bologna which reportedly included 'two hundred maids, wives and widows, with many nuns'. He claimed to have seduced hundreds of women there. Many of the wives who stayed in the Cardinal's palace were later put to death by their jealous husbands or families who felt they had been dishonoured.

Cardinal Cossa taxed prostitutes and gambling houses, as well as bakers, flour millers and wine sellers. He preyed on nobles and, with democratic impartiality, ground down the poor.

'Day after day,' it was said, 'such multitudes of persons of both sexes – strangers as well as Bolognese – were put to death on various charges that the population of Bologna seemed dwindled down to that of a small city.'

Leonardo Aretino, Cossa's secretary during the Cardinal's nine-year rule in Bologna, said that those who survived prospered. Cossa's iron will brought peace and those who remained alive were inclined to co-operate.

Cardinal Cossa was a man with great administrative skill and business acumen, but his spiritual standing, Aretino says, should be 'zero, or minus zero' for he preferred preying to praying. It is also said that he had never been to confession or taken the sacraments and did not believe in the soul's immortality, the resurrection of the dead or, for that matter, God.

Alexander V made the mistake of visiting his protégé in Bologna and died soon after. Not surprisingly, Cossa was accused of poisoning him. It hardly mattered, though. The conclave for the election of his successor was called in Bologna in May 1410. It was surrounded by Cossa's troops. He was amply supplied with money for bribes, if they were needed.

When Cardinal Cossa entered the conclave, he asked for the stole of St Peter to be brought in. 'I will place it upon the man who most deserves it,' he said. When it arrived, he took it and put it on himself.

'I am pope,' he told the other cardinals. No one dared oppose him. Bribery was unnecessary. Without further ado, they crowned one-time pirate Baldassare Cossa John XXIII.

Just one day before his consecration, Cossa became a priest. In those days, it was possible to be a cardinal – a prince of the Church – without taking holy orders. John XXIII was enrolled with much pomp and circumstance. As he was being carried around the streets in triumph, a Jew gave him a copy of the Old Testament. Examining it, he said: 'Your religion is good, but ours is better.' John flung it in the road behind him. Two hundred of his men-at-arms went into the ghetto armed with leather mallets to beat the Jews. Celebrations went on for eight days with feasting, dancing and music.

In the papacy, John XXIII was extravagant. His secretary said that he hacked his way through the papal throne with an axe of gold. Those he could not bribe, he had seduced by the prostitutes that were under his control.

'At dice, he would call upon the devil and in merriment carouse a cup of wine to his devilship,' it was said. It was widely rumoured that he was an atheist. He was also fond of mutilating his cardinals: 'some he deprived of their tongues, some of their fingers, hands and noses.' Sexually, he was fairly depraved too. He was said to have 'had wicked company with two of his own sisters'.

There were still three popes at this time, but John XXIII managed to establish himself in Rome, sidelining

Gregory, only to be forced to withdraw when Ladislas of Naples attacked him.

John XXIII had risen to the papacy by force of arms, but his support within the Church soon dwindled. The cardinals who formed the Council of Pisa that had elected Alexander V represented the main body of Church believers. They thought that they could re-unite the Church under Alexander, but there was certainly no chance of doing that under John XXIII. Gregory XII and Benedict XIII were blameless by comparison. Somehow the three separate strands of the Church government had to be brought back together again.

The man who eventually healed the Great Schism was an extremely unlikely character. His name was Sigismund, a Luxemburger, King of Hungary and the Holy Roman Emperor. An educated man who spoke several languages, he was renowned for his wit. He was also a heavy drinker and found his way in and out of an astonishing number of beds. 'Never was a man less wont to keep his marriage vows,' says one early report of him.

In 1396, when the Turks reached the Danube, he led the Christian forces against them, at the behest of Boniface IX, the Pope of Rome, and survived defeat at the hands of the Sultan of Nicopolis. Later he was deposed and imprisoned in Hungary. After he regained his throne, he nearly died of fever. As part of the cure, he was hung by the heels for twenty-four hours so that the fever would trickle out of his mouth.

His wife, Barbara of Styria, was a famous beauty who was as unfaithful as he was. He never repudiated her, though, accepting that 'those who make the horns must not refuse to wear them'. She was an unbeliever who mocked Christianity and called the afterlife a foolish dream. She found stories of the fasting and penances of virgins martyred for the faith particularly amusing. Pleasure was all there was to life, she said. When Sigismund died, she was asked to observe an appropriate period of chastity, 'like a turtle dove mourning its mate'. She said she thought that doves were stupid birds and she much preferred sparrows.

Sigismund saw that the only way to resolve the Great Schism was to call the three rival popes and all the other interested parties together, which he did in 1414 at the Council of Constance. The city of Constance was chosen because of its generosity to Sigismund on previous visits. He had once publicly thanked the authorities for making the brothels free to his men while he was there.

John XXIII had no choice but to attend the Council of Constance. Since he had been forced out of Rome, he had sought refuge with Sigismund. But he knew what it took to win a fight like this – money. Before the Council, he went back to Bologna where he sold prospective bishoprics and archbishoprics over and over again. He headed for Constance with nearly a million ducats.

Sigismund met him in Milan and accompanied what he knew to be the most dangerous of the three popes across the Tyrolean Alps. On the way, John XXIII – who knew the dangers of his position as well as anybody – was thrown from his cart. Asked if he was hurt, John replied: 'No, I am all right, but this fall is a sinister warning that I should have done better to remain in Bologna.' When he finally looked down on the city of Constance, John said: 'So here is the pit where they catch foxes.'

The Council of Constance was a huge affair. It drew some 2300 princes and knights; 18,000 prelates, priests and theologians; and 80,000 laymen – including 45 gold-smiths and silversmiths, 330 retail merchants, 242 bankers, 75 confectioners, 250 bakers, 70 shoemakers, 48 furriers, 44 apothecaries, 92 blacksmiths, 48 money-changers, 228 tailors, 83 tavern-keepers dispensing Italian wine, 65 heralds at arms or public criers, 346 buffoons, jugglers and tumblers, 306 barbers and 700 prostitutes.

This was an absurdly low number of prostitutes to cater for the number of churchmen present. But the ones listed here are only the ones who had a fixed place of business. Another list mentions 1500 who were working the streets without a fixed abode. There were probably more. Reports show that business was so brisk that some of them saved up enough money to retire.

A contemporary account says of the clergymen who attended the Council: 'The freer they are, the more licentious they are, giving themselves over to all vices. A single woman does not suffice for a canon; and besides the one who lives with them in their home as their wife, they further have a large number of young girls for concubines.'

One business-minded citizen of Constance took advantage of the situation. He sold his wife to the employees of Sigismund's chancery. She fetched 500 ducats, with which he bought a house.

One chronicler, Benedict de Pileo, declared that Venus herself reigned in Constance 'so great is the host of most dainty dames and damsels who surpass the snow in the delicacy of their colouring'.

The poet Oswald von Wolkenstein also attended and wrote:

Women here like angels wooing,
  They have been my heart's undoing,
They possess my dreams at night, jewels rare,
  In their auburn tresses, their blushing faces,
When sorrow trips and leaves no traces.

He also lamented that the money-grubbers took all his money. The local riffraff were kicked out of the town, but still two people were murdered in street brawls and, in all, 263 bodies were fished out of the lake. Churchmen took the opportunity to settle old scores.

With so much sinning going on, and so many foreigners in town, confessionals had to be marked with languages the confessor understood. The Ethiopians were out of luck, though; they were denied absolution because no one understood their tongue.

The grand opening of the Council – delayed by an outbreak of *noli me tangere*, a contagious ulceration of the face which especially attacks the nose – was finally set for 3 November. But with everyone robed and in their place, Pope John feigned illness, so the Council was delayed again. Two days later, on 5 November 1414, it at last got underway.

Despite what he took to be evil omens, John XXIII still felt he was in with a chance. After all, the other two contenders Benedict XIII and Gregory XII had not even dared show their faces in Constance. Many of the clergy who attended the Council were as corrupt as he was, if not so good at it. It was generally accepted that the priests were worse than the people – Chaucer made the comparison of 'a shiten sheperde and a clene sheep'.

In England, the civil authorities even stepped in to try and clean up the Church. In 1414, King Henry V asked the University of Oxford to prepare articles for the reform of the Church. Article 39 began: 'Because the carnal and sinful life of priests today scandalizes the entire church and their public fornications go completely unpunished...' The good gentlemen of Kent had their own, radical, solution for clerical incontinence. They suggested enforced castration as a rite of ordination.

In France, Nicolas de Clemanges, rector of the University of Paris and archdeacon of Bayonne, deplored priests 'softened by an effeminate excess, they then had to satisfy three masters: wantonness, which required the delights of wine, of meat, of sleep, of splendid games, of whores and panders. Pride, which desired tall houses, towers and castles, costly garments, horses bred for speed. Avarice, which had carefully amassed great treasure to pay for these things.' The result, he said, was that 'every stroke of the pen had its price' and a clergy who 'would rather suffer the loss of ten thousand souls than of ten *sols*'. There were twenty sols to the old French *livre.*

De Clemanges also drew attention to a perennial problem in the Church, saying: 'What are the convents of girls today if not execrable houses of Venus?'

John XXIII felt comfortable among the company of such clergymen. He also felt those cardinals who had convened the Council of Pisa were bound to support his claim to the papacy as he was the uncontested successor to their choice Alexander V. Better still, John's arch enemy King Ladislas had died.

In fact, John felt that he was in such a strong position that he could thwart the Council by not attending their meeting. But the proceedings now had a momentum of their own. Delegates had come from thousands of miles.

They were not going to leave Constance without a decision.

He soon learnt that, in a secret session, the Council was planning to expose his vices and impeach him. John moved quickly. He appeared before a general session of the Council and abdicated. But his abdication would only be valid, he said, if the other two popes abdicated too. The Council would be then free to pick a new pope.

Of course, he knew that the Avignon anti-pope Benedict XIII was not going to abdicate. He had stood his ground for twenty years. He had even spent five years imprisoned in Avignon, before escaping in 1403. And he had denounced the abdication of a lawful pope as sinful. So John's abdication was no abdication at all.

But it was a good move, while he retained his backing. However John had fallen out with Sigismund. While remaining superficially polite, John had described Sigismund behind his back as a drunkard, a savage and a fool. Sigismund was more direct. 'You Italians seem to think that you lead the world in knowledge and power,' he said. 'But I call you the dregs of the earth.'

This provoked John to more open hostility. 'Do you imagine that you sit on the same bench as me because you are a Luxemburger?' he asked Sigismund. 'If you were not King of the Romans, you would be sitting at my feet. I only grant you this honour as an Italian, not as a barbarian.'

With that remark, John XXIII overstepped the mark. The Council wanted to see meekness and humility in its popes, not the arrogance of a tyrant. He quickly tried to claw back support by bestowing a Golden Rose, the symbol of papal recognition, on Sigismund. But it was too late. The Pope's character had become the burning issue again.

Reviewing John XXIII's many crimes, Robert Hallum, Bishop of Salisbury, spoke for the vast majority of the Council when he said quite simply that John 'ought to be burnt at the stake'.

When things started going badly against him, John XXIII slipped out of Constance dressed as a groom, with a scarf tied over his mouth and carrying a crossbow. The Pope sought safety at Schaffhausen with his ally Duke Frederick. Sigismund, frightened that John might end up in Avignon multiplying their problems, attacked Frederick, defeating him decisively.

Meanwhile the Council ruled, for the first time, that you could depose a pope 'as you might pluck a sword from a madman'. They insisted that John return to Constance and, with nowhere else to go, he said he would be delighted to.

On 14 May 1415, at the tenth session of the Council of Constance, a truncated list of John's crimes was read out. One commentator wrote: 'Never probably were seventy more awful accusations brought against a man than against the Vicar of Christ. Before the final decree, sixteen of those of the most indescribable depravity were dropped, out of respect not for the pope, but for public decency.' That still left fifty-four. Edward Gibbon wrote in *The Decline and Fall of the Roman Empire*: 'The most scandalous charges were suppressed; the Vicar of Christ was only accused of piracy, murder, rape, sodomy and incest.'

Pope John XXIII was accused of being '...untruthful, addicted to every vice, [he] had led Pope Boniface IX astray, bought his way into the College of Cardinals, cruelly misgoverned Bologna, poisoned Pope Alexander V, believed in neither the resurrection nor in a life to come, was given over to animal pleasures, was a mirror of infamy, a Devil incarnate, fouled the whole Church with simony...' Incest and sodomy were also mentioned, as was 'having hired and maintained a sacrilegious intercourse with three hundred nuns; violated three sisters; and imprisoned a whole family in order to abuse the mother, son and father'. The Council then suspended him from his papal office 'as a murderer, a sodomite, a simoniac and a heretic'. All Christian folk were ordered to withdraw their obedience. He was formally deposed on 29 May. Shortly afterwards he abdicated and handed over the papal seal and fisherman's ring.

Pope John XXIII actually admitted to murder, adultery, incest and atheism. But that did not rule out a continued career in the Church. After three years imprisonment in Bavaria, he bought his freedom for a huge sum and returned to Italy, where he was appointed Cardinal Bishop of Tusculum (now known better as Frascati). Soon after, he was made Dean of the Sacred College and went to live in splendour in Florence courtesy of his friend, the banker Cosimo de'Medici. John died in 1419 and lies in the octagonal baptistry of Florence Cathedral in a tomb designed by Donatello which bears the simple inscription: 'Here lies the body of Baldassare Cossa, John XXIII, who was pope.'

In the twentieth century, there was another Pope John XXIII (1958–63). This was not a mistake. It is common for the Catholic Church to obscure the misdeeds of one pope by giving another one the same name. There have been two Benedict XIIs, two Benedict XIVs, two Clement VIIs and two Clement VIIIs.

146

After the fall of the fifteenth-century John XXIII, Gregory XII got sick of all the wrangling. He re-convened the Council of Constance as pope, then abdicated. In exchange, he was made the Cardinal Bishop of Porto and permanent Legate of the Holy See at Ancona.

And then there was one. Pope Benedict XIII became the only pope of Western Christendom. Sigismund went to visit him and begged him to make a *pro forma* abdication so that the Council could assert its authority and re-elect him, healing the schism. But Benedict refused. He claimed to be a valid pope. He pointed out that he was the only Cardinal still alive who had been appointed before the schism. And as the only legitimate cardinal, no Council on earth had greater power to elect a pope than he did himself.

The Council disagreed. They deposed him and his political support evaporated. Martin V (1417–31) – ironically a supporter of John XXIII – was picked as the next pope.

12

Papal pornography

During the Renaissance, the popes became great patrons of the arts and writing.

Martin V employed the bawdy writer Poggio Bracciolini as his chief secretary, famous for a collection of salacious stories written at his desk in the papal offices. These were circulated in manuscript form. Later they were published and twenty-six editions printed in less than a quarter of a century. When the *Index of Forbidden Books* was begun by Pope Paul IV (1555–59), his work was referred to the censors for expurgation.

Martin V, no prude when it came to a lewd story, loved Bracciolini's work. In a letter to a friend, Bracciolini says the Pope was 'greatly amused' when an abbot told him that he had five sons who would fight for him. It was said at the time: 'Scarcely one priest in every thousand would be found to be chaste: all live in adultery or concubinage or something worse.'

'Something worse' in this context means incest or sodomy. Bracciolini himself admitted having fourteen children but, like most fashionable writers at the time, he wrote openly in praise of sodomy which other, more censorious writers say, 'raged like a moral pestilence in the larger towns of Italy'.

Bracciolini also wrote praising the goings-on in the baths in Baden saying: 'There are nuns, abbots, friars and priests, and they often behave less decently than the others.' Pope Martin V's impressions are not recorded.

Despite his taste in literature, Martin tried to clamp down on clerical immorality. In a letter, he wrote that concubinage, simony, neglect of sacred functions, gambling, drinking, fighting, buffoonery and kindred pursuits were the prevalent vices of the ministers of Christ. The Bishop of Angers agreed. He admitted in 1428, that licentiousness had become so habitual among his clergy that it was no longer considered a sin.

Meanwhile, priests in the fifteenth century condemned from the pulpit the latest décolleté fashion. Women, apparently, were coming to church with their breasts exposed. 'When you come to church, it seems from the pompous, indecent and open-breasted clothing that you are at a ball. When you go to a dance, to a feast, or the baths, dress as you please,' said one clergyman of the period, 'but when you come to church, I beg you, make some difference between the house of God and that of the Devil.'

Others condemned the social mores of the time altogether. 'How rare is shame among men of this century. They do not blush when in public they blaspheme, gamble, steal, take usury, perjure themselves, utter unseemly words, or even sing them. And the women leave their arms, neck and breasts uncovered, and exhibit themselves thus before me in order to excite them to the horrible crimes of adultery, fornication, rape, sacrilege and sodomy.'

A Brother Maillard also spoke out against the fashion, asking: 'And you women, who show your fine breasts, your neck, your throat, would you wish to die in that condition? Tell me, foolish women, do you not have lovers who give you bouquets and do you not, for love of them, place these bouquets on your bosom?' Their punishment, Brother Maillard said, would be the attack of 'a toad which vomited forth torrents of fire'.

At the same time, there was a fashion for men to wear a codpiece that fitted around the virile member like the finger of a glove. 'What is the purpose of that monstrosity that we to this day have fixed to our trousers?' said the essayist Michel de Montaigne. 'And often, which is worse, it is beyond its natural size, through falseness and imposture.'

In England the clergy were still going their own sweet way. In the parish of St John Zachary in London, a brothel opened that catered exclusively for friars and priests. You had to be tonsured to get in. No doubt the ladies working there felt they had a special calling.

Martin V's successor, Eugene IV (1431–47) was deposed by the anti-pope Felix V (1439–49). Felix was not even a priest before his election. He was Duke of Savoy, though he abdicated his dukedom when he became pope. As Duke Amadeus VIII, he was married with two sons, but the death of his wife and his older son deeply affected him and he withdrew to govern an order of knights-hermit near Thonon, on Lake Geneva, leaving the administration of the duchy to his surviving son Lodovico.

Although his papacy made little impact outside Savoy,

he employed Enea Silvio Piccolomini as his secretary. Piccolomini was another literary figure of the day who specialized in pornographic subjects. Felix V abdicated in 1449 in favour of the new Roman pope Nicholas V (1447–55) and was rewarded with the post of Cardinal Bishop of St Sabina and a substantial pension. He was also appointed papal legate to Savoy, where he had once been duke.

Once in office, Nicholas V gave more than £1000 to the poet Francesco Filelfo for writing a book of stories described as 'the most nauseous compositions that coarse spite and filthy fancy ever spawned'. But Nicholas liked his work, paid Filelfo well and employed him regularly.

Around the same period the writer Lorenzo Valle wrote an essay called 'On Pleasure', which scorned the very idea of chastity. But he did not get into trouble with the papacy until he attacked the Church directly.

In fact, between 1400 and 1550, many Italian writers, some of them cardinals and many employed by the popes wrote poems, stories and comedies 'as advanced sexually as you will find in any literature of the world,' according to historian Joseph McCabe. It was not just cardinals and writers employed by the popes who wrote these earthy classics. One well-known erotic author actually got to sit on St Peter's chair.

Pius II (1458–64), before he became Pope, had been the aforementioned lewd writer Enea Silvio Piccolomini. He was a man of the world. His father, Silvio Piccolomini, was a soldier. His mother, Vittoria, was said to be so fruitful that she often bore twins. She had eighteen children in all, though there were never more than ten alive at the same time. Enea was born in 1405 and brought up in poverty in the town of Corsignano, in the valley of the Orcia. When he was still a child, the town was hit by plague which wiped out most of his siblings. Only Enea and his two sisters Laodamia and Catherina survived.

Enea was an accident-prone child. At the age of three, he fell off a high wall on to a rock. At eight, he was tossed by a bull and escaped death, he says, 'more by the help of Heaven than through any human aid'. Nevertheless he showed more than just a talent for survival.

At eighteen, he went to Siena and Florence to study poetry and oratory, but a war between the two cities forced him to give up his literary studies. Loath to re-turned to small-town Corsignano, he took a job as the private secretary of Bartolommeo Visconti, Bishop of Novara. This soon gave him an insight into the workings of the medieval Church. After a five-day visit to his uncle Niccolo Piccinino, a distinguished general, he returned to discover that Bartolommeo had been accused on 'grave offences' in his absence and was on trial for his life.

Enea took another job with Cardinal Niccolo of Santa Croce and began honing his writing skills. He became the Cardinal's roving ambassador and travelled to Scotland. 'The women there are fair, charming and easily won,' he wrote. 'They think less of a kiss than a touch of the hand in Italy.' Indeed, they were so easily won that he sired a boy-child by a Scottish lass. To his deep distress, the baby died.

Travelling on to England, he was stranded with his two servants, a guide and a hundred women. Two of the young women took him to a chamber strewn with straw, 'planning to sleep with him if they were asked, as was the custom of the country,' Pope Pius says in his *Secret*

Memoirs, which he writes in the third person. But he stoutly 'repulsed the girls' fearing that, if he made love to them, he would forget to watch out for robbers. Later, there was a barking of dogs and a hissing of geese. The women scattered as if attacked by an enemy, but no robbers appeared. Pius thought that this was the reward for his continence. Well, that was the story he told in the memoirs.

Back in Italy he became more hot-blooded. In Naples, he fell under the spell of the 'divine' Lucrezia di Alagno – 'a beautiful woman or girl, the daughter of poor but noble Neapolitan parents (if there is any nobility in poverty),' he says. Unfortunately King Alfonso of Naples was desperately in love with her. 'In her presence he was beside himself and could neither hear nor see anything but Lucrezia. He could not take his eyes off her, praised everything she said, marvelled at her wisdom. He had given her many presents, had given orders that she was to receive the honours of a queen, and at last was so completely dominated by her that no one could get a hearing without her consent.'

'Marvellous, the power of love,' comments Pius.

Lucrezia promised Enea that she would not have sex with the king. 'Never with my consent shall the king ravish my maidenhood,' she told him. 'But if he should attempt force, I shall not imitate Lucretia, the wife of Collatinus, who endured the outrage and then took her own life. I will anticipate the outrage by my death.'

But noble acts are not so easy as noble words, reflects Pius in his memoirs, 'nor did her afterlife bear out her protestations'. After Alfonso's death she defected to the camp of the Piccinino's where she became the mistress of a certain secretary and had a child by him. Later

Lucrezia turned up in Rome. But while many of the cardinals flocked to see her. Only the broke-hearted Enea stayed away.

On the last page of his *Secret Memoirs*, Pius mentions ruefully that Lucrezia had eloped to Dalmatia with her latest lover. He was never to see her again. Enea continued his career as a diplomat, becoming secretary to the anti-pope Felix V. He was sent to Strasbourg in early February 1442. Although nearing forty he still possessed the passion of youth and 'grew hot and burned for a woman there'. She was a Breton named Elizabeth, married with a five-year-old daughter. She was charming, witty and vivacious. He was lonely and he fell head over heels in love with her. Her husband was away briefly on business and Enea begged her to go to bed with him. She resisted him stoutly for three days, but on 13 February, the night before she was to leave to join her husband, she left her door unbolted. Enea was overjoyed when he later heard that Elizabeth had conceived. Their son was born on 13 November 1442.

Enea, delighted by this, wrote to tell his father, but his father must have been less than enthusiastic about the news, for Enea wrote to him again, saying:

You write that you do not know whether to be glad or sorry, Father, that the Lord has given me a child... But I see only cause for gladness and none for sorrow. For what is sweeter to mankind than to beget in one's own likeness, and, as it were, continue one's stock and leave something after one's own death. What on earth is more blessed than to see your children's children? For my part, I am delighted that my seed has borne fruit and that some part of me will survive when I die: and I thank God who has made this woman's child a boy, so that another

*little Enea will play about my father and mother, and give to his
grandparents the comfort which his father should have supplied.
For if my birth was a pleasure to you, who begat me, why should
not my son be a joy to me? But perhaps you will say it is my
offence you mourn, because I have begotten a child in sin. I do
not know what idea you have of me. Certainly you, who are
flesh, did not beget a son of stone or iron. You know what a cock
you were and I am no eunuch, nor to be put in the category of
cold-blooded. Nor yet am I a hypocrite who wants to seem better
than he is. I firmly confess my error, for I am no holier than
David the King, nor wiser than Solomon.*

Enea was to see Elizabeth again in Basel, but the child
died at the age of fourteen months, robbing the Church
of a future cardinal, no doubt. Enea never saw the child.

Enea moved on to the Diet of Frankfurt, where King
Frederick III of Germany noticed his astonishing oratory
and literary skills and crowned him poet laureate. So
Enea quit Felix's service and indulged himself in the
more 'humanist' atmosphere of Frederick's court. He
was especially close to Frederick's chancellor, Caspar
Schlick. Enea's widely read pornographic novel, *Lucretia
and Euryalus,* is based on Schlick's amorous adventures.
Later, Enea achieved even greater literary fame for his
erotic comedy *Chrysis.*

Enea Piccolomini was one of a number of quite unrestrained writers of the fifteenth century, who in their
frequent quarrels, accused each other of homosexual
practices although they often championed homosexuality in their work. During his time in Frederick's court,
the future Pius II certainly practised what he preached.
His letters show that he advocated and enjoyed total
sexual freedom, fathering at least two more bastards.

The historian Gregorovius claims he fathered twelve illegitimate children in all.

The Emperor Frederick sent him as ambassador to Rome to try to effect a reconciliation with Pope Eugene IV (1431–47). And there, as a means of advancement, he took holy orders. When he was ordained a deacon, he spoke to a friend of his worries about giving up his former licentious ways for a life of chastity. 'I do not deny my past,' he said. 'I have been a great wanderer from what is right, but at least I know it and hope that the knowledge has not come too late.'

Not that the burden of clerical celibacy was necessarily onerous at that time. In 1432, a General Council was called in Basel, which demanded that 'all priests from the highest or lowest rank shall put away their concubines, and whoever within two months of this decree neglects its demands shall be deprived of office, though he be the Bishop of Rome'.

Although it is not recorded whether the Bishop of Rome at that time, Eugene IV, had any concubines, he did not react well to this proclamation and convened his own Council in Florence. It decried the Council of Basel as 'a beggarly mob, mere vulgar fellows from the lowest dregs of the clergy, apostates, blaspheming rebels, men guilty of sacrilege, jailbirds, men who without exception deserve only to be hunted back to the devil whence they came'. Plainly the Council of Basel had touched a raw nerve.

Enea had not given up the literary life completely. He retired to the baths at Viterbo, where he began his *History of Bohemia.* Two years after becoming a priest, he was appointed bishop; from there, his ascent to the papacy was effortless.

However, on reaching the papal chair, he had to recant the erotic works of his youth and did as much as he could to conceal his literary past, which is hardly mentioned at all in his *Secret Memoirs*.

'Reject Enea and accept Pius,' he wrote on his coronation. But, although he was reformed, he did not entirely forget that he had once been a lecherous youth. During an uprising against his papacy, a gang of about three hundred young men went on a rampage of rape in Rome. One of them kidnapped and raped a girl on the way to her wedding. When order was restored, Cardinal Tebaldo demanded that men guilty of 'such atrocious crimes' should be tortured before they were put to death. Pius intervened. Death was punishment enough, he said, and he wept from pity when they were hanged.

Pius II allowed his nephew to marry the illegitimate daughter of Ferrante, son of King Alfonso, but this was a purely political move. The crown of Naples was dominant in Italy and the marriage gained the young boy princely status.

He also seems to have taken rather a shine to Queen Charlotte of Cyprus, who threw herself on his mercy after her throne had been seized by her illegitimate half-brother. In his *Memoirs*, Pius talks of her 'sparkling eyes' and her extraordinary complexion 'between blonde and brunette'. She was, he says, 'not without charm', then recounts lovingly how she kissed his feet. Politically, Charlotte of Cyprus got everything she asked for from Pius II.

Pius was certainly not happy about being celibate. He said that matrimony had been forbidden to priests for good reasons, but there were much better reasons to restore it. It would be much better for priests to marry, he wrote, since many of them would probably be saved in the conjugal state, which he hardly thought possible in celibacy. This was at a time when many local people would not accept a curate unless he came with a concubine – they were afraid that otherwise he would debauch their wives.

As if to highlight the problem, Pius II had to dissolve the nunneries of St Bridget and St Clara, 'lest the nuns should harbour under religious habits lascivious hearts'. But he had a harder time cleaning up Rome – the only city in the world to be run by bastards, he said. The bastards were, of course, the illegitimate children of the senior clergy.

13

Our ladies

Pius II used to call Cardinal Pietro Barbo of St Marco – his successor – 'godly Mary' as a joke. Barbo, the future Paul II (1464–71) liked to see naked men being racked and tortured.

He was gay and wore a papal tiara that, according to one source, 'outweighed a palace in its worth'. He plundered the papal treasury to satisfy his love of glitter and finery. Handsome and vain, he loved to be surrounded by beauty and splendour. He would sleep during the day and spend the night looking over his jewels and precious stones. He also loved a party and promoted sports, entertainments and carnivals in Rome, at the expense of the city's Jews who were forced to stump up the money.

Known to his cardinals as 'Our Lady of Pity', he would burst into tears at the slightest provocation. Paul II allegedly died of a heart attack while being sodomized by one of his favourite boys.

The election of Paul's successor Sixtus IV (1471–84) was secured by lavish gifts to the influential Duke of

Milan. He was renowned as a 'bountiful benefactor towards whores'. To pay for his war against the Turks, he built a noble 'lupanar' or brothel-house in Rome for both sexes. And every whore in Rome paid him a Julius – a silver coin worth around 2 ½ p – 'which amounted yearly to four hundred ducats'. Other sources put his income higher, saying that courtesans paid him 'every week a Julio of gold and made an annual revenue of 26,000 ducats'.

Sixtus IV also 'devoted all his care and solicitude to increasing his own riches'. He increased taxes, including the one on priests who kept mistresses, and he found a new source of income – selling rich men privileges to 'solace certain matrons in the absence of their husbands'.

Sixtus was bisexual and very probably engaged in incest. He made six of his close relations, 'nephews' or illegitimate sons, cardinals. Two of his beautiful young nephews, Pietro Riario – said to be Sixtus's son by his own sister – and Giuliano della Rovere were also 'the instruments of his infamous pleasure'. By all accounts Riario was charming and witty, and Sixtus made him a millionaire by plundering the papal treasury. But in 1474, Riario 'succumbed to his dissipations'. Giuliano went on to become Pope Julius II (1503–13).

Sixtus did not keep his pleasures to himself. According to one chronicler of the age: 'The following most execrable act was alone sufficient to render the memory of Sixtus IV forever infamous: the family of the Cardinal of St Lucia having presented to him a request to be permitted to commit sodomy during the three hot months of the year – June, July and August – the pope wrote on the bottom of the petition: "Let it be done as requested".'

After the death of Pietro Riario, his place was taken by his brother Giulamo, who dragged the Pope into a conspiracy against Lorenzo and Giuliano de'Medici. He sent another brother, Raphael Riario, to Florence to organize their assassination. During a solemn mass in Florence Cathedral, and at the moment when the cardinal was raising the host, the conspirators stabbed Giuliano de'Medici with their poniards. Lorenzo defended himself courageously and succeeded, though wounded, in reaching the sacristy. Meanwhile, the congregation turned on the conspirators, disarmed them and hanged them naked at the church windows. This started a pointless war between the papacy and Florence, which plunged the whole of Italy into a bloodbath.

Sodomy, whoremongering and ill-advised acts of violence did not take up all the Pope's time. Sixtus also found a moment to sanctify the erotic and blasphemous vision of a monk named Alano de Rupe. A version of the vision published in Germany at the time says: 'Upon a time the ever-blessed Virgin Mary entering the cell of Alano de Rupe, being locked, she took a hair of his head and made a ring, with which she espoused the father, and made him to kiss her and handle her breasts, and, in a word, grew in a short time as familiar with him as women used to be with their husbands.'

Sixtus is, of course, best known for the building of the Sistine Chapel, where popes are now crowned, but he also left a rather less civilized legacy. In 1478, he issued the papal bull sanctioning the Inquisition in Castile and he appointed the infamous Torquemada as its Inquisitor General. In no time Torquemada got to work. In 1482, the Spanish Inquisition burnt 2000 'heretics' in Andalusia alone – enemies of the Church were burnt because it neatly got round the biblical injunction against shedding blood.

The prosecution of a typical case was described in Henry Charles Lea's classic *History of the Inquisition of Spain.* He tells of a young pregnant woman named Elvira del Campo arrested for being a 'crypto-Jewess'. She had a baby in jail before being brought before the Tribunal of Toledo the following year.

The witnesses against her were two workmen who lodged in her house. They said that she did not eat pork and changed her underclothes on a Saturday. For reporting such suspicious behaviour to the Inquisition, they were rewarded with three years' indulgence.

Elvira protested her innocence. She was a Christian. Her husband was a Christian. Her father was a Christian but, it seems, her mother had some Jewish ancestry. From the time she was eleven, she simply took against pork. When she tried to eat it, it made her sick. Her mother had taught her to change her underclothes on a Saturday, but she saw no religious significance in it.

The Tribunal warned her that she would be tortured if she did not tell the truth. She had nothing to add to the story. She was stripped naked and her arms bound. The cord was twisted until she screamed that they were breaking her arms. On the sixteenth turn, it snapped.

Then she was tied down on a table with sharpened bars running across it. The ropes tying her were tightened again. In agony and desperation, she cried out admitting that she had broken the law.

'What law?' she was asked.

When she could not come up with the details of which

of God's laws she had broken, a piece of cloth was rammed down her throat with a rod and the water torture began. When it was over, she was unable to speak, so the torture was suspended for four days, during which time she was kept in solitary confinement.

When the next session began, all she could do was beg for her nakedness to be covered before she broke down completely.

Eventually, she admitted that she was Jewish and begged for mercy. And the judges were merciful. They confiscated her property and sentenced her to a further three years in jail. She was released after six months, having gone insane. There is no record of what happened to her child.

The Spanish Inquisition was treating hapless victims this way – and far worse – for over three centuries. It was still going about its gruesome business in 1808, when Napoleon invaded. Under the Dominican monastery in Madrid, the French found torture chambers full of prisoners, all naked and mostly insane. This turned the stomachs of even the battle-hardened French troops. They evacuated the dungeons and blew the monastery up.

Even that was not the end of the Inquisition in Spain. It was eventually suppressed in 1813, but continued its work in other countries for another twenty years.

Beginning the Spanish Inquisition was a heinous crime. Bishop Creighton said simply of Sixtus that: 'He lowered the moral tone of Europe.'

Another commentator was less mealy mouthed. Pope Sixtus, he said, 'embodied the utmost possible concentration of human wickedness'.

Sixtus was not even popular in Rome. When he died

the papal apartments were so thoroughly ransacked that Sixtus's chaplain had to borrow a cassock to cover the Pope's corpse.

His successor, Innocent VIII (1484–92), was not innocent at all. It was said that 'his private life was darkened by the most scandalous proceedings. Having been educated among the people of King Alfonso of Sicily, he had contracted the frightful vice of sodomy. His uncommon beauty had introduced him, in Rome, into the family of Philip, Cardinal of Bologna, to serve his pleasures; and after the death of his protector, he became the favourite of Paul II and Sixtus IV, who created him cardinal.'

Both these popes were gay. However, there was no clear distinction between straight and gay at that time. It was not uncommon for men who were basically heterosexual to use homosexual liaisons to advance their careers. Nor was it odd for those homosexually inclined to father numerous children.

Innocent had 'eight bastard sons and as many bastard daughters'. A poem written in Latin about him goes:

> He begot eight sons, with as many daughters;
> And Rome might with good reason call him father.
> But, oh Innocent VIII, wherever you lie buried,
>   Filthiness, gluttony, covetousness and sloth will lie with thee.

It loses something in the translation, but the sentiment is still there.

Unlike most other popes, Innocent VIII openly acknowledged his illegitimate children at court. He baptised them, officiated at their weddings and found suitable jobs for them. His reign was known as the 'Golden Age of Bastards'. His sons and daughters, critics said, 'he raised to riches and honour without a blush, being the first pope that had dared so to do publicly without any previous pretence of their being nephews, nieces or the like.'

When he was made a cardinal by Sixtus IV, he offered his children for marriage to princely houses. One of them married Maddalena, the daughter of Lorenzo de'Medici. Having survived the assassination attempt in Florence Cathedral, Lorenzo was determined that such a thing would never happen again. He backed Innocent, his father-in-law, for the papacy and, in office, Innocent did whatever Medici told him. The year after Innocent became pope at the age of fifty-two, he saw his granddaughter Peretta married in the Vatican with full papal pomp. At the wedding breakfast, in the papal apartments, his daughters and their mother were present. Later, his second granddaughter was married off in similar splendour to a Neapolitan prince. Catholic historians say Innocent gave up his mistress when he became pope, but it was widely rumoured that he kept on a few concubines. 'His Holiness rises from the bed of harlots,' it was said, 'to bolt and unbolt the gates of purgatory and heaven.'

The Pope also tolerated the excesses of his son Franceschetto, who was an 'unbridled rake'. One day Franceschetto complained to his father that Cardinal Riario had cheated him out of £50,000 the night before when they were gambling. Instead of chastising his son, the Pope made Cardinal Riario give his winnings back.

But gambling was the least of Franceschetto's sins. He would roam the streets at night breaking into people's houses and raping any woman that took his fancy without a single word of censure from his father.

Innocent had another ward on his hands – Djem, the younger brother of the Ottoman Sultan Bayezid II. The Sultan paid the Pope 40,000 ducats (£60,000) a year and the Holy Lance, which is supposed to have pierced Christ's side during the crucifixion, to keep Djem in 'every luxury and the instruments of vice'. Djem had been driven from Constantinople and, thus distracted, he would be unlikely to return to Turkey to oppose Bayezid.

Innocent's court, like Sixtus's, was as colourful and loose as any Italian prince's and his cardinals, mostly Sixtus's creations, were worldly *grand seigneurs*. The Church was little better. In 1489, Morton, Archbishop of Canterbury, visited the abbey at St Albans to find that the monks had turned out the nuns and had filled their quarters with prostitutes to which they were 'publicly resorting, indulging in all manner of shameless and riotous living'. The place, he said, was 'a riot of seed and blood'. It was suggested to Innocent that he might have another try at stopping priests having mistresses. Innocent replied that it was a waste of time. 'It is so widespread among priests, even among the Curia, you will hardly find one without his concubine.'

On the papal throne, Innocent VIII 'gave himself up to idleness and pleasure, which are wont to be attended by vanity, pomp, profuseness, gluttony, luxury and like vices and sins.'

He was very fond of money and condemned eight men and six women as heretics because they said that the Pope, as the Vicar of Christ, should 'imitate him in his poverty'. He also issued an edict expelling from Spain all Jews who would not convert to Christianity. A hundred thousand left, but as many stayed. Unconvinced that they had truly converted, the Spanish Inquisition set about putting their faith to the test in the most bloodthirsty fashion.

In his dissipation, Innocent VIII also became very concerned about the outbreak of witchcraft that seemed to be engulfing Christendom. He wrote a papal bull which said:

> *Men and women straying from the Catholic faith have abandoned themselves to devils,* incubi *and* succubi *[male and female demons who have sex with people while they are asleep] and by incantations, spells, conjurations, and other accursed offences, have slain infants yet in the mother's womb, as also the offspring of cattle, have blasted the produce of the earth...they hinder men from performing the sexual act and women from conceiving, whence husbands cannot know their wives nor wives receive their husbands.*

This Bull appeared as the preface to a book called - *Malleus Maleficarum [The Witches' Hammer]*, a handbook for the discovery and punishment of witches. It was written by Heinrich Krammer and James Sprenger, two Dominican monks to whom Innocent VIII personally gave supreme authority as inquisitors. Krammer and Sprenger were particularly interested in copulation with Satan. This was not uncommon according to Sprenger.

'A woman is carnal lust personified,' he wrote. 'If a woman cannot get a man, she will consort with the devil himself.' Sprenger himself did not like women much. 'I would rather have a lion or a dragon loose in my house than a woman.'

He was much more concerned with the male sexual organ, for theological reasons, of course – 'the power of the devil lies in the privy parts of men,' he wrote. And these parts must be protected, especially by Dominicans. *The Witches' Hammer* reports a story related by a Dominican Father. 'One day,' he says,

> *while I was hearing confessions, a young man came to me and, in the course of his confession, woefully said that he had lost his member. Being astonished at this, and not being willing to give it credence easily...I obtained proof of it when I saw nothing, on the young man's removing his clothes and showing the place. Then, using the wisest counsel, I asked him whether he suspected anyone of having so bewitched him. And the young man said that he did suspect someone but that she was absent and living in Worms. Then I said: 'I advise you to go to her as soon as possible and try your utmost to soften her with gentle words and promises.' And he did so. For he came back after a few days and thanked me, saying that he was whole and had recovered everything. And I believed his words, but again proved them by the evidence of my own eyes.*

Men losing their penises, apparently, was not an uncommon phenomenon during the papacy of Innocent VIII.

> *Witches...collect male organs in great numbers, as many as twenty or thirty members together, and put them in a bird's nest, or shut them up in a box, where they move themselves like living members, and eat oats and corn... It is all done by devil's work and illusion... For a certain man tells me that, when he lost his member, he approached a known witch to ask her to restore it to him. She told the afflicted man to climb a certain tree and take that which he liked out of a nest in which there were several members. And when he tried to take a big one, the witch said: 'You must not take that'; adding, 'because it belongs to the parish priest.'*

With Innocent's blessing these two witch-finders set about their work. They 'traversed the land, leaving behind them a trail of blood and fire', but the regular sadistic fare of stripping, flogging, racking and thumbscrews which Krammer and Sprenger used was not considered 'real torture'. For that you had to turn to the *Tariff of Torture*, drawn up by the Archbishop of Cologne during Innocent's pontificate. He, thoughtfully, laid out a list of charges that the victim's family would have to pay the papal torturers. These included separate charges for squeezing thumbs, toes and legs in vices. It cost five times as much, for example, to have a victim's tongue cut out and red-hot lead poured in their mouth than to have a straightforward whipping. It is not recorded what happened to those who did not pay, but the tariff certainly gave a witch an incentive to own up before she bankrupted her relatives. And if she confessed straightaway, she would be strangled before she was burnt.

Under torture, of course, hapless women victims told these two perverted Dominicans anything they wanted to hear. Not surprisingly, there was a high sexual content to their confessions. Kramer and Sprenger particularly liked stories about orgies and black masses. One of the key tricks, *The Witches' Hammer* advises all would-be witch-finders, was to promise their victims a minor penance if they confessed, give them a minor penance and then burn them. Another recommended ploy was to promise a witch a pardon if she gave the names of other witches, then get another inquisitor to condemn her. These were serious misogynists.

That such things were going on throughout Christendom did not worry Pope Innocent VIII in the least. Languishing on his death bed, he craved only one thing for nourishment - woman's milk. A wet nurse was found. Perhaps, like Casanova, what he really wanted was the comfort of the breast before he went to meet his maker. In a last ditch attempt to keep him alive, Innocent's chaplain Johann Buchard paid three youths to give their blood for a transfusion. All three died during the operation and Buchard prised the money out of their hands before their bodies were disposed of.

Innocent VIII paved the way for the Borgias. He made Cesare Borgia a bishop at the age of eighteen and let his cardinals strut around Rome dressed as soldiers or cavaliers, wearing plumed hats and brightly coloured jackets. He also made the fourteen-year-old son of his patron Lorenzo de'Medici a cardinal. He went on to become the gay Pope Leo X (1513–21).

14

A Borgia orgy tonight

*T*he Spanish pope Alexander VI (1492–1503) was born Rodrigo de Borja y Borja in Játiva, near Valencia, on 1 January 1431. Borgia was the Italian spelling of his name. Rodrigo was probably the illegitimate son of his maternal uncle Alfonso de Borja, Archbishop of Valencia, who went on to become Callistus III (1455–58), by his sister Joanna. She was married to Geoffrey Lenzuolo, but the Pope wanted his son to have his name and forced his brother-in-law to give up his own surname and take the name of Borja, or Borgia.

Rodrigo was spoilt from birth. He was reputed to have committed his first murder when he was twelve. A chronicler recorded:

As Rodrigo grew in years, so he also grew in pride and haughtiness, cruelty and tyranny, showing himself stern, implacable, vindictive and unpredictable in his actions. It is said that when only twelve years old, he killed another boy in Valencia – his equal in age, but of low birth – by driving his scabbard again and again into his belly, to punish him for having uttered some indecent words. This was the first test of his pride, and the first incident that forced people to recognize the stuff he was made of, the kind of spirit and temper he had.

As a youth, Rodrigo was also notoriously promiscuous. He had numerous mistresses and at least six illegitimate sons in Spain. Not a bad start if you wanted to be a Renaissance pope.

As a youth he was said to have been handsome, tall and strong, with penetrating eyes. By the time he was Pope he was ugly and fat, but women were still impressed by his charm and intellect, and his eye for pretty women did not fade, even in old age.

In Spain, he was educated by the best professors. 'He is of aspiring mind,' a contemporary wrote, 'of ready and vigorous speech, of crafty nature but above all of admirable intellect where action is concerned.'

The newly elected Pope Callistus brought the young Rodrigo to Italy to study law in Bologna, like his rival in iniquity John XXIII. His tutor in Bologna, Gaspare de Verona, also described the young Rodrigo:

He is handsome; with a most cheerful countenance and genial bearing. He is gifted with a honeyed and choice eloquence. Beautiful women are attracted to love him and are excited by him in a quite remarkable way, more powerfully than an iron is attracted by a magnet.

Callistus was considered a pious and austere man, but he nevertheless appointed two of his 'nephews' cardinals. One of them was Rodrigo. He also installed Rodrigo as Archbishop of Valencia – his own former See – in 1456, when Rodrigo was just twenty-five. Valencia was the wealthiest See in Spain at that time and this appointment marked the beginnings of the Borgias' great wealth.

Rodrigo enjoyed the trappings of wealth and power that Valencia gave him so much that he scandalized the Church and embarrassed his uncle even in those free-wheeling times. He had a large number of illegitimate children during his career as a churchman – so many that it is not possible to put together an accurate record.

Around this time he met a Spanish widow of astonishing beauty. After seducing her, he also ravished her two daughters and 'initiated them into the most hideous voluptuousness'. Soon after, the mother died. Rodrigo forced the elder daughter to join a convent and kept the younger, more appealing one with him. She gave him three children whom he acknowledged – Pedro Luis, born in 1462, and two girls, Isabella and Girolama, in 1467 and 1471. Isabella's great-great-grand-son became Pope Innocent X (1644-55).

Through his uncle Callistus, Rodrigo picked up a string of bishoprics and abbeys and, in 1457, became vice-chancellor of the Holy See. This was a particularly lucrative office, which he held under the next four popes. It made him a conspicuously wealthy man. The salary alone was 12,000 crowns a year – on top of the 30,000 ducats he already got from the papal estates, plus the lucrative Church offices he had to sell.

In Rome, Rodrigo took advantage of his good looks and was notorious for his voracious sexual appetite, cutting a swathe through the willing matrons of Rome.

When Callistus died, Rodrigo expected to succeed him. But the Church was not ready for him just yet. The pornographer Pius II was elected instead, acceding to the papacy with the words: 'I renounce the frivolity of humanism, and take on the burden of the Church.' One of the great burdens he had to take on was his vice-chancellor Rodrigo Borgia. When the papal court met with the secular princes at Mantua, an eyewitness to the event wrote: 'The vice-chancellor is twenty-five [in fact, he was twenty-eight] and looks capable of every wickedness; when he goes to the pope's court he is accompanied by 200 or 250 horses and great pomp.'

Rodrigo stayed with the Marchesa of Mantua, who shared his passion for hunting and for sport. He also entertained himself with the stunning wife of a dim-witted nobleman. Pius II, now a reformed character, was outraged by the behaviour of his prelates. He withdrew to Siena where he condemned their immorality.

You do not preserve the dignity and sanctity belonging to this eminence. Judging from the manner of your life, you seem not to have chosen to govern the state of the Church, but to enjoy pleasure. You do not abstain from hunting or games, or from intercourse with women; you give dinners of unseemly magnificence; you wear costly clothes; you have an abundance of gold and silver plate, and you keep more horses and servants than any man can need.

But Rodrigo took no notice. After Pius left Siena, he and the ageing Cardinal Estouteville disported themselves in a most licentious way at a christening party held in a Sienese garden on 7 June 1460. After the baptism, at which the two Cardinals were honoured guests, the party adjourned to a walled garden, where only the Cardinals, their servants and the ladies were admitted. Men – the husbands, fathers, brothers and other male kin – were specifically excluded and soon all Italy was buzzing with gossip.

On 11 June, Pius sent Rodrigo a severe reprimand:

Beloved Son: We have learned that your worthiness, forgetful of the high office with which you are invested, was present from the 17th to the 22nd hour, four days ago, in the gardens of Giovanni de Bichi, where there were several women of Siena, women wholly given over to worldly vanities. Your companion was one of your colleagues, whose years, if not the dignity of his office, ought to have reminded him of his duty. We have heard that the dance was indulged in, in all wantonness; none of the allurements to love were spared, and you behaved yourself as if you were one of a group of young laymen. In order that your lust might be all the more unrestrained, the husbands, fathers, brothers, kinsmen of the young girls were not invited; you and a few servants were the leaders and inspirers of this orgy. It is said that nothing is now talked of in Siena but your vanity, which is the subject of universal ridicule. Certainly, here at the baths, your name is on everyone's tongue. Our displeasure is beyond words.

This was no isolated incident. Pius II also had cause to ask Rodrigo whether it was consistent with his position as Cardinal 'to court young women, to give those who you love presents of fruit and wine, and to give no thought to anything but sensual pleasure'. No puritan himself in the past, Pius could only ask Rodrigo not to appear at an orgy again in his Cardinal's vestments.

The Mantuan envoy to Siena, Bartomeo Bonatti, commented that 'if all the children born within the year arrive dressed like their fathers, many will appear as priests and cardinals.'

Bonatti also reported to his mistress, the Marchesa of

Mantua, that Rodrigo was to be seen 'in the company of the most beautiful woman that ever was'. She was Nachine, a wealthy courtesan, whose liaison with Cardinal Borgia was well known. Even by the standards of the time, Rodrigo Borgia's behaviour was scandalous. But Pius II's rebuke did deter him as he positioned himself for a renewed bid for the papacy.

Rodrigo met the Roman beauty Vannozza Catanei at Mantua during the Council of 1461. She was eighteen. He called her Rosa. He had already slept with her mother and, possibly, her sister, but Vannozza was to become his long-term lover. She was an extraordinarily beautiful woman with an oval face, almond eyes and a small, well-shaped mouth. She also had a passionate nature and a mercurial temper which seemed to fascinate him.

Mindful of Pius II's attitude to his openly licentious lifestyle, he installed her in Venice while he went back to Rome. He visited her often and for nearly twenty years maintained a regular correspondence with Rosa. In one letter he wrote: 'Rosa, my dear love, follow my example, remain chaste till the day in which I shall be allowed to see you, and blend our affection in endless voluptuousness. Till then, let no lips profane thy charms, let no hand lift those veils which cover my sovereign blessings. A little more patience and I shall have what he whom they called my uncle has left me for an inheritance, the See of St Peter. Meanwhile take particular care of the education of our children, because they are destined to govern nations and kings.'

They had four children together – Cesare, born 1475; Juan, born 1477; Lucrezia, born 1480; and Jofré, born 1481. There was no great scandal attached to this as

Rodrigo took the precaution of having Rosa set up in marriage.

Meanwhile, Rodrigo was building his power base. A contemporary, dazzled by his wealth, wrote:

> *His papal offices, his numerous abbeys in Italy and Spain, and his three bishoprics of Valencia, Porto and Cartagena, yield him a vast income, and it is said that the office of vice-chancellor alone brings him in 8000 gold florins. His plate, his pearls, his stuffs embroidered in silk and gold, and his books in every department of learning are very numerous, and all are of a magnificence worthy of a king or pope. I need not mention the innumerable bed-hangings, the trappings for his horses, nor his magnificence wardrobe, nor the vast amount of gold coin he possesses.*

He spent a huge amount of money on the palace he was building in Rome. Pius II compared it to Nero's house, both for its splendour and for what went on there.

'The palace is splendidly decorated,' wrote Cardinal Ascanio Sforza. 'The walls of the great entrance hall are hung with fine tapestries; the carpets on the floor harmonized with the furnishings which included a sumptuous day bed upholstered in red satin with a canopy over it, and a chest on which was laid out a vast and beautiful collection of gold and silver plate. Beyond this there were two more rooms, one hung with fine satin, carpeted, and with another canopied bed covered with Alexandrine velvet; the other even more ornate with a couch covered in cloth of gold. In this room the central table was covered with a cloth of Alexandrine velvet and surrounded by finely carved chairs.'

Despite his manoeuvrings, Rodrigo did not succeed Pius II. Paul II did. Then when Paul II died, Rodrigo was still thought to be too young to be pope. Nevertheless he wielded enormous influence. He used it to secure the election of Francesco della Rovere as Pope Sixtus IV and received even more power and wealth in return.

Under Sixtus IV, Rodrigo bought the wealthy abbey of Subiacco and became papal legate to Aragon and Castile. But, while back in Spain, he and his men committed so many rapes and murders, that they were expelled by Henry the Feeble, King of Castile.

On his return to Rome, Rodrigo saw no reason for further discretion. He sent for Vannozza Catanei and their children. He bought her a palace in a quiet part of the city. She took the title of Countess Ferdinand of Castile, from the name of his agent who passed himself off as her husband. Every night, on the pretext of visiting his fellow countryman, Rodrigo went to stay with her.

When Sixtus IV was replaced by Innocent VIII, Rodrigo's earthy activities passed unnoticed among the general debauchery of the time. Rome had become one great brothel, with over 50,000 prostitutes working there. The streets were full of pickpockets, ruffians, banditti and cut-throats. Things were so bad that when the conclave was called on the death of Innocent VIII, soldiers had to be stationed at the cardinals' mansions to prevent them being looted while they were away. The roads to the Vatican had to be barricaded with timbers and guarded by cavalry and infantry.

Under Rodrigo's influence as vice-chancellor, Rome had become a public market, where all sacred offices were up for sale. Even the papacy went to the highest bidder. When Pope Innocent VIII died in 1492, Cardinal de la Rovere, who later became Pope Julius II (1503–13), was favourite to take over. He had 100,000 gold ducats from the Republic of Genoa and 200,000 from the King of France to back his claim.

But Rodrigo Borgia had been vice-chancellor of the Holy See under four popes and, in this position, had become hugely wealthy. The bribes he offered were staggering. He would give away wealthy abbeys, luxurious villas and whole towns to secure a cardinal's vote.

During the five-day conclave that August, Rodrigo used the promise of rich preferments and out-and-out bribery to win the election. Some cardinals wanted palaces; others castles, land or money. Cardinal Orsini sold his vote for the castles of Monticelli and Sariani. Cardinal Ascanio Sforza wanted four mule-loads of silver – and the lucrative chancellorship of the Church to secure his vote. Cardinal Colonna got the wealthy abbey of St Benedict, with its domains and rights of patronage, for himself and his family, in perpetuity. The Cardinal of St Angelo wanted the bishopric of Porto, the castle there, and a cellar full of wine. Cardinal Savelli was given the Civita Castellana.

One uncommitted elector was Cardinal Gherardo of Venice. He was ninety-five and probably senile. He neither asked for, nor took, a bribe. But he voted for Rodrigo anyway.

Rodrigo still found himself one short of victory. The clinching vote belonged to a Venetian monk. All he wanted was 5,000 crowns and a night with Rodrigo's daughter, the lovely twelve-year-old Lucrezia. The deal was done and with the vote of twenty-two cardinals in his pocket Rodrigo Borgia was proclaimed Pope Alexander VI (1492–1503).

The cardinals who had elected Alexander VI were under no illusions about what they had done. Giovanni de'Medici, the future Leo X, said to Cardinal Cibò: 'We are now in the clutches of perhaps the most savage wolf the world has ever seen. Either we flee or he will, without a doubt, devour us.'

Cardinal della Rovere sensibly fled to France and spent much of Alexander VI's reign in hiding. Others kept a low profile or found their careers prematurely curtailed. But Rodrigo did not worry about what people were saying. He had got what he wanted.

Gibbon described Alexander as the 'Tiberius of Christian Rome'. Alexander's contemporary, the Florentine statesman Francesco Guicciardini took a less moralistic view. He said: 'The goodness of a pontiff is commended when it does not surpass the wickedness of other men.' Another critic called Alexander 'a most luxurious tyrant; no pen is able to register the beastly qualities of this impious knave'.

It was said that Alexander VI made a pact with the devil to procure the papacy. But the most consistent charge was that he 'was familiar with his impudent daughter Lucrezia'.

After the ceremony of the bottomless chair – unnecessary in Rodrigo's case, one would have thought – and his coronation, Alexander held a huge parade through Rome. The streets were decked with flowers and the public buildings hung with flags. All the princes of Christendom sent envoys. Only Ferdinand, King of Naples, refused to open diplomatic relations with him.

Although Rodrigo Borgia was crowned Alexander VI, he should technically have been Alexander V. The Alexander V who had been elected by the Council of Pisa in

1406 was no longer on the official roll of popes. Since the deposition of John XXIII at the Council of Constance in 1415, he had been reclassified as an anti-pope. But as the Pisan anti-pope had been well known for his retinue of women, he was obviously very much a man after Rodrigo's heart and the new Pope tacitly acknowledged his lascivious predecessor.

Rodrigo delighted in sponsoring entertainments featuring nude and nubile women. Sometimes they interrupted Mass. On one occasion, he brought giggling women up to the altar and the sanctified Host was trampled under foot. He would take any excuse for a party, which would inevitably mean packing the papal apartments with courtesans. Wherever he travelled he took with him an entourage of scantily clad dancing girls.

Alexander was sympathetic to others' sexual excesses. As Pope, he gave his blessing on the funeral of a fifteen-year-old Florentine lad who had died, it was said, from an excess of intercourse. He had had sex with a young girl seven times in one hour - though others said it was eleven times in one night - then succumbed to the fever and passed away.

At the same time, Alexander tried to adopt the censorious attitudes befitting a pope. In 1496, he issued a papal bull trying to reform the Benedictines, describing 'both sexes in that ancient and honoured institution as indulging in the most shameless profligacy'.

Beyond his twin passions of money and women, Rodrigo loved his children. Boccaccio said: 'Ten papacies would not be enough to satisfy these relations.' Once Pope, Alexander VI set about advancing his illegitimate children, particularly the four favourites he had had by Vannozza Catanei.

On the day of Alexander's coronation, his vicious seventeen-year-old son Cesare was appointed Archbishop of Valencia. Later, in a consistory that also promoted Vannozza Catanei's brother and fifteen-year-old favourite Ippolito d'Este, Cesare became a cardinal.

Alexander skilfully got round the stipulation that a cardinal must be legitimate. He issued two papal bulls. One, distributed publicly, declared that Cesare was the son of Vannozza Catanei and her 'husband'. The second, published secretly, acknowledged Cesare as his own.

Initially, Alexander thought it wise to keep Cesare away from Rome and sent him to Siena to attend the Palio, the famous horse-race around the city square. Cesare ensured victory by the simple expedient of bribing the judges. But after about a month, once Alexander had his hands firmly on the levers of power, Cesare returned to Rome, took over a palace near the Vatican and began entertaining a string of girlfriends and hordes of prostitutes there.

'The day before yesterday I went to find Cesare at his house in the Trastevere,' wrote Boccaccio. 'He was on the point of going out for the hunt; he was wearing a worldly garment of silk and had his sword at his side. He had only a little tonsure like a simple priest. I rode at his side and conversed with him at length. I am on intimate terms with him. He has the manners of a great prince; being very modest, his bearing is much better than that of the Duke of Gandia, his brother.'

As Pope, Rodrigo moved his mistress and his daughter into the Vatican. He commissioned a full-length portrait by Pinturicchio, showing him swathed in sumptuous brocade and opulent jewellery, which hung in his apartment in the Apostolic Palace. He also began to build up the political power of the papacy again, which had been in decline since the exile in Avignon.

Alexander's other ambition in office was to recoup the money he had expended on bribes to obtain the pontificate. This was easy. With murders running at about fourteen a day in Rome, Alexander simply let the culprits off – for a fee. After all, the Pope pointed out: 'The Lord requires not the death of the sinner but rather that he should pay and live.'

Simony was another good source of income. Anyone who wanted to become a cardinal could simply buy the position. To increase the turnover, Alexander took to poisoning cardinals once he had elevated them. Not only did he have their cardinal's hat to sell all over again, their property naturally reverted to the Church – that is, to Pope Alexander. He simply carried on as he had when vice-chancellor, selling other benefices and indulgences. He charged one nobleman 24,000 gold pieces for permission to commit incest with his sister. Peter Mendoza, Cardinal of Valencia, bought permission to name his catamite his natural son.

'It is necessary to be a good prince,' said Alexander, 'and in conscience we cannot refuse to our subjects a permission which we may have many times granted ourselves.'

Murder was another source of income. Tiring of the threat of his brother who was still a refugee in the Vatican, the Ottoman Sultan Bayezid II sent Alexander 40,000 gold ducats to kill Djem. But the honour of Alexander was not to be bought so cheaply. He waited. Another 200,000 ducats turned up. Then Alexander had Djem poisoned.

By the time Rodrigo Borgia had settled into the

papacy, his long-time mistress Vannozza Catanei had become old and her beauty faded. So the fifty-eight-year-old Alexander VI took another mistress, fifteen-year-old Giulia Farnese. She was so beautiful that Romans knew her as 'Giulia Bella' – Julia the Beautiful.

Alexander had officiated at her marriage to Orsino Orsini, in 'the room of stars' at the Borgia palace. He took the young couple under his wing. But soon after, he bedded the young bride. This was part of an arrangement Alexander made with Giulia's brother Alessandro. He arranged for the Pope to enjoy her favours in exchange for a pardon for a forgery. Like a good Roman husband, Orsino Orsini tolerated the arrangement. He was blind in one eye and, it is said, he knew when to blink the other.

Although Alexander's liaison with Giulia Farnese began as a casual affair, genuine passion began to creep into their relationship. To maintain his hold on the beautiful Giulia, the Pope gave Alessandro Farnese, still only nineteen, a cardinal's hat. This earned Alessandro the nickname 'Cardinal Petticoat'. He went on to become Pope Paul III (1534–49).

Throughout Italy, Giulia became known as the 'Bride of Christ' or 'the Pope's Whore'. But everyone who set eyes on her dazzling beauty understood Alexander's infatuation. She was the 'heart and eyes' of the Pope, one diplomat said. Alexander had her immortalized in a painting of the Madonna with Giulia's face. They had children together, but Alexander tried to pretend that their first daughter Laura was the child of Orsino Orsini, Giulia's husband. The Florentine ambassador was not fooled. He wrote home: 'The child's resemblance to the

Pope is such she just has to be his.' They also had a son, Rodrigo, who was born just before Alexander VI died.

Giulia and Alexander's daughter Lucrezia became firm friends. They would take their sport in flirting with the visitors to the papal apartments. Alexander grew jealous and decided that it was time to get Lucrezia married off. She was a beautiful woman, with blonde hair and blue eyes. Alexander loved her dearly and all who met her were affected by her gaiety.

'She had a smile that lit up her features in a thousand different ways,' wrote Boccaccio, who was then the Ferrarese ambassador to the papal court. 'Never did a gentle creature seem happier to be alive.'

Another visitor wrote: 'She is of middle height and graceful of form, her face is rather long, the nose well-cut, hair golden, her mouth is rather large, the teeth brilliantly white, her neck is slender and fair, her bosom admirably proportioned. She is always gay and smiling.'

Alexander betrothed her a couple of times, then arranged an advantageous match to Giovanni Sforza, Lord of Pesaro. One of the prior fiancés, Don Gasparo de Procida, kicked up a fuss about this.

'There is much gossip about Pesaro's marriage,' wrote Boccaccio. 'The first bridegroom is here, raising a great hue and cry, as a Catalan, saying he will protest to all the princes and potentates of Christendom; but will he, nil he, he will have to submit.'

Rodrigo simply paid him off with 3,000 gold ducats. Don Gasparo dropped his claims to Lucrezia's hand and went back to Spain.

Lucrezia was married in style in the Salla Reale. She was attended by Pope Innocent VIII's granddaughter, Giulia Farnese and 150 other Roman women who had reputedly caught the eye of Alexander. At the wedding feast, the place of honour was taken by the Pope and his mistress. Alexander outdressed even the bride. He wore a gold Turkish robe whose train was carried by an African slave girl.

'On the occasion of the marriage there were festivals and orgies worthy of Madam Lucrezia,' records Stefano Jufessura. There was dancing and feasting, a 'worldly comedy' and much uproarious behaviour. The Pope, particularly, took delight in throwing confetti down the low-cut bodices of the ladies' dresses.

'In the evening, his Holiness, the Cardinal Borgia [Cesare], the Duke of Gandia [Juan], some courtiers and some noble ladies, sat down to supper, where appeared buffoons and dancers of both sexes, who gave obscene representations, to the great amusement of the guests,' one chronicler recorded. 'Towards morning Alexander VI conducted the young couple into the nuptial chamber, in the middle of which had been set up a gorgeous bed without curtains. There such shocking and hideous scenes took place, as no language can convey or describe. The Pope performed the part of matron for his daughter; Lucrezia, that Messalina who, even while a child, had been by her father and brothers initiated into the most hideous debauchery, played, in this instance, the part of an innocent, in order to prolong the obscenities of the comedy; and the marriage took place in the presence of the pontifical family.'

But after her marriage, Lucrezia refused to follow her husband to Pesaro and continued to live in the Vatican. According to Buchard: 'She never left the apartments of the Pope, either day or night.' Eventually, Lucrezia was prevailed on to go and visit her husband and the beautiful Giulia accompanied her. This only doubled the Pope's pain.

Alexander grew excruciatingly jealous when Giulia, writing from Pesaro, praised, too fulsomely, Caterina Gonzaga, a relative of Lucrezia's husband Giovanni Sforza.

The Pope wrote back:

We know well that your expatiating and dilating the beauty of this person, who is not worthy so much as to tie your shoe, is due to the modesty you affect, in this as in all other matters. We are well aware, too, why you act thus; so that you, being informed that all who wrote to us said that beside you she seemed but a lantern held against the sun, we might the more appreciate your beauty, of which, to tell the truth, we never doubted. And we would wish that just as we know this clearly, so you for your part were wholly destined and made over, with no reserves, to that person who loves you more than anything else in the world.

Plainly, he missed her. But when he wrote again, Lucrezia wrote back informing him that Giulia and Alexander's cousin Adriana del Mila, who had been Lucrezia's governess, had gone to Capodimonte, the Farnese home, where Giulia's brother Angelo lay dying.

Alexander was furious and wrote back chastising Lucrezia. 'But of a truth, Don Giovanni and yourself have displayed very little thought for me in this departure of Madonna Adriana and Giulia, since you allowed them to leave without our permission,' he wrote. 'For you should have remembered, indeed, it was your duty, that such a sudden departure without our knowledge would cause us the greatest displeasure. And if you say that they did so because Cardinal Farnese commanded it, you ought to have asked yourself whether it would have pleased the

187

pope. However, it is done. But another time, we will be more careful, and will look about to see where our interests lie.'

A jealous letter to Giulia at Capodimonte followed. She wrote back to him: 'Since Your Holiness writes exhorting me strongly to act as befits me, to watch my virtue, in these matters I can at once set Your Holiness's mind at rest. Be assured that day and night I have no other thought in my mind – both for my own honour and for love of Your Holiness – than to show myself another St Catherine.'

St Catherine was a virgin martyr, but how Alexander took this allusion one cannot be sure. In his Vatican apartments, he had had Pinturicchio paint a fresco called 'The Disputation of St Catherine'. In it, Rodrigo Borgia appeared both as an admiring young bishop and as the pious Pope Alexander VI, while St Catherine herself was modelled on Lucrezia.

To further reassure Alexander, Giulia wrote that Adriana de Mila, who had been his children's governess, would also confirm her faithfulness. There then followed a furious exchange of letters. 'Giulia, my dearest daughter,' wrote Alexander, 'I received your letter which, if it had been longer and more prolix, would have made me even happier.'

She replied gushingly: 'To my one and only lord.' Then she dismissed all talk of the fun she had been having away from him by saying: 'And since perchance Your Holiness may believe, reading the above-mentioned things, that we are in great joy and happiness, we do certify this as a great error, since being absent from Your Holiness, and all my happiness and well-being depending thereupon, I cannot taste such delights with any satisfaction. Wheresoever my treasure is, there shall my heart be also. And he who says the contrary is right foolish. So we beseech Your Holiness, do not forget us…and if Your Holiness pleases to remember us, bring us back soon to kiss the feet we miss and long for.'

Alexander then heard that Giulia's husband, Orsino Orsini, had left his military post and returned to the family estate at Bassanello, claiming illness. The lovelorn Pope suspected that the young Orsini might be making an attempt to reclaim his bride and wrote to Giulia, forbidding her to go to Bassanello. She wrote back saying that there were political reasons for going there.

So Alexander wrote to Cardinal Alessandro Farnese and demanded that he intervene. When he dithered, Alexander wrote again in a more threatening tone saying: 'You know well how much we have done for you, and with how much love. Never would we have believed how swiftly you were to forget our favours, and to set Orsino above ourselves. We beseech and exhort you not to repay us in such coin, since thus you do not satisfy those promises you so often gave us, much less your own honour and welfare.'

To receive such a letter from a monster like Alexander VI must have had Farnese quaking.

That same day, Alexander wrote to Giulia, blasting her. Under the Greek initials of Jesus Christ, Alexander wrote:

Ungrateful and treacherous Giulia, we have received a letter of yours, by the hand of Navarico, in which you signify and declare that your intention is not to come here unless Orsino wills it; and though hitherto we understood well enough both your wicked inclinations, and from whom you sought advice, nevertheless in consideration of your feigned and pretended assurances, we could not wholly persuade ourselves that you were capable of treating us with such ingratitude and disloyalty (having so often sworn and given your word to us that you were at our command, and would not keep company with Orsino) as now to do the contrary and go to Bassanello, at open peril of your life; nor can I believe that you are acting thus except to get yourself pregnant a second time by that horse of Bassanello. And we hope that very soon both you and Madame Adriana, most ungrateful of women, will acknowledge your fault and suffer condign punishment for it. And moreover, as regarding the present we command you, on pain of excommunication and eternal malediction, that you do not stir forth from Capodimonte, much less go to Bassanello for matters concerning our state.

This was a bit much. In Renaissance Italy, under law of both Church and state, Giulia had to obey her husband without question. It was a matter for theological debate whether her duty to obey the orders of the Pope came above that.

Adriana de Mila also got a blast. 'At last, you have revealed all the evil and malice in your heart,' Alexander wrote. 'Rest assured that you will suffer most condign punishment for your deceit.'

If she left Capodimonte without his permission, he said, he would confiscate everything she owned and consign her to eternal damnation. And just in case Cardinal Farnese was having difficulty making up his mind about what to say to Giulia, Alexander sent him a papal brief, lending the full weight of the Church's authority to preventing Giulia visiting Orsino – 'that monkey' as Alexander was now calling him.

The emissary carrying the brief was told to impress on

Giulia and Adriana that they risked excommunication. Another emissary rode to Bassanello and told Orsino that he, too, risked excommunication if he failed to turn up in Rome in three days. But Orsino's confessor warned Alexander that the young man felt so humiliated by his wife's affair with the Pope that he would now risk anything to get her back.

Alexander did not find his anguish any easier to cope with without Lucrezia around. He wrote to her chidingly: 'For several days, we have had no letter from you. Your neglect to write to us how you and Don Giovanni, our beloved son, are, causes us great pain. In future, be more heedful and diligent.'

Lucrezia was sympathetic in her response. 'We understand that things are going badly in Rome,' she wrote. With the French army invading Italy and demanding passage through the papal states to attack Naples, this was something of an understatement. 'I implore Your Beatitude to leave and if that is not practical, to take the greatest possible care, and Your Beatitude must not impute this to presumption but to the very great love I bear and be certain, Your Holiness, that I will never be at peace unless I have frequent news of Your Holiness.'

But the crisis had passed – the romantic one at least. Giulia and Adriana were too afraid of Alexander to travel to Bassanello. When Orsino heard they were not coming, he returned to his unit.

In November 1494, Giulia and Adriana did risk leaving Capodimonte, though. They headed to Viterbo, which is just north of Rome, to see Cardinal Farnese, who had just been appointed papal legate there. But on the way they were captured by advanced detachments of the French army. King Charles roared with laughter when he heard that he had just captured Alexander's 'heart and ears'.

Alexander paid 3,000 gold ducats in ransom to get the two women back. They were returned by an honour guard of four hundred French cavalrymen. Alexander received them wearing a black doublet bordered with gold brocade, Spanish boots, a Spanish belt carrying a sword and dagger, and a velvet biretta. An observer said he looked 'very gallant'. That night Alexander slept with his beloved Giulia in his arms in the Vatican apartments again.

Even though he was fiercely jealous, that did not mean he was at all faithful to Giulia. Ludovico Sforza told the Milanese Senate that, within a week of their reunion, Alexander had slept with three other women – 'one of them a nun from Valencia, another a Castilian, a third a very beautiful girl from Venice, fifteen or sixteen years of age'.

But Alexander VI had bigger problems. The King of France was at the gates of Rome. He threatened to depose Alexander and charge him with adultery, incest and murder, among other things. With no forces coming to his defence, Alexander threw open the gates to Rome, though Cesare put up some brutal and futile resistance. To ensure safe passage, King Charles took Cesare with him as the French army marched on Naples. But after a couple of days, Cesare escaped, dressed as a stable boy, leaving his scarlet cardinal's cape tossed, contemptuously across his bed. Furious, Charles ordered the destruction of a nearby town in revenge, but Cardinal della Rovere, who had been travelling with the French, pointed out that it would only delay their march south.

When the French army reached Naples, the city's resistance soon crumbled. Once inside, so did that of the French troops. They quickly succumbed to the beautiful, hot-blooded Neapolitan women. Unfortunately they were infected with syphilis, known locally as 'the sickness of Naples'. It was virtually unknown in the rest of Europe at the time, but it soon became known as 'the French disease' and spread from the toe of Italy to the English Channel. In 1494, seventeen members of the Pope's family and court, including Cesare Borgia, came down with syphilis in just two months.

That same year, Jofré Borgia married the King of Ferrante's beautiful green-eyed granddaughter Sancia, sealing another alliance. Their nuptial banquet continued until three in the morning when the bridal couple were escorted to the bedroom, undressed by the bridesmaids and put to bed together naked. Then, in the time-honoured fashion, King Alfonso and Cardinal Borgia-Lanzol, turned up in the bedroom to watch the thirteen-year-old prince and the twenty-year-old princess kiss and cuddle. The couple, it seemed, showed no embarrassment. When it was deemed that the marriage had been consummated, the two older men withdrew, leaving the newlyweds to enjoy the rest of the night together.

In his report to Alexander, Cardinal Borgia-Lanzol said that Jofré's performance had been gracious and full of spirit and mentioned that others would have paid plenty to see the young bridegroom in action as he had.

But, apparently, Jofré's performance was neither graceful nor full of spirit enough for Sancia. Soon her amorous adventures around Rome were the talk of the town. Alexander wrote to her, accusing her of gross immorality. Her steward leapt to her defence, saying that the only man who had entered her bedroom apart from her husband was 'a man of good will, well past his sixtieth birthday'. As Alexander was well past sixty himself, this cannot have been much of a comfort – especially as Jofré's brothers, Juan and Cesare, were competing for her attentions. Soon the sensuous, by now twenty-two-year-old Sancia was entertaining them both in her bed, while Jofré, still only fifteen, consoled himself with a spending spree.

The first impact of syphilis on Europe was devastating, causing havoc and confusion in every community. It was then a killer disease. People had no resistance and its transmission rate was extremely high. Each act of intercourse with a sufferer gave a fifty percent chance of catching the disease. There had never been anything like it before.

But the disease itself was not the only hazard. Rome was rife with quack cures. When the pedlars were caught, the anger was intense. On one occasion, six turbaned rustics were beaten through the streets of Rome with sticks. They had an oil which they claimed cured the pox. People paid to bathe in it. But it was discovered that, once the bath was done, the canny salesmen put the oil back in jars and used it again.

The Dominican friar Girolamo Savonarola declared that syphilis was a punishment from God. Alexander, a sufferer, was not amused. From the pulpit of the Duomo in Florence Savonarola railed:

> *Come hither oh degenerate church. I gave you fine raiment, saith the Lord, and you have made it an idol. Your vessels you turn to pride, and your sacraments to simony. In lasciviousness, you have become a shameless whore. You are worse than the*

beasts, you are a monster and an abomination. Time was when you felt shame for your sins, but no longer. You have built a house of public ill-fame, a common brothel.

The clergy, in particular, were his target.

They sell benefices, they sell the sacraments, they sell nuptial Masses, they sell everything. And then they are frightened of excommunication. When evening comes, one will betake himself to the gambling table, another to his concubine. This poison has reached such a height in Rome that France, Germany, the whole world are sickened by it. Things have come to such a pass that we must counsel all men to keep clear of Rome, and say, 'Do you want to ruin your son? Then make him a priest.' The time is drawing near when we will turn the stopcocks and open the jakes [privies], and then such stinking filth and fetid matter will issue from the city of Rome as will spread throughout the length and breadth of Christendom.

And he zeroed in on Pope Alexander.

I assure you that this Alexander is no pope, nor can be considered as such. Leaving aside the fact that he purchased his pontifical throne through simony, and that he assigns the ecclesiastical benefices to those who pay highest for them; and leaving aside his other vices, well known to all men, I assert that he is no Christian, and does not believe in God's existence.

Alexander ordered Savonarola to hold his tongue. When he did not, he offered him a cardinal's hat – for free. Savonarola refused. So in 1498 Alexander had him burnt at the stake as a heretic, celebrating the death with an orgy and the baptism of his child by Giulia Farnese. Afterwards he annulled the marriage of Lucrezia and Giovanni Sforza on the ludicrous grounds of non-con-

summation, even though he had seen the marriage consummated with his own eyes.

Giovanni Sforza did not take this well. He publicly
announced that he had consummated the marriage, not
once but, he said, 'an infinite number of times'. However, he was not very brave and did not relish standing
up to Alexander, who was probably plotting to poison
him. Sforza was given two choices. He could confess to
impotence, or have his marriage declared illegal because of Lucrezia's prior engagement to Don Gasparo
de Procida. This would have meant that Giovanni would
have had to pay back the dowry he had already received,
which he was not in a position to do. However, being an
Italian, and proud, he was not going to admit impotence
under any circumstances.

'I would prefer to lose my estate and my life rather
than my honour,' he said.

Giovanni fled Rome and went to see his cousin,
Ludovico Sforza, Duke of Milan. Ludovico advised
Giovanni to challenge the Pope by having him send Lucrezia to a neutral location where he could prove his
potency by making love to her in public. If the Pope did
not want to put his daughter through that sort of humiliation, Giovanni was equally willing to prove his mascu-
linity with prostitutes in the brothels of Milan, witnessed
by the papal legate to Milan, who was Alexander's
nephew, Cardinal Borgia-Lanzol.

This may seem like a crude spectacle, but it was not
uncommon in those days for men to undergo such potency tests. The bottom line was that Ludovico was not
prepared to back his cousin with force of arms.

Giovanni lashed out at the Pope, claiming that he
'wanted his daughter for himself' and 'had known her

carnally on countless occasions'. The whole of Italy was on Giovanni's side. Alexander's claim only stood up if Lucrezia could be shown to be a virgin. The very idea was laughable. Lucrezia herself was terrified that she would have to be examined by a midwife to prove that she was *virga intacta* and locked herself up in a convent.

Cardinal Ascanio Sforza tried to mediate. But it did no good. Alexander and Cesare were hell-bent on the divorce. Lucrezia was required for another important alliance. Cardinal Sforza had to write, reluctantly, that although he 'would have liked this marriage to be a lasting one…it had remained unconsummated as a result of impotence'.

In the end, Giovanni had to back down. For the remainder of Lucrezia's dowry, some 31,000 ducats, he signed a confession of impotence.

Lucrezia was brought from the convent and swore to a papal commission that she was still a virgin. This brought hoots of derision. Many of the papal commissioners knew of her incest and her numerous sexual affairs with members of the Vatican establishment. But the commission duly annulled the marriage on that basis – 'a conclusion that set all of Italy laughing,' wrote one chronicler. 'It was common knowledge that she was the biggest whore there ever was in Rome.'

To cap it all, when the divorce was finally granted, Lucrezia found that she was pregnant. The father was probably Perotto Calderoni, Alexander's handsome Spanish chamberlain and the Pope's favourite. Infuriated that Alexander's plans might be ruined, Cesare stabbed Calderoni in the papal apartments and his body was dumped in the Tiber.

Paolo Capello, the Venetian envoy to Rome, wrote

home: 'With his own hand, and under the mantle of the pope, Cesare murdered Master Perotto so that his blood spattered in the face of the pope.'

Alexander had tried to shelter his young favourite under his papal cape. But that did not stop Cesare. He hacked the unfortunate chamberlain to pieces, leaving his father, the Pope, drenched in blood.

Calderoni may have been a favourite of the Pope, but his wife, it seems, was even more of a favourite. Alexander was said to be the father of the son she bore in 1497.

The murder of Calderoni did not end the gossip. The Ferrarese envoy reported some months later: 'It has been vouchsafed from Rome that the daughter of the pope gave birth to a child.'

The baby was hidden away but, in 1501, Lucrezia appeared with a three-year-old child named Giovanni, known popularly as *Infans Romans*. However, historians still dispute who the father was. Calderoni is one candidate and Cesare obviously thought so. But two papal bulls were issued: one named Cesare as the father; the second named Alexander VI himself – which seems more likely.

There is no doubt that Lucrezia and her father were very close. She ran the papacy like a regent when he was away from Rome. She opened official letters, attended to the business and called the meetings of the Holy College. Often, after a revel, she would preside over the council of cardinals dressed as a Bacchanalian, with her breasts naked and her body scarcely covered with a see-through muslin robe. She would then 'propose for discussion luxurious subjects'. And, according to Buchard, she was not ashamed to give or to receive 'indecent caresses' before the whole council.

Johann Buchard was Alexander's major duomo and he noted in his journal: 'Today the Pope, in order to amuse Madam Lucrezia, had some mares, loaded with boughs, brought into the little yard near the principal entrance of the palace, and ordered the stallions of his stables, free from bits and bonds, to be let loose on them. They rushed upon the mares, neighing in a dreadful manner; and, after a terrible struggle with their teeth and feet, the poor mares were overwhelmed and subdued, with great applause from Madam Lucrezia and the Pope, who contemplated the scene from a bedroom window, which was above the door of the palace.'

Afterwards, Buchard notes, the Pope and his daughter retired to an interior room and remained locked up together for more than an hour.

If Alexander did indeed have an incestuous affair with his beautiful daughter Lucrezia, he is probably the only Pope to have enjoyed three generations of women – grandmother, mother and daughter.

Alexander's object in engineering Lucrezia's divorce was to marry her off to King Federigo in Naples. Cesare was sent to make the overture, but Federigo, who feared a Borgia takeover, refused to marry a woman who was 'commonly reputed to have slept with her brothers'.

He was even more alarmed when he witnessed Cesare's behaviour in his court. Cesare threw off his cardinal's robes and satiated himself with the beautiful women of Naples. A handsome and athletic man, he attracted the attention of every woman at court. He fell in love with Maria Diaz Garlon, the daughter of an Aragonese count. The affair foundered because the symptoms of syphilis Cesare was exhibiting became so gross. When he returned to Rome the symptoms abated.

He thought he was cured, but the disease was simply going into its secondary, more dangerous, phase.

Meanwhile, Juan Borgia, the Duke of Gandia, had in 1493 married a Spanish princess, King Ferdinand's cousin, but instead of uniting Italy and Spain as planned, Juan managed to alienate Ferdinand even further. Alexander had warned him against gambling and womanizing. A bishop and two of the Pope's most trusted servants had been sent to try to keep the young Duke out of trouble, but by Christmas of 1493, Alexander was receiving reports that Juan was gambling heavily and was spending his nights in the brothels of Valencia and Barcelona. Worse, it was rumoured that he had failed to consummate his marriage.

Alexander wrote to Juan telling him that nothing was calculated to offend a woman more than not making love to her. Failing to consummate the marriage would be a catastrophic insult to Ferdinand.

Cesare also wrote, begging him: 'Try to fulfil the hopes which His Holiness has always founded on you, if you wish him a long life, in which is all our good, our life and exaltation; and if you have compassion for me, see that these reports that give His Holiness such pain should cease.'

Juan wrote back that the rumours of his scandalous behaviour came from people 'with little brain or in a state of drunkenness'. He also claimed that he had consummated his marriage not once, but many times. And eventually Alexander received news that his daughter-in-law, the duchess, was pregnant.

The Pope was shattered when Juan was murdered, probably in 1497. Cesare, who was jealous of his father's special affection for Juan, was suspected. For years they had vied with each other for their father's favours by supplying the old man with stimulating beauties for his private harem and Juan had found an exotic Spanish girl who moved Alexander to ecstasy. Cesare was a sore loser. He was also put out when Lucrezia turned her incestuous affections to Juan, leaving Cesare out of the ménage.

After a party at their mother's house, Juan and Cesare rode back to the Vatican together. Juan said he was 'going in search of further pleasure' and rode off with a groom and a masked man. The next day his body was fished from the Tiber. He had been stabbed eight times and his throat was cut. His hands were tied together and a stone was tied to his neck to weight the body. The motive for the murder was certainly not theft. He was still fully dressed. His gloves were tucked in his belt and he had thirty gold pieces on him.

Juan's last few hours were spent in the arms of a woman. In one account, she was the notorious Roman courtesan Madonna Damiata. In another, he was lured to his death by a Roman nobleman's beautiful daughter with whom he had fallen in love.

The first suspect was Jofré. It was suggested that he had killed his brother in jealousy over his wife Sancia. Another suspect was Giovanni Sforza, his motive jealousy over Lucrezia. But it was the Florentine political maestro Niccolo Machiavelli who fingered Cesare. His deductive process was simple – he looked at who had most to gain. With his rival Juan out of the way, Cesare could monopolize the love of his father Pope Alexander and his sister Lucrezia, and take over his brother's position as head of the papal armies.

When Juan's body was fished out of the river and lain

at the Pope's feet, a cynic whispered: 'At last, a fisher of men.'

Grief-stricken the Pope repented his wicked ways and swore to dedicate himself to the Church's business. All clerical concubines, he decreed, were to be dismissed within ten days. But he himself could not give up his voluptuous pleasures so easily. Buchard records: 'Then he dried his tears and consoled himself in the embraces of Madam Lucrezia, the very cause of the murder.' Giulia Farnese gave him a child the following year.

Anyway, things between Cesare and his father were soon patched up. In celebration, Cesare organized a hunting party. The two churchmen set out to Ostia, followed by a great number of courtesans and prostitutes, dancers and minions, all protected by five hundred knights and six hundred infantrymen.

'They passed four entire days in the woods of Ostia,' records the historian Thomas Tomasi, 'amusing themselves in surpassing all that imagination could invent in lewdness and debauchery. They then returned to Rome, which they had converted into a den of brigands and iniquity.'

Tomasi adds despairingly: 'It would be impossible to enumerate all the murders, the rapes and the incests, which were every day committed at the court of the pope. Scarcely the life of a man could be long enough to register the names of the victims murdered, poisoned, or thrown alive into the Tiber.'

Simply to preserve their own lives the prelates had to prostrate themselves before Alexander VI, praise his incestuous connections with his children and flatter Cesare.

Although King Federigo had refused the hand of Lucrezia, he thought it diplomatic to arrange another match for her. She was to marry Alfonso, Duke of Bisagilia, the son of Alfonso II, Duke of Aragon, who controlled Sorrento. At last Alexander had a Neapolitan alliance, which would greatly increase his power in Italy. With Lucrezia and Alfonso, it was love at first sight. When he arrived in Rome, a chronicler reported that he was the 'handsomest young man every seen in the Imperial City'. And, in Lucrezia's eyes, he was very different from the uncouth Giovanni Sforza.

Alexander was delighted that Lucrezia had found happiness, but stipulated in the wedding contract, that the couple must live in Rome throughout their marriage. He could not go through another separation from his beloved daughter.

The wedding feast was a comparatively quiet affair, though there was a fight between Cesare's servants and those of Princess Sancia. Afterwards there was a play in which Cesare appropriately played a unicorn, that horny symbol of chastity.

The papal master of ceremonies, Johann Buchard confirmed that the marriage was consummated on the first night and soon afterwards Lucrezia became pregnant. She miscarried after frolicking in a vineyard belonging to one of the cardinals, but was soon pregnant again.

Lucrezia and Alfonso named the baby Rodrigo after her father. The Pope was so excited by the event he got ambassadors out of their beds to announce to the whole of Europe that he was a grandfather. In a baptismal robe of gold brocade, the child was christened in the Sistine Chapel before a crowd of dignitaries. The Venetian diarist, Girolamo Priuli wrote: 'There was much murmuring through all Christendom and it was said that the pontiff, the head of the Christian religion, was making a public demonstration of his love and affection for his family, and that the pope was officially declaring himself the father of his children.'

Politically, the tide had turned against the Neapolitan alliance. Alfonso, wisely, had fled back to Naples, but he was enticed back to Rome for the christening. After a celebratory meal, five men attacked him with swords and knives on the steps of St Peter's. His gentlemen in waiting rescued him and carried him back up to the papal apartments where he was nursed by his loving wife, Lucrezia.

Cesare, now the Church's military commander, mounted a guard. Anyone carrying a weapon in the Vatican was to be executed. Lucrezia and Sancia prepared Alfonso's food, so they could be sure it was not poisoned. The doctor was watched like a hawk. But just when Alfonso seemed to be pulling through, he was found strangled. Everybody thought that Cesare had done it.

After the murder of Lucrezia's second husband, Alexander was with three prelates one evening, discussing the profits from the forthcoming Jubilee when a storm broke. Lightning struck the roof of the Vatican, which caved in. The three bishops were struck and killed by the falling beams. The Pope alone escaped. Still, many saw it as God's comment on the Borgias' unscrupulous matchmaking.

Cesare Borgia was Machiavelli's model for the utterly ruthless statesman he portrayed in his classic political theory *The Prince*. In fact, Machiavelli acknowledged his countrymen's debt to the Borgia family and their Church. He wrote: 'The Italians owe a great debt to the Roman church and its clergy. Through their example,

we have lost all true religion and become complete un-
believers. Take it as a rule, the nearer a nation dwells to
the Roman Curia, the less religion it has.'

Florentine statesman Francesco Guicciardini was
more afraid of Cesare than of Alexander. He wrote that
Cesare had been born so that 'there might be in the
world one man vile enough to carry out the designs of
his father, Alexander VI'.

The rest of the Church establishment were little better, Guicciardini concludes: 'One cannot speak badly
enough about the Roman Curia but it deserves more, for
it is infamous, an example of all that is vicious and nasty
in the world.'

By all accounts Cesare was handsome, virile, athletic,
charming, intelligent and utterly without scruple.
Throughout his life only one good deed was every attributed to him. He opened a retirement home for ageing
prostitutes – although there may have been a little self-
interest involved.

Cesare particularly enjoyed being his father's hench-
man. When King Ferdinand and Queen Isabella of
Castile complained that Bishop Florida of Cosenza had
granted a licence for the heiress of the throne of Portugal to leave the convent where she was a nun to marry
the natural son of the late King John II – thus preventing
Castile from seizing Portugal – Alexander had Bishop
Florida seized, stripped and thrown naked into the dungeons of Castel Sant'Angelo where he sank to his knees
in filth. He was given two pounds of bread, a bucket of
water, a phial of oil and a lamp, and was informed that
his provisions would be replenished only once a week.

After two months, Cesare felt that the prelate's resolve
might have weakened. He promised that the Bishop

would not go to the gallows and would be reinstated if he signed a declaration that he had forged the marriage licence he had given the Portuguese princess. Seeing no other way out, the Bishop signed. Alexander, claiming he knew nothing of the agreement stripped him of his bishopric and handed him over to the civil authorities for punishment.

Cesare fulfilled part of his promise, though. He saved Bishop Florida from the gallows by the simple expediency of poisoning him in his cell before he was taken to the scaffold. Meanwhile, the Bishop's property, positions and benefices were sold to the highest bidder.

Even with a Borgia in the papal chair, sexual attitudes in Rome were not that liberal – at least, not for those who were not rich and powerful. Johann Buchard reported the punishment meted out to a black transvestite, who called himself Spanish Barbara, and a prostitute named Cursetta. First they were led about the city. He wore a dress that was pulled up so that his genitals were exposed and there could be no mistaking he was a man. She wore a full-length tiger-skin coat which was held closed only by a belt.

After one circuit of the city, Cursetta was released. But Spanish Barbara was thrown back in jail. A few days later, he was led out with two thieves. At the head of the parade was a man seated on a donkey. He held up two testicles tied to the point of a stick. They had been cut off a Jew who been caught having sex with a Christian woman.

Spanish Barbara was stood on a pile of wood. A rope was put around his neck, looped though the branch of a forked post and twisted tight with a stick. Then the wood was set on fire. Unfortunately, it had been raining and the wood did not burn very well. But eventually it caught fire well enough to burn away Spanish Barbara's legs.

Cesare was certainly bloodthirsty enough to fulfil his father's ambitions. With Spanish flair he killed five bulls in St Peter's Square with a lance. A sixth he decapitated with a single blow of his sword.

'It was so agreeable to him to see blood shed that, like the Emperor Commodus, he practised butchery in order to keep alive his thirst for blood,' wrote Buchard.

> 'One day he went so far as to have the square of St Peter enclosed by a palisade, into which he ordered some prisoners – men, women and children – to be brought. He then had them bound, hand and foot, and being armed and mounted on a fiery charger, commenced a horrible attack upon them. Some he shot, and others he cut down with his sword, trampling them under his horse's feet. In less than half-an-hour, he wheeled around alone in a puddle of blood, among the dead bodies of his victims, while his Holiness and Madam Lucrezia, from a balcony, enjoyed the sight of that horrid scene.'

And he exceeded his father even in the pursuit of women. Once he abducted a man's wife, raped her and, when he was done with her, had her murdered. As he grew more pox-ridden, he became unmoved by grace or beauty – 'the only favour which he granted to the young ladies was that of their serving a few days for his debaucheries, and afterwards he threw them in the Tiber'.

Cesare was never very happy as a churchman. He preferred hunting and seducing women to saying Mass. With Juan dead, he was eager to step into his shoes as head of the papal armies. But first he needed a title and position. He also thought that it was his duty to perpetuate the house of Borgia by having children.

While in Naples negotiating Lucrezia's second marriage, Cesare had met Carlotta, King Federigo's legitimate daughter. He offered to marry her, but King Federigo pointed out that he was a cardinal. Federigo told the Pope: 'If you can find a son who can marry my daughter and remain a cardinal, I would then consider it.'

In fact, Federigo was just stalling. He knew full well that if Cesare married his daughter, he would risk being murdered as he would be the only thing that stood between Cesare and the throne of Naples.

At the age of twenty-two, Cesare asked to quit the Sacred College, still aiming to marry Carlotta. Alexander approved because Cesare's face was already covered in the weals and dark blotches of secondary syphilis. One cardinal remarked that if they were all allowed to resign for such trivial reasons there would be no one left.

Carlotta was in France at the time. King Louis XII of France promised Cesare his help in exchange for a divorce from his current wife Jeanne de Valois. He wanted to marry Anne of Brittany. So the hapless Jeanne was pressured into saying that the marriage had not been consummated because of a malformation of her genitals and Cesare did the rest.

Having cast off his cardinal's hat, Cesare was created Duke of Valentinois and went to Paris, where he tried to impress Carlotta. A fortune was squandered on wedding gifts and other luggage. Six French galleys were needed to transport the load from Civitavecchia to Marseilles. Cesare was accompanied by an entourage of nearly two hundred. He was dressed in velvet and damask, and his charger was shod with silver. His pages were dressed in tunics of silk embroidered with gold. They wore necklaces of emeralds and sapphires and their shoes were adorned with pearl. Even the mules that carried their provisions, when they approached Paris, were shod with gold, though many of them lost their shoes.

But Carlotta was not impressed. She turned Cesare down. Her father opposed the match, she knew. But the clinching factor was that Carlotta was in love with a Breton nobleman and she said that she would never marry the bastard son of a priest. Alexander wrote demanding that the wedding take place, or the Borgias would become the laughing stock of Europe. The truth was that Carlotta was not particularly attractive, which did not matter to Cesare, who wanted only power from the match. However, he was judged to be the 'handsomest man of his age' by the French court, despite his syphilitic dry skin and unsightly brown rash. Nevertheless, a snub by such a plain woman was a deep humiliation.

Matters got worse when emissaries from King Federigo turned up. They brought a message that said: 'To the bastard son of the pope, the King not only would not give his legitimate daughter, but not even a bastard child.'

To take the sting off such an insult, Louis of France offered the beautiful seventeen-year-old Charlotte d'Albret, daughter of the Duke of Guyenne, who had caught Cesare's roving eye. The wedding took place on 12 May 1499 in a private chapel at Blois Castle. A sumptuous wedding breakfast was held in silk tents in the fields just outside the castle walls. The marriage was consummated twice that afternoon and six times more in the evening. A messenger left for Rome the next morning with the glad tiding that Cesare had given his wife 'eight marks of his virility'. Buchard also notes in his diary that the consummation was made eight times in succession. King Louis wrote admiringly of Cesare's virility, and Cesare himself wrote to his father with the news. This was not done boastfully. It was a normal correspondence between two men of similar erotic interests. Cesare obviously fancied his young bride a great deal, because the amorous events of their nuptial night had been cut short. Some brave practical joker substituted laxatives for the aphrodisiac pills Cesare had ordered from the chemist. According to Charlotte's ladies in waiting, who watched events through the keyhole, Cesare spent as much time on the commode as in bed.

Robert de la Marck, Lord of Fleurange, recorded in his memoirs: 'To tell you of the Duke of Valentinois's wedding night, he asked the apothecary for some pills to pleasure his lady, from whom he received a bad turn, for, instead of giving him what he asked for, he gave him purgative pills, to such an effect that he never ceased going to the privy the whole night, as the ladies reported in the morning.'

Cesare was happy, though. He told Alexander that he was 'the most contented man in the world'. However, despite the fact that Alexander ordered bonfires to be burned throughout Rome in celebration, Buchard recorded that the marriage was no cause for rejoicing, but rather 'a great dishonour', another snub from Naples to the Holy See.

The marriage lasted just four months. Cesare had to return to his duties with the papal army in Italy, which was now in a state of permanent warfare. Charlotte gave birth to a daughter named Luisa several months later. His only legitimate offspring, Cesare never saw her or his bride again, though he wrote often and sent expensive gifts. Charlotte was twenty-five when she heard of her husband's death. She went into mourning that ended only with her own death, seven years later.

Cesare, naturally, comforted himself with other women during his separation from his wife. In 1500, he captured the Romagnan stronghold of Forli and, with it, thirty-seven-year-old Caterina Sforza. For years, she had fought courageously against every foe that had come against her. She was a beautiful woman who rode into battle in armour with a specially designed breast-plate to accommodate her splendid figure. Two of her husbands had been assassinated before her eyes and when a mob threatened to murder her two children, she stood on top of the battlements of her castle, pulled up her shirts and shouted: 'Look, I have the mould to make some more.'

She had fought valiantly to defend her lands against Cesare and the papal armies. Then, when all seemed lost, she sent the Pope a letter of surrender, which had been painstakingly infected with plague germs. When Cesare found out, he rushed to Rome to save his father. Alexander had the messengers, still holding the message, burnt at the stake.

To prevent further resistance, Cesare was determined to humiliate Caterina publicly. He returned to Forli and, after a final assault in which four hundred men were killed in less that half-an-hour, Caterina was captured. Cesare whipped her and raped her, then put it about that she had defended her castle more strenuously than she had defended her virtue.

Caterina seems to have thought that she had met her perfect partner in Cesare. On their way to Rome they seem to have become lovers. The affair was brief. When they arrived in Rome, she was led into the city in manacles.

There is also a story that Cesare abducted and raped the most beautiful young man in Italy. During his conquest of the Romagna, Cesare besieged the city of Faenza, which was defended by sixteen-year-old Astor Manfredi. Several assaults were repelled, but the city was finally surrendered, provided the life and property of the young prince were respected. But young Manfredi's beauty awoke Cesare's lust. Once he had tired of the young man, he sent him to Alexander along with his brother and another good looking young man. These men, it is said, were used for some time by the Pope. But the evidence is thin. As the victims were found in the Tiber with stones tied around their necks, they could not tell their side of the story.

They were probably better off dead. The symptoms of the pox became so severe that Cesare began wearing a black silk mask in public, which further enhanced his demonic reputation, and he would venture out only at night.

Finally, with the help of the French, Cesare captured the whole of the Romagna, becoming its Duke in 1501.

Alexander VI travelled from Rome with his mistresses and courtesans to inspect the newly extended papal states. On the island of Elba, he invited the prettiest girls of the island to perform their dances at his palace.

'That party with a Borgia could not end otherwise than with orgies,' says the historian Gordon, 'and therefore licence was carried to its excess, and at the supper they had no scruple, though in Lent, to eat every kind of meat. His Holiness, however, baptised the chicken and venison with the name of turbots and sturgeon.'

Despite the pox, Cesare had taken up with the beautiful and cultured Florentine courtesan Fiametta de'Michelis in 1500. She played the lyre, sang beautifully, recited poetry in Greek and spoke fluently. Her favours were so much in demand that she had become a wealthy woman.

But Cesare rarely paid for his pleasures. He usually took what he wanted. In 1501, he kidnapped Dorotea Malatesta Caracciolo, one of the most beautiful women in Italy, who was on her way to see her husband, a Venetian army officer. 'If the duke has done this,' cursed Alexander, 'then he has lost his mind.' Offending the Venetians so crassly risked a diplomatic incident that would plunge the papal states back into war. When accused of the abduction, Cesare said he knew nothing about it and blamed one of his officers. Cesare kept Dorotea Malatesta prisoner for two years and used her as a sex toy. When he grew tired of her, he sent her back to her husband.

Meanwhile father and son were attempting to appropriate the whole of central Italy, funding their efforts by selling high offices and by assassinating anyone who stood in their way and seizing their property.

Alexander arranged a third marriage for his beloved Lucrezia. Again it was a political match. Her third husband, Alfonso d'Este, Duke of Ferrara was not a particularly appealing catch. He was ugly, with a big nose and a bull-neck, and he was not very bright. His first wife, Anna Sforza, had died in childbirth, but he was reputed to have spent more time in brothels that with her anyway.

To celebrate the forthcoming nuptials Cesare invited his father Pope Alexander and his sister Lucrezia to what he called 'The Joust of Whores'. Fifty prominent Roman prostitutes were invited to Cesare's apartment in the apostolic palace. Even Johann Buchard, who thought he had seen it all, was outraged when the women danced, first scantily clad, then naked, around the Pope's table.

'This marriage,' wrote Buchard,

> has been celebrated with such unexampled orgies as were never before seen. His Holiness gave a supper to the cardinals and grandees of his court, placing at the side of each guest two courtesans, whose only dress consisted of a loose garment of gauze and garlands of flowers; and when the meal was over, those women, more than fifty in number, performed lascivious dances – at first alone, afterwards with the guests. At last, at a signal given by Madam Lucrezia, the garments of the women fell down, and the dance went on to the applause of His Holiness.
>
> They afterwards proceeded to other sports. By order of the Pope, there were symmetrically placed in the ballroom, twelve rows of branched candelabras covered with lighted candles; Madam Lucrezia threw upon the floor some handfuls of chestnuts, after which those courtesans, entirely naked, ran on all fours, contending to gather the most, and the swifter and more successful obtained from his Holiness presents of jewels and silk dresses. At last, as there were prizes for the sports, there were premiums for lust, and the women were carnally attacked at the pleasure of the guests; and this time Madam Lucrezia, who presided with the Pope on a platform, distributed the premiums to the victors.

Whoever had sex with the greatest number of prostitutes won a prize.

The 'Joust of Whores' was, no doubt, the pinnacle of

papal excess; but for some time, it had been the talk of the Roman diplomatic corps that twenty-five prostitutes were taken every night into the Vatican to entertain Alexander, Cesare and the cardinals. 'The Pope,' it was said, 'keeps his permanent little flock there so that the whole place is being openly converted into a brothel for every kind of depravity.'

Tales of the Pope's drunken orgies abounded. One day when he put off official engagements because of a cold, the Florentine envoy, Francesco Pepi, wrote 'this did not prevent him on Sunday night, the eve of All Saints' Day, from staying up till twelve o'clock with the Duke of Valentinois, who had brought prostitutes and courtesans into the Vatican; and they passed the night with dancing and laughter.'

Although similar stories had spread through Alexander's reign, things began to get out of hand when a letter detailing his excesses began to circulate. Translated into every European language, the so-called 'Letter to Silvo Savelli' purported to be addressed to a Baron Savelli whose lands had been confiscated by Alexander. It called the Pope an 'infamous beast' and a 'monster' and accused him of murder, theft and incest.

Who is not shocked to hear tales of the monstrous lasciviousness openly exhibited in the Vatican in defiance of God and all human decency? Who is not repelled by the debauchery, the incest, the obscenity of the children of the Pope, his son and daughter, the flocks of courtesans in the palace of St Peter? There is not a house of ill fame or a brothel that is not more respectable. On the first of November, All Saints' Day, fifty courtesans were invited to a banquet at this pontifical palace and gave the most repug-

nant performance there. Rodrigo Borgia is an abyss of vice and a subverter of all justice, human or divine.

It also had a go at Cesare.

His father favours him because he has his own perversity, his own cruelty. It is difficult to say which of these two is the most execrable. The cardinals see all and keep quiet and flatter and admire the Pope. But all fear him and, above all, fear his fratricidal son, who from being a cardinal has made himself into an assassin. He lives like the Turks, surrounded by flocks of prostitutes, guarded by armed soldiers. At his orders or decree, men are killed, wounded, thrown into the Tiber, poisoned, robbed of all their possessions.

Alexander took no notice of such criticism, but the letter annoyed Cesare. One man circulating it was thrown in jail. So that he could neither write nor speak, Cesare had his right hand amputated and his tongue cut out. As a warning to others, the hand and tongue were hung on the front of his cell where visitors could see them. Alexander, as always, found an excuse for such barbarism. 'The duke is a good-hearted man,' he said, 'but he cannot tolerate insults.'

As part of Lucrezia's dowry, Alexander threw in a few minor benefices. The wedding was performed by Alexander in the absence of the bridegroom. His brother performed as proxy. To celebrate, Alexander had a medal struck. Lucrezia was on one side; the other bore the legend: 'Chastity, a thing most precious for virtue and beauty.'

Lucrezia had to leave her children behind in Rome as no Renaissance prince would take on another man's children. Cesare insisted that she travel to Ferrara via the cities of the Romagna that he had conquered and Alexander even postponed the start of Lent so that the people of Ferrara could celebrate.

When she arrived in Ferrara, her new husband took her direct to the nuptial chamber. The following morning, Duke Ercole wrote to Alexander: 'Last night our son, the illustrious Don Alfonso, and Lucrezia kept company and we are convinced that both parties are thoroughly satisfied.'

But Alfonso was no Cesare. Alfonso's sister told her husband: 'From what I have been given to understand, Don Alfonso took her three times.'

Happy though the marriage may have been, Cesare kept a loving eye on his little sister. When she was ill, he broke off a military campaign to be by her side.

In August 1503, Alexander died. At dinner with a cardinal who had fallen into disfavour, both the Pope and Cesare fell ill. Cesare pulled through. It was said that they had malaria, but it is more than likely that they were victims of poison that Cesare had intended for the cardinal.

The Borgias' poison of choice was cantarella, made up largely of white arsenic, though Alexander preferred straightforward strangling and bludgeoning. The arsenic, it is said, created a fireball in Alexander's stomach. His eyes were bloodshot and his complexion turned yellow. He lay on his bed for hours, unable to swallow. Slowly his face turned mulberry-coloured and his skin began to peel off. The fat on his belly turned to liquid and he bled from both ends.

Doctors had very few techniques at their disposal. Both emetics and bleeding worsened the situation. Eventually, the last rites were administered and Rodrigo Borgia, Pope Alexander VI, was dead.

From his sick-bed, Cesare quickly ordered his father's apartments sealed before they were ransacked by greedy cardinals. The Pope's body was laid on a trestle. It had turned black and putrefaction set in almost immediately. The body swelled until it was as broad as it was long. The tongue swelled up and fluid spewed from the gaping mouth. The Venetian ambassador described Alexander's corpse as 'the ugliest, most monstrous and horrible dead body that was ever seen, without any form or likeness of humanity'.

'It was a revolting scene,' says Raphael Volterrano, 'to look at that deformed, blackened corpse, prodigiously swelled, and exhaling an infectious smell; his lips and nose were covered with brown drivel, his mouth was opened very widely, and his tongue, inflated by poison, fell out upon his chin; therefore no fanatic or devotee dared to kiss his feet or hands, as custom would have required.'

While the chaplain washed the body ready for burial, Cesare himself oversaw the looting of his father's apartment. His henchmen stole the gold and silver ornaments, the opulent vestments, the rugs and hangings. They even prised the rings off the corpse's swollen fingers.

By the time they had finished stripping the apartments, the body was leaking putrid fluids from all its orifices. Papal porters pegged their noses and tried to get the body into a coffin. Scared to touch the corpse because of the infection it might contain, they tied a rope around the feet that had so often been kissed by princes and pretty women and hauled the corpse into the box. The hugely swollen corpse would not fit and the chaplain Johann Buchard had to push and beat it into the coffin as best he could. Then he covered the papal remains with a bit of old carpet. That was all Cesare's men had left in the apartments.

The clergy at the Basilica refused entry to the coffin. A fight broke out and the papal porters managed to lodge the coffin in the crypt. No Mass was said over the body. Pope Julius decreed that it was blasphemy to pray for the damned, so any service would have been sacrilege.

On the day of his election Julius II said: 'I will not live in the same rooms as the Borgias lived. He desecrated the Holy Church as none before. He usurped the papal power by the devil's aid, and I forbid under pain of excommunication anyone to speak or think of Borgia again. His name and memory must be forgotten. It must be crossed out of every document and memorial. His reign must be obliterated. All paintings made of the Borgias or for them must be covered over with black crepe. All the tombs of the Borgias must be opened and their bodies sent back to where they belong – to Spain.'

The Borgia apartments in the Vatican were sealed off and remained closed until the nineteenth century. In 1610, Pope Alexander VI's body was removed from the Basilica. It now rests in the Spanish Church in the Via di Monserrato, awaiting judgement day.

However, after Alexander VI died, Vannozza Catanei was honoured as the Pope's widow. And when she herself died at the age of seventy-six, she was buried with elaborate ceremony in the church of Santa Maria del Popolo. The entire papal court turned out as if they were attending the funeral of a cardinal.

Without his father to protect him, Cesare was in trouble. He had tried to block the election of Julius II. Arrested, he escaped twice and ultimately found safety with his brother-in-law, the King of Navarre. He died bravely when he rode into an ambush in Viana, Spain, in 1507. His attackers stripped off his armour and left him naked except for a stone strategically placed on his genitals. There were twenty-three wounds on his body. He was just thirty-one years old.

He was buried in the simple parish church of Santa Maria at Viana. The inscription on his tomb reads: 'Here, in a scant piece of earth, lies he whom all the world feared.'

A French soldier who fought alongside him added: 'Of his virtues I shall say no more, for they have been talked about enough, but I must say he was a good comrade and a brave man.'

But perhaps his finest epitaph is the dedication in a book on syphilis called *Tractatus contra Pudendarga*. It was written by Cesare's Spanish doctor. Cesare had given permission for the dedication and he had allowed the doctor to try out some new cures for the disease on him. The doctor gratefully notes in the dedication that 'in Your Person, you have afforded mankind the chance to find a cure for this illness'.

Cesare left two children by his extra-marital affairs, one of whom, Gerolamo, inherited his father's ruthless character. He married the daughter of the Lord of Capri in 1537 and their daughter, Camilla Lucrezia, became a nun and, apparently, led a saintly life.

Lucrezia's third marriage could be judged a success. With Alexander and Cesare dead, there was no political advantage in it, but Alfonso refused to divorce her, though he kept a mistress on the side. Lucrezia gave Alfonso an heir and took a number of lovers herself. One of them was the Venetian poet Pietro Bembo, who wrote poems celebrating her beauty and elegance.

Lucrezia also had an affair with Francesco Gonzaga, who had taken Cesare's place as military commander of the Church. She particularly relished this affair as Gonzaga was married to Alfonso's sister Isabel, whom she hated. The affair got a little out of hand when Gonzaga attempted to invade Ferrara and carry Lucrezia off – he even had rooms prepared for her – but the French army arrived in the nick of time and drove him off.

When Alfonso was away, Lucrezia acted as regent. She made Ferrara one of the centres of letters of the Renaissance. In later life she turned to religion. She died in childbirth at the age of thirty-nine.

15

Holy fathers

*P*ope Pius III (1503) was hardly a worthy successor to Alexander VI. He had even angrily refused Rodrigo's handsome bribe at the conclave of 1492 and protested to the Sacred College when Rodrigo gave a substantial part of the papal states to his son Juan. But then Pius III reigned for just twenty-six days.

Although Julius II (1503–13) quickly distanced himself from Alexander VI, he was much more in the Borgia mould. He was the father of a family and a hard-drinking, hard-swearing, swashbuckling pederast. Handsome and syphilitic, he had many mistresses, one of whom had given him the pox. As Cardinal Giuliano della Rovere, he fathered three daughters and was nicknamed 'Il terrible' – an awesome reputation to have gained in the reign of a Borgia pope.

He had been Alexander's rival for the papacy and feared assassination throughout his reign, most of which he had spent in France. He tried to turn Charles VIII of France against Alexander and set up a council to depose the Pope. But Alexander was wily enough to block those plans and the future Pope Julius had to remain in hiding until Alexander's death. After the brief papacy of Pius III, he bribed his way into office in a conclave that lasted a single day. Once on the papal throne he decreed that, from then on, anyone who bribed the conclave should be deposed.

As well as loving sex, he loved his food. Even during Lent he would eat the best caviare, tunny, prawns and lampreys from Flanders. He also liked a drink. The Emperor Maximilian said straightforwardly: 'Julius is a drunken and wicked pope.'

It is said that with Julius, religion was not even a hobby. He had a volcanic temper and used to hit anyone who annoyed him with a stick he always carried.

He is remembered as the pope who forced the thirty-one-year-old sculptor Michelangelo to abandon the stonemason's craft and paint the ceiling of the Sistine Chapel. Michelangelo was as grumpy as his patron and they frequently exchanged blows. The two men had something else in common. While he was a cardinal, leading nobles openly accused Julius of 'unnatural vice'. Michelangelo, of course, was gay. It was said that Julius wore himself out in two years leading a hectic life 'amongst prostitutes and boys'.

Contemporary authors said he was a 'great sodomite'. And according to a seventeenth-century tract, 'this man abused two young gentlemen, besides many others'. The two young gentlemen were, apparently, two noble youths 'whom Anne, Queen of France, had sent to Robert, Cardinal of Nantz, to be instructed'. What they were to be instructed in, the author does not say, but the curriculum was plainly not meant to include 'that act'.

Julius II was also said to have seduced a German youth. His conquest is commemorated in verse:

> *To Rome, a German came of fair aspect,*
> *But he returned a woman in effect.*

He was a liberal when it came to other people's pleasures. He issued a papal bull on 2 July 1510 establishing a brothel where young women could ply their trade. Leo X and Clement VII also condoned this establishment, on the condition that a quarter of the goods and chattels of the courtesans who worked there should belong, after their death, to the nuns of Sainte-Marie-Madeleine. It was Julius who gave Henry VIII the dispensation that allowed him to marry his brother Arthur's widow, Catherine of Aragon.

Julius's main interest, however, was not religion or art or sex, but war. In defiance of canon law, he donned armour and rode a charger into battle at the head of the papal army. When they took Mirandola from the French, he clambered over frozen ditches and through a breach in the wall in full armour. Claiming the town for Christ, he yelled: 'Let's see who had the bigger balls, the King of France or the Pope.' In Italian, it is clear that he was not talking about cannon balls.

The humanist Erasmus wrote a satirical sketch in which Pope Julius turned up at the Pearly Gates in full armour. But St Peter did not recognize him. So Julius whipped off his helmet and donned the papal tiara. But St Peter still did not recognize his successor. In desperation, Julius held up his papal keys, said to be the keys to the Kingdom of Heaven. St Peter examined them carefully and shook his head.

'Sorry, but they will not fit anything in this Kingdom,' he said.

When Michelangelo had finished painting the ceiling of the Sistine Chapel, he got out his chisels again and sculpted a statue of his patron. When Pope Julius II saw it, he said: 'What's that under my arm?'

'A book, Holiness,' said Michelangelo.

'What do I know about books?' yelled the Pope. 'Make it a sword instead.'

But by 1508, Julius II had to give up his man of action image and the Master of Ceremonies at the papal court had to prevent distinguished visitors kissing the papal foot, it was so riddled with syphilis.

After Julius died, Cardinal Farnese rushed out of the conclave into St Peter's Square, screaming 'Balls! Balls!' The crowd knew immediately what he meant. The new pope was to be Giovanni de'Medici – *palle* or balls were a prominent part of the Medici coat of arms.

Giovanni de'Medici became Pope Leo X (1513–21). He also had several bastards, but it was the bastard son of his illegitimate brother, Giuliano de'Medici who followed him on to the papal throne as Clement VII (1523–34).

When elected, Leo said to Giuliano, who was a cardinal: 'God has given us the papacy. Let us enjoy it.' He certainly did that. Even the *Catholic Encyclopædia* admits that Leo X 'looked upon the papal court as a centre of amusement'.

The Roman people were a little surprised to find that Leo X did not bring a mistress with him to Rome but, despite his illegitimate offspring, his first preference was not heterosexuality. Florentine statesman Francesco Guicciardini reported that the new pope was excessively devoted to the flesh, 'especially those pleasures which cannot, with delicacy, be mentioned'. According to Joseph McCabe, Leo X was 'a coarse, frivolous, cynical voluptuary, probably addicted to homosexual vice in the Vatican'.

'He was much given to idleness, pleasure and carnal delights, whereby he had many bastard sons, all of whom he promoted to be Dukes and great Lords, and married them to the prime quality,' contemporary accounts say. He was 'a lover of boys' and loved his liquor. He was also the patron of Michelangelo and Raphael.

His homosexuality may have originated in the fact that he had been locked up in various abbeys and priories since he was a child. He was made an abbot at the age of seven, took over the famous abbey at Monte Cassino at eleven and became a cardinal at thirteen – the youngest ever, though Benedict IX had become pope by the age of twelve.

As a cardinal, he started how he meant to go on, immediately selling indulgences to enrich his family. He seems to have been discreet about his sexual proclivities, only 'coming out' when he was pope. Soon his proclivities were well known. His friend and biographer Bishop Giovio said openly: 'Nor was he free from the infamy that he seemed to have an improper love of some of his chamberlains, who were members of the noblest families of Italy, and to speak tenderly to them and make broad jokes.' He had plainly been a practising sodomite for years. When he was elected he was suffering from chronic ulcers on the backside and had to be carried into the conclave on a stretcher.

His coronation was more like that of an Emperor than a pope. Cardinal Farnese put the papal tiara on Leo X's head and said: 'Receive the tiara adorned with three crowns and know that you are father of princes and kings, victor of the whole world under the earth and Vicar of Our Lord Jesus Christ to whom be honour and glory without end.'

Then Leo, dressed in woven gold cloth and covered with jewels, rode on a white Turkish horse at the head of a procession of 2500 troops and 4000 kings, princes, prelates and nobles along a route bedecked with banners, bunting and statues of the saints interspersed with Roman gods, past the Forum and the Colosseum to the Lateran Palace. For this coronation procession, he had an arch erected which bore the legend: 'Mars has reigned, Pallas has followed, but the reign of Venus goes on forever.'

The evening was given over to feasting and fireworks. The whole extravaganza cost him 100,000 ducats. That night, he celebrated his coronation privately in the Castel Sant'Angelo with his lover Alfonso Petrucci of Siena, whom Leo made a cardinal.

Leo lavished entertainments on his lover. A great hunter and a gourmet, he kept a game reserve near Rome for the exclusive use of himself and his cardinals – ten square miles of forest. Any trespassers found there were to have their hands and feet cut off, their homes burned and their children sold into servitude.

He loved giving masked balls for his cardinals and their ladies, and he put on huge banquets where naked boys would appear from the puddings. One meal, attended by the Venetian ambassador, consisted of sixty-five courses, with three dishes per course, served with remarkable speed.

'Scarcely had we finished one delicacy than a fresh

plate was set before us,' wrote his Excellency, 'and yet everything was served on the finest of silver of which his Eminence has an abundant supply. At the end of the meal we rose from the table gorged with rich food and deafened by the continual concert, carried on both in-side and outside the hall and proceeding from every instrument that Rome could produce – fifes, harpsi-chords and four-stringed lutes as well as the voices of a choir.'

Dishes included monkeys' brains, parrots' tongues, live fish from Constantinople, apes' meat, quails and venison, all prepared in exquisite sauces and served with aromatic wines and fruit from three continents. Im-mensely wealthy, Leo would save on the washing up by having the silver dishes thrown into the Tiber after each course was finished.

He acquired a reputation for being wildly extravagant. Among other things, he would play cards with his cardi-nals, allow the public to sit in as spectators and toss huge handfuls of gold coins to the crowd whenever he won a hand. The expense of both his cultural and military en-deavours, along with his taste for increasingly ornate pa-pal gowns, eventually drove the papal treasury into bankruptcy.

Leo was also a practical joker. He once had carrion covered in a strong sauce. Pretending it was a papal deli-cacy, he served it to the poor. He had an old priest called Baraballo, who was proud of his terrible verse, made poet laureate. After Baraballo was crowned, he was pa-raded around the Capitol on a white elephant, recently given to the Pope by the King of Portugal.

Leo liked to keep tabs on the misdemeanours of others for the purposes of blackmail. One night a

Roman nobleman, Lorenzo Strozzi, invited Cardinal Cibò and three other cardinals to a private party. The guests arrived to be ushered into a mortuary, full of skulls, naked bodies, blood, pigs' heads and instruments of torture. Next they were taken into an opulent dining hall, where exquisite food was served by beautiful waitresses and handsome waiters. While they ate they were entertained by clowns, jesters and musicians. The climax of the evening was provided by Rome's most sought-after prostitute, Madre Mia, and her stable.

A report on the goings-on at Strozzi's party was on Leo X's desk by 7 a.m. the next day. He sent for Cibò and asked about the origin of the Spanish expression 'Madre Mia'. Did it refer to the mother of Christ, perhaps? Cibò, still hung over, got the point.

Leo also put on plays in his palace, but he preferred broad comedies and more or less indecent Rabelaisian farces to serious dramatic works. One of the authors of these lewd plays was a senior churchman, Cardinal Bibbiena.

At one spring carnival, Leo himself produced a play that involved eight hermits and a 'virgin'. The woman, naked, prayed to Venus and the hermits became her lusty lovers, then they killed each other for love of her.

'It is difficult to judge whether the merits of the learned or the tricks of fools afford most delight to His Holiness,' said Pietro Aretino, who enjoyed Leo X's patronage. A well-known Renaissance pornographer, Pietro Aretino was famous for the bawdy sonnets he wrote to accompany the graphic drawings of sixteen known sexual positions by Raphael's gifted student, Giuliano Romano, a man also responsible for many of the frescoes in the Vatican. The work was notorious in Rome at the time.

In 1516, Aretino wrote a mock will for Hanno, Leo X's pet elephant, which left the animal's substantial genitals to one of the Pope's more lascivious cardinals.

That same year, while the fun was at its height in Rome, a general chapter was held, which denounced the intolerable abuse indulged in by some abbots who threw off all obedience to the rule of celibacy and dared to keep women under the pretence of requiring domestic services. Leo X himself made a feeble effort at reform by banning the systematic sale of concubinage licences to the clergy. It did not help. The Renaissance artist Benvenuto Cellini, who suffered from syphilis, reported regretfully that the 'illness was very common among priests'.

Leo raised simony to a new height to raise the funds for his new project. Against all advice, he decided to pull down Celestine's Basilica, which had been standing for twelve hundred years, and build a new one. Even though there were 7000 registered prostitutes in Rome for a population of less than 50,000, the papal brothels were not bringing in enough cash. So Leo was happy to sell cardinal's hats to atheists, if they could come up with the right price. They fetched anywhere from 24,000 to 70,000 ducats.

Leo's lover Alfonso Petrucci did not have to pay for his, of course, but once he was a cardinal, he realized that he was then just one small step from the papacy himself. He bribed a Florentine doctor, Battista de Vercelli, to poison Leo by sticking venom up his back passage while operating on his piles. Unfortunately, the Pope's secret police intercepted a note outlining the plan. Under torture, de Vercelli confessed and was hanged, drawn and quartered.

Realizing that his number was up, Petrucci fled. But Leo sent the Spanish ambassador to him, guaranteeing him safe conduct provided he return to Rome immediately. Petrucci stupidly agreed. As soon as he arrived in Rome, Leo had him thrown into the infamous Sammarocco dungeon beneath the Castel Sant'Angelo. There, he was tortured daily on the rack. When the Spanish ambassador complained that his word of honour, which had guaranteed Petrucci's safe passage, had been besmirched, Leo told him: 'No faith need be kept with a poisoner.'

In his confession, extracted under torture, Petrucci admitted: 'Eight times I, Cardinal Petrucci, went to a consistory with a stiletto beneath my robes waiting for the opportune moment to kill de'Medici.'

Petrucci was sentenced to death. But as the Pope could not allow a Christian to lay a finger on a prince of the Church, he had Petrucci strangled by a Moor. With due respect to Petrucci's station in life, a silk cord in cardinal's crimson was used to choke the life out of him.

Four other cardinals who were in on the plot were absolved, but only after they had come up with huge reparations.

Afterwards Leo comforted himself with the boy singer Solimando, who was the grandson of Sultan Mehmet, the Turk who took Constantinople in 1453. Solimando's father was Sultan Djem, who had been murdered by Alexander VI on the instructions of his brother Sultan Bayezid.

Leo X was said to have been an atheist. After hearing Cardinal Bembo speaking on the joyful message of our

Lord, Leo commented that it was well known to the world through all ages how greatly the fable of Christ had 'profited us and our associates'.

This cynical attitude to the papacy was the last straw. During the reign of Leo X, Martin Luther nailed his ninety-five theses to the door of the church in Wittenburg, denouncing the sale of indulgences, simony and corruption. Later, he rebelled against clerical celibacy as well.

After the death of Leo X, the Dutchman Hadrian VI (1522–23) was Pope briefly. He told the Diet of Nuremberg in 1522 that: 'For many years, abominable things have taken place in the Chair of Peter, abuses in spiritual matters, transgressions of the commandments, so that everything here has been wickedly perverted.' But after that brief and boring interlude, the fun started again.

Clement VII (1523–34) was 'a bastard, a poisoner, a sodomite, a geomancer, a church robber'. The chronicler Paulus Jovius relates 'divers abominations'.

He was the bastard son of Giuliano de'Medici, by his mistress Fioretta. Being illegitimate should have made him ineligible for the papacy, but his uncle Pope Leo X straightened that out. Like his uncle, Clement VII was an atheist and he brazenly bought the election by distributing 60,000 ducats around the conclave cardinals.

He took a black woman as his mistress. The Italian historian Gino Capponi described her as 'a Moorish or mulatto slave'. She was the wife of a mule-driver who worked for his aunt. Clement had a son by her, Alessandro, who became the first hereditary Duke of Florence after Clement abolished the city's old constitution. He was known to the Florentines as 'The Moor' and the *Encyclopædia Italiana* says that his skin colour, lips and hair all revealed his African ancestry. His portrait by Bronzino shows this to be true and Benvenuto Cellini, who worked for Alessandro, says that it was well known that Alessandro was the son of the Pope.

Clement was another patron of the erotic writer Aretino and his 'lewd life' was commemorated in verse:

> *Vile Rome, Adieu;*
> *I did thee view,*
> *But thee no more will see*
> *Till pimp or punk,*
> *Or lewd or drunk,*
> *I resolve to be.*

Clement so enraged Emperor Charles V that Rome was given up to pillage for two entire months. In May 1527, the Imperial forces of Charles V entered the city, virtually unopposed. Emperor Constantine's golden cross was stolen and never recovered; so were the tiara of Nicholas I and the Golden Rose of Martin V. Romans who took shelter in churches were slaughtered out of hand. Five hundred men were massacred on the altar of St Peter's and holy relics were burned or destroyed. Priests were stripped naked and forced to perform blasphemous Masses. Men were tortured by having their genitals bound until they revealed the whereabouts of hidden treasures. Others were forced to eat their own testicles, roasted.

Nuns were raped, sold at auction on street corners or used as stakes in games of chance. Parents were forced to watch, or even assist, in the multiple rape of their daughters. Convents were turned into brothels, staffed by upper class women who had been dragged there.

'Marchionesses, countesses and baronesses served the unruly troops,' wrote the Sieur de Brantome, 'and for long afterwards the patrician women of the city were known as "the relics of the Sack of Rome".'

Clement VII remained safe in the Castel Sant'Angelo and eventually escaped to Orvieto, where the ambassador from Henry VIII caught up with him. But it was not a good time to ask the Pope to annul the King of England's marriage to Catherine of Aragon. His refusal to consider the matter led to the establishment of the Church of England.

Meanwhile, in Germany, Clement had even more problems. Martin Luther had just discovered sex. In 1525, Luther married Katherine von Bora, one of the twelve nuns he had kidnapped from the convent at Nimbschen. Sex, he said, was okay. Luther later wrote that he could find nothing but godliness in marriage.

Luther soon found that making clerical marriage legal in the Protestant Church was a popular move and the disaffected clergy rallied to him. According to one commentator: 'To turn the mistress into the honourable wife, to turn the bastards into honourable children, was the momentous single gift bestowed upon the clergy by Protestantism. Apart from higher considerations, it was said that, before his marriage to Katherine von Bora, Luther's bed had not been made for a year.'

16

Pope Petticoat

*A*lessandro Farnese succeeded Clement VII, under the name of Paul III (1534–49). He was a man of sagacity and experience but 'his morals were no higher than the debased age in which he lived'.

One commentator despairs at the task of relating 'the many enormous and horrible parricides, thefts, sorceries, treacheries, tryannies, incests and unparalleled whoredoms of this pope'. Nevertheless, we will have a go.

When he joined the Sacred College, he was known as 'Cardinal Petticoat' because he gave his sister Giulia 'to Alexander VI to be deflowered'. The lucrative offices that came along with his elevation allowed him to keep a noble Roman mistress, who bore him three sons and a daughter. He broke off with her in 1513, when the tide began to turn against the excesses of the Borgias and the Medicis. From then on, he tried to be more discreet.

There are numerous accounts of how he poisoned his mother and his niece to gain the whole of the family's inheritance. 'Adding a double incest to parricide, he caused the death of one of his sisters from jealousy of her other lovers.' Then he 'committed incest with his own daughter Constancia and poisoned her husband Bosius Sforza, that he might the more freely enjoy her; but pressing on his niece, Laura Farnese in the like nature, her husband Nicholas Quercen, taking him in the act, gave him a mark that he carried to his grave.'

He did not confine his amorous attentions to his own family.

> *Being legate in Ancona under Pope Julius II, he over-persuaded a young lady, under pretence of marriage, to yield to his lust, she verily thinking she had to do not with the legate but with one of his gentlemen. But on discovery of the illusion ran almost mad, yet brought him forth that monster in nature, Pietro Aloysius, afterwards Duke of Parma and Placentia.*

The Duke of Parma and Placentia had quite a reputation of his own.

> *This Peter being the darling of his father, insomuch that when he was told of any of his vile doings he would smile, saying his son had not learnt those things from him.*
>
> *Every one knows the detestable abominations this person committed on the body of Cosmo Cherio, Bishop of Fano, which I abhor to relate. At length this Duke's own domestics being not able to endure any longer his tyrannies and filthy abominations got rid of him out of the way in the year 1548.*

When Pietro was murdered, Paul III made his son-in-law Ottavio Duke of Parma and Placentia in his place.

After 'prostituting his sister to the Spanish pope, for his cardinal's cap', Paul was accused of using the assistance of astrologers and other necromancers to get himself elected. He was also accused of being an atheist, of poisoning two cardinals and a Polish bishop over a theological point, and of keeping 'a roll of forty-five thousand whores, who paid him a monthly tribute'. The city of Rome only had a population of around 100,000 inhabitants at the time.

He celebrated his election by striking a new gold coin. As the greatness of the Farnese family was based solely on his sister's adultery with Pope Alexander VI, on the reverse side, the coin shows a naked Ganymede watering a lily. Ganymede, in mythology, was the lover of Jupiter.

Despite having shed his mistress, Paul III enjoyed a party and liked to have beautiful women at his table. The Vatican resounded to masked balls and brilliant feasts. And he commissioned Michelangelo's Last Judgement in the Sistine Chapel.

But Paul III's prime aim in the papacy was the advancement of the Farnese family. He 'tried in all ways imaginable to enrich his bastards, of which he had many'. One of them, named Pietro Lodovico 'was the most detestable sodomite who every lived', according to the Italian historian Cypriano de Valera. Two of his grandchildren were created cardinal at the ages of fourteen and sixteen.

Paul excommunicated Henry VIII and placed England under an interdict – no Catholic services could be said there. In retaliation, Henry ordered his principal adviser Thomas Cromwell to investigate life in the cloisters. Cromwell sent one of his men, a Dr Leighton, to visit Langdon Abbey in Kent where, after breaking down the door, he found the abbot in bed with his mistress. The woman had been smuggled into the abbey in men's clothes. Leighton found her disguise hanging up in the wardrobe.

In all, 144 monasteries and convents were investigated by Cromwell. His report says that they displayed the viciousness of Sodom, that nuns were served by 'lewd confessors' and that monks went with married women as well as prostitutes.

This gave Henry the excuse to suppress the monasteries. He sent one monk to the scaffold without benefit of clergy because he refused to abandon his wife. Thomas Cranmer, Henry's Archbishop of Canterbury, got the message. He had just been married secretly for the second time and sent his new wife off to safety in Germany.

While Henry VIII's England embraced the Reformation, Paul III managed to hold on to Scotland. He appointed the notorious Cardinal David Beaton Archbishop of St Andrews and Scottish Primate. Beaton was a widower with three legitimate children, but it was widely known that he still exercised 'the talent God gave him'. It is estimated that he had eleven sons and four daughters who were mentioned in the official lists as the 'bastards of the Archbishop of St Andrews'.

Archbishop Hey, bemoaning Paul's appointment of Beaton, wrote:

I often wonder what bishops were thinking about when they admitted such men to the handling of the Lord's holy body, when they hardly know the order of the alphabet. Priests come to the holy table who have not slept off yesterday's debauch...? I will not treat the riotous living of those who, professing chastity, have invented new kinds of lusts, which I prefer to be left unknown rather than be told by me.

Nevertheless, Paul III would not hear a word said against Beaton. He was plainly a man after the Pope's heart. Beaton's behaviour was certainly not unusual for the time. Priests specialized in seduction during confession. Boxes were not introduced until the middle of the sixteenth century and not widely used until they were made compulsory in 1614. Until then, penitents would sit beside their confessor, or kneel at his feet. In the dark corner of a church, it was all too easy to make an amorous move. Even if a penitent denounced a priest, the ecclesiastical court usually went easy on the cleric. In February 1535, the parish priest in Almodovar was accused of a number of sexual offences. These included frequenting brothels and soliciting in the confessional. He had refused to give a young woman absolution until she had had sex with him. His punishment was a trifling fine and being confined to his house for thirty days.

Heresy was a different altogether. Paul III viciously persecuted Protestants. It is said that his son the Duke of Parma and his grandson Cardinal Farnese shed so much blood in their war against the Lutherans 'that their hordes should be able to swim in it'.

Another account says: 'After he became infuriated against the unfortunate Lutherans, his nephews became the executors of his cruelty, and were not afraid to boast in public of having caused rivers of blood to flow deep enough to swim horses. During the time of those butcheries, the pope indulged in voluptuousness with his daughter Constancia.'

Despite his own shortcomings, Paul III began a new Inquisition to suppress heresy in Rome. He appointed Cardinal John Peter Carafa – the future Paul IV (1555–

59) – and a dozen other cardinals to investigate all those who had erred from the one true path.

'The guilty and the suspects are to be imprisoned and proceeded against up to the final sentence,' said Paul III. The irony was that with his mistresses, illegitimate children, double incest, divers poisonings, and the gift of cardinal's red to his teenage grandsons, the Pope might have considered himself a prime suspect for the Inquisition.

Carafa went about his duties with a will and he wrote a *Consilium* for Pope Paul III. This was an 'advice note' spelling out the details of the corruption that he had found in the Church. But the document was leaked.

It said, among other things: 'In this Rome, harlots go about in the city like married women, or ride on their mules, followed from the heart of the city by nobles and clerics of the Cardinals' household. In no city have we seen such corruption, except in this, an example to all.'

The Protestants were delighted when they got their hands on it because it confirmed everything that they said about the corruption of the papacy. The leak was plainly a disaster. So when Cardinal Carafa became pope, he took the only logical step. He put his own *Consilium* on the *Index of Forbidden Books*.

Julius III (1550–55) Paul III's successor, 'used one innocent as his minion and created him Cardinal, and abstained not of the Cardinal himself'. So read the charges against Pope Julius.

Another chronicler says: 'He fulminated an anathema against the Lutherans, persecuted them to death, and, adding depravity to cruelty, elevated to the cardinalate a young boy, who performed in his house, the double part of keeper of a monkey and minister to the infamous pleasures of the pope.'

In fact, he took as his lovers both his bastard son, Bertuccino, and his adopted son, Innocente, a fifteen-year-old youth he had picked up in the streets of Palma. He made the two of them cardinals, along with another 'sodomite boy' he had known when he was legate in Bologna. The other cardinals were not pleased, especially by this last appointment, and asked him what he could see in the lad to lavish on him such high office. Julius replied: 'And what could you see in me to make me pope? Fortune favours whom he pleases and this boy perhaps might have as much merit as I.'

Afterwards the people of Rome called the boy-cardinal Ganymede and the Pope Jupiter. This was more appropriate than portraying Giulia Farnese as Ganymede, as his predecessor had done. Ganymede was the mythological king of Troy who was carried off by the gods for his beauty and used as a catamite by his heavenly kidnapper.

Naturally indolent, Julius devoted himself to pleasurable pursuits. He was generous to relatives and devoted to banquets, the theatre and hunting. He was also renowned for his bad temper and his propensity to swear. He got really angry once because a roast peacock was served to him cold. After his tirade of filth was over, he was asked why he got so angry about a trifle. He said that if it pleased the Lord to get angry about an apple, expelling Adam and Eve from the garden of Eden over one, then a pope could get angry over a peacock.

He appointed numerous other handsome teenage boys as cardinals, and allegedly enjoyed bringing them together for orgies where he would watch them sodomize one another. Cardinal della Casa's famous poem 'In Praise of Sodomy' was dedicated to him. Poets could hardly resist celebrating the depravity of Julius and his pontificate:

> *What's Roma? Even that preposterous order shows,*
> *What's that? What he that spells it backward knows.*
> *Backwards "tis Amor, love; What love? Nay, hold*
> *Why, male love, and that odious to be told.*

Julius, the erotic writer Aretino's third papal patron, came within a stone's throw of giving him a cardinal's hat for his contribution to bawdiness.

17

The Sistine goes pristine

*P*aul IV (1555–59) was the real herald of the era of sexual sobriety for the popes. As John Carafa, he was chosen by Hadrian IV (1522–23) to spearhead the counter-reformation. To do so, he gave up a number of lucrative bishoprics to head an order dedicated to poverty. Then as Cardinal Carafa, he had been Inquisitor General under Paul III – his reward for dreaming up the idea of having a new Inquisition, this time in Rome itself. He was the perfect man for the job. 'If my own father were a heretic,' Paul wrote, 'I would personally gather the wood to burn him.'

Feeling that, under his predecessors, priests who solicited in the confessional were getting off too lightly in the Bishops' Tribunals, he decided that this was a job for the Inquisition. Such behaviour was surely an indication of heresy. He was not concerned for the women who might be coerced into sex by an unscrupulous priest, but rather that the sacrament might be defiled if the priest handled it afterwards.

Once the Inquisition got involved, they had to define what exactly was meant by soliciting. Was it touching hands, or playing footsie? Passing love letters or making lewd suggestions? Or did the priest have to fondle the penitent's breasts or grope her? For example, when a woman fainted during confession and the priest seized the opportunity to rape her, the Inquisition found that this, technically, was not a case of soliciting.

According to the records of the Inquisition, a huge number of complaints were made against priests, especially those holding high office in the Church. Many clergymen thought of it as one of the perks of the job.

There were numerous instances of the priest, acting as *flagellant*, ordering a penitent to take off her clothes so that he could whip her. Sometimes the confessor decided that he was a sinner too. Both of them took off their clothes and whipped each other.

One priest in Ypres persuaded nine nuns in a Cistercian convent to strip off and beat each other, while he applied his whip to their peccant parts. Presumably this happy little bunch had to mortify the flesh in a similar fashion all over again after their fresh transgression. Apparently the priest got so inflamed that he had sex with all nine of them.

But very few of the clerical offenders were punished. The Inquisitors reckoned that for men who had been deprived of sex since they joined a seminary in their early teens, sitting in the dark listening to some attractive young lady confess the details of her sexual misdemeanours was more than flesh and blood could stand.

Once pope, Paul IV indulged in the usual practice of promoting relatives to profitable positions, but when he discovered that they were indulging in the same unprin-

244

cipled behaviour as other churchmen he sacked them. This made him very unpopular.

Unlike nearly all his predecessors, Paul was narrow minded. While the Renaissance popes had encouraged the new flowering of literature, in 1557 he began the *Index of Forbidden Books*. One of the first titles on it was Boccaccio's literary classic the *Decameron*, which stayed on this list until it was expurgated by the papal censors. Rabelais' bawdy *Gargantua and Pantagruel* was banned completely, even though Rabelais was a monk.

Of course, the papal censorship of books did not begin with Paul IV. Thr faithful were forbidden to read *The Acts of St Paul* in AD 150. Only part of that work survives. It is called *The Acts of Paul and Thecla*. Thecla, apparently, was a woman who held a prominent position in the early Church and the men who headed the Church in the second century wanted knowledge of her success suppressed.

The Council of Nicæa in AD 325 banned *Thalia* by Arius, a satirical work, because it quoted a couple of popular jokes about the divinity of Jesus. In AD 398, the twenty-one-year-old Emperor Arcadius was persuaded to threaten anyone who read the works of Eunomius with the gravest of penalties. Eunomius was, of course, the chief critic of the Church establishment.

In AD 446, Leo I came up with a long list of works which the faithful were required to burn. The Spanish Church began burning authors instead. This was found to be much more efficient. The Emperor Justinian and his wife, the former courtesan, Theodora, atoned for their sins by ordering anyone who even touched a banned book to have their hands cut off.

Many of the early bannings had to do with heresy and

the suppression of other versions of the Gospel stories, many of which may have been more authentic than the official ones. Pope Damasus (366–84) and Pope Gelasius I (492–96) both came up with lists of prohibited books. But soon literacy in Europe dropped to such a level that further banning was unnecessary. Only a relatively few people in the inner core of the Church could read, and they were easily policed.

Around 1050, toward the end of the Dark Ages, intellectual life was re-established in Europe. Literature, particularly, was full of sexual candour and bawdy tales of the goings on in monasteries and convents. The Church reacted predictably by burning books and their authors.

With the invention of printing in the fourteenth century, the problem, as far as the Church was concerned, got worse. Up until then, writers had had to depend on copyists and the Church had most of those. But the printing presses gave humanist writers a chance to publish books exploring all of human experience and the Church was quick to pounce any book that seemed to promote 'unchastity'. It was the Church's duty, popes reasoned, to protect its flock from eternal damnation. The irony was that the man doing much of the banning was Pope Gregory XI, whose papal court in Avignon was notorious for its sexual corruption and luxury.

Under Clement VII and Paul III the only books to be banned were those supporting the Protestant 'heresy'. Given those popes' morals they could hardly ban erotic literature. Clement VII staged immoral plays in the Vatican gardens in the evening before going off to bed with his page boys, so he would have had to ban his own work.

One German critic pointed out that if the popes of

that time had to ban 'unchaste' literature they would have had to suppress a book of poems by Cardinal della Casa which glorified sodomy. Cardinal Bembo was another man with a velvet pen, but he too was a close friend of the popes.

So it was Paul IV who took on what he saw as the sea of filth, and began banning any book that he took offence at.

As governor of Rome, Paul IV tried to stamp out public immorality. He confined Jews to their ghettos and forced them to wear distinctive headgear. But his draconian attitudes were not at all popular in the city. When he died in the summer of 1559, the Inquisition jail on the Via Ripetta was burnt down. His statue was toppled. The mob spat on it and kicked it around. And Jews put a yellow hat on its severed head. Finally, the fragments were thrown in the Tiber. The crowds started baying for Paul's corpse, but the Catholic authorities took the precaution of burying it secretly in St Peter's in the middle of the night and mounting an armed guard.

Paul's original *Index* was dismissed as a piece of ignorance and folly, even by contemporary Catholics, and when he died a special Commission of four archbishops and nine bishops was set up to sort it out. They did a better job, but they still ordered the destruction of the classic books by Machiavelli, Guicciardini and Dante.

In 1560, at the Council of Trent, set up in 1542 to find ways of resisting the Reformation, the Emperor Ferdinand begged Pope Pius IV (1559–65) to allow priests to marry in the hope that they would behave. 'For although all flesh is corrupted,' he said, 'none the less, the corruption of the priesthood is worse.'

But as ever, the Council saw the reasoning behind

clerical celibacy – it secured the loyalty of the clergy and preserved the assets of the Church. In 1563, the Council once again asserted that virginity or celibacy was better than marriage. Celibates, it declared, were in 'the state of perfection' and anyone who said otherwise was a heretic. Pius IV took on the job of revising the *Index of Forbidden Books* personally. He also created the Congregation of the Index with seven cardinals to vet new books.

Pius IV's successor, Pius V (1566–72) had three children and his private life was a source of endless gossip. However, he had been Paul IV's Grand Inquisitor and had given up sex in later life. His principle aim was to turn the Vatican into a monastery and he even threatened to excommunicate his cook when he was discovered putting forbidden ingredients into his soup on days of fasting.

When Pius V was crowned Pope, he said that he found Rome as immoral as at the height of the Renaissance. He was particularly offended by the number of prostitutes there and demanded they be expelled, especially those who earned vast sums catering to the prelates. earning vast sums. The Roman Senate resisted, arguing that licentiousness always flourished where there was celibacy, and if the prostitutes left, no respectable woman would be safe from the attentions of the priests.

But Pius V was determined to clean things up. He ordered that all the prostitutes in Rome be either married or whipped. Those who died under the lash were to be buried in a dungheap. The survivors were confined to special areas where they would not be seen by His Holiness – out of sight, out of mind. He also issued a bull banning ecclesiastical property being inherited by the illegitimate children of priests.

Next Pius V cracked down on clerical incontinence. But he found that this resulted in a disastrous increase in the incidence of sodomy among the clergy and he soon wearied of the campaign.

Pius tried to destroy all the ancient monuments around Rome on the grounds that they were the work of heathens. He also banned Romans from entering taverns. Blasphemers had their tongues pierced with a red-hot poker and hundreds of heretics were burnt alive.

Bachelors were forbidden female servants and nuns were not allowed to keep male dogs. Sexual misconduct of any kind was punished with the utmost ferocity and sodomites were burnt. Adulterers of both sexes were flogged in public. He was only dissuaded at the last minute from making adultery a capital offence. Doesn't he know anything about papal history, one cardinal commented.

While he was often too busy to attend other functions, Pius V never missed a single Thursday meeting of the Holy Office of the Inquisitor and constantly urged them to create more and more offences worthy of the death penalty.

Pius hated women with a passion. When Elizabeth I came to the throne of England he excommunicated her immediately. He also declared her to be a servant of vice and charged her with seventeen counts of infidelity. This forced her hand and, once again, England turned Protestant.

Pius was persuaded to defer the question of clerical marriage. Instead he took his frustrations out on the Jews. They were given an even harder time than under Paul IV. Jews were confined to the ghetto, forced to wear

249

badges and were excluded from all honourable positions and many occupations.

Under Pius V's successor, Gregory XIII (1572–85), matters returned to normal. He openly kept a mistress in Rome before he was pope and had many bastards, before and during his reign. It was said that 'having therefore such certain proofs of the Pope's manhood, the See of Rome could have no further use of the chair of trial' – that is, the groping chair.

After he was elected he was a bit more discreet, but he had so many of his children living with him that they 'diverted him with their prattle'. His favourite was his eldest son Philip Buoncompagni, on whom he settled 6000 crowns a year. With typical papal flair, he made another son, Giovanni, a cardinal.

St Bridget told Gregory: 'The clergy are less priests of God than the pimps of the devil.' But he took no notice. Contemporary writers talked of priests who spent their days in the tavern and their nights in the arms of their concubines. Members of the Curia all had their mistresses, it was argued, so concubinage must be all right.

Gregory lifted his predecessor's ban on prostitutes and huge numbers flocked to Rome because of all the 'celibates' there. Under Gregory, one courtesan, who was the toast of the city, made £150,000. Convents were converted back into brothels; respectable women had to carry daggers with them to confession to fend off the advances of their confessors; and the finest Roman choirs sang songs so filthy that the cardinals considered banning all singing in church.

Cosimo de'Medici, the first Medici monarch, was deeply fond of Boccaccio's masterpiece the *Decameron* and he asked Pope Gregory if he could find a way of taking it off the *Index of Forbidden Books*. Gregory was a liberal man by nature and he got the papal censor, Vincenzo Borghini, to look into it. Borghini was brilliant when it came to compromise. The book was deeply scatological, but he could see that it was a work of genius. So he simply went through it and changed all the misbehaving priests to laymen. In this form the *Decameron* was republished, this time with a preface that included a papal bull and two *Imprimaturs*, one from the supreme court of the Inquisition and one from the Inquisitor-General of Florence. To that, the Kings of France and Spain added their recommendations.

Gregory XIII's successor, Sixtus V (1585–90), knew how to deal with this sort of thing. He was a Franciscan monk who attacked heresy and vice with a passion. He executed thousands, including monks and their mistresses who, after the previous popes had banished whores from Rome, hired out their own daughters.

Errant nuns, of course, could be saved from their indecent reveries by regular flagellation.

Sixtus was a little easier on his own family. During his reign, his sister, a peasant, became the richest woman in Rome.

Sixtus V had a new torrent of filthy books to deal with that were cascading from the printing presses of Europe. He split the Congregation of the Index into fifteen committees, dividing the work of censorship among them, which caused confusion. The Spanish Congregation, for example, banned a number of Catholic prayer books, because they carried an illustration showing the martyrdom of St Ursula and the virgins. She and her nubile companions are shown quite naked, surrounded by pagan soldiers who are taking an indelicate interest in their persons.

Once the *Index* was published, anyone printing a banned book would be branded on the public scaffold with a cross-shaped iron, have one eye gouged out by the public executioner or have one hand amputated. The bookseller would face simple execution. And those would did not turn banned books over to the Inquisition would be beheaded or burned. Meanwhile, the Inquisitors, the Church's censors and the Pope could, of course, peruse banned books at their leisure.

Under Sixtus the writer François Rabelais – with his extraordinarily scatological tales involving discussions of bum-wiping, sexual intercourse in the privy and the advantages of co-educational monasteries and convents – came off the *Index* because he was a friend of the Pope's. However, books that described the sexual behaviour of the Popes went on the *Index* and stayed there.

Urban VII (1590) seemed a more tolerant soul. But he was struck down by malaria on the night of his election and died before his consecration could take place. He left his personal wealth of 30,000 scudi to provide dowries for impoverished Roman girls.

During the reign of Paul V (1605–21), the clergy still kept their mistresses. The Archbishop of Salzburg said that it was perfectly okay for his priests to maintain their concubines and children, provided they kept them outside a six-mile exclusion zone around the city.

To his everlasting credit, Paul V's successor, Gregory XV (1621–23) remained faithful throughout his time as pontiff to the mistress he had first seduced as a cardinal.

In the Church, the devil was still at work. Even by the seventeenth century, the Cathar tradition had not died out completely. In 1633, the French priest Urbain Grandier, well known as a womanizer and a deflowerer of virgins, was accused of seducing nuns into devil worship. With the nuns from his local convent, he had organized orgies in his own church in the name of the Persian god Asmodeus. His home was searched and a pact with the devil was found. It was written backwards in Latin and signed in Grandier's own blood.

Around the same time, there was an outbreak of satanism at the Monastère de Saint-Louis de Louvier in Paris. Father David, the confessor there, encouraged the nuns to go about their devotions in the nude. They took communion stripped to the waist and performed lesbian acts in the chapel. When Father David died, his place was taken by Father Mathurin Picard. He introduced the Black Mass, where the nuns had sexual intercourse with a devil figure – priests dressed as animals, reading from 'a book of blasphemies'. Communion wafers would be stuck to the penises of the priests as they entered the nuns. A new-born baby was crucified and two men who had come along to watch were murdered when they tried to leave. When the nuns gave birth, the babies were killed, cooked and eaten. Plainly, the Inquisition still had work to do.

Under Innocent X (1644–55), elected to the papal chair in 1644 at the age of seventy-two, 'the influence of a bad and reckless woman once more became conspicuous within the walls of the Vatican'. The reckless woman in question was his sister-in-law Donna Olimpia Maidalchini who was known for her 'insatiable ambition and rapacity'.

There were suggestions that their relationship was more intimate than that of brother-in-law and sister-in-law. Certainly Innocent was no celibate. Before his elevation, the Venetian ambassador reports that Innocent had devoted himself chiefly to 'knightly exercises and the pleasures of love'.

'This pope granted a dispensation to Casimir, King of Poland,' says Cypriano de Valera, 'which is no wonder if it is true that he himself had been too familiar with his brother's wife, the infamous Donna Olimpia.'

If she was not his mistress, she certainly acted that way. He made no important decision without consulting her, and her son Camillo Pamfili was made a cardinal. She entertained on the Pope's behalf, signed papal decrees and was First Lady in all but name. She organized the simony for him, selling benefices and fixing promotions. The period was know as 'the Pontificate of Donna Olimpia'.

Innocent and Olimpia were so open about their relationship that a medal was struck in Florence, showing Donna Olimpia on one side dressed in the papal robes. On the other side was Innocent X, wearing a woman's bonnet and sitting by a spinning wheel.

When Cardinal Pencirillo, Innocent's aide, drew his attention to the scandal he was causing, the Pope protested that he found Donna Olimpia indispensable.

However, Innocent X was a terrible prude. He had a horror of displays of nudity in art. He paid for fig leaves and metal tunics to be placed on statues around Rome, and he had Pietro da Cortona clothe a nude figure of the child Jesus by the baroque painter Guercino.

During the last few weeks of Innocent's life, Donna Olimpia never left his side. He died in 1655, at the age of eighty, with his head resting on her bosom.

Innocent's successor, Pope Alexander VII (1655–67),

was an intellectual and a poet. He took great pride in converting Queen Christina of Sweden from Protestantism after her abdication in June 1654. She settled in Rome in the Palazzo Farnese, turning the palace into an intellectual centre, though this was a great burden both to Alexander personally and to the treasury – her allowance alone was 12,000 crowns a year. She hung the walls with extremely indelicate pictures and had the fig leaves removed from the statues there.

An extraordinary woman, she wore men's clothing and shocked visiting dignitaries by introducing her intimate friend Ebba Sparre as her 'bedfellow' and assuring one and all that Ebba's mind was as lovely as her body. On formal occasions, even when she was entertaining cardinals, she would put aside her male attire and wear extremely provocative dresses. Pope Alexander called her 'a woman born a barbarian, barbarously brought up and having barbarous thoughts'.

Alexander's successor, Clement IX (1667–69), liked her, though, and visited her often. He invited her to dinner at a time when it was unheard of for a pope to eat with a woman. And he gave her a generous pension. But then Clement IX was a realist.

'Alphonso, King of Portugal, being deposed and divorced on the grounds of impotence, this pope granted a dispensation for his brother Don Pedro's marrying his Queen,' reports Cypriano de Valera. 'But to put a better colour on this extraordinary action, 'tis said he was necessitated to it, the marriage being already consummated, and the Queen big with child.'

Under the protection of Clement IX and Queen Christina, women appeared on the Roman stage again, after being banned by previous papal edicts.

This period of liberalization did not last long, though. Innocent XII (1691–1700) put 'certain ladies' in prison for playing the card game basset and demanded that preachers should be more 'decent and modest' in their sermons. He continued the work of putting fig leaves on statues. The breasts of Guido Reni's Madonna were painted over. Public theatres were closed. Women were again banned from the stage, being replaced by castrati. The carnival was strictly limited. Romans called Innocent XII 'Papa No'. Queen Christina fell into disfavour.

Clement XI (1700–21) faced scandal in 1703. An earthquake had destroyed a large number of houses, the Tiber had burst its banks and disease was rife. Clement, a charitable man, did his best to help out by allowing widows and young girls to stay in the palaces of prelates where, it was rumoured, the homeless women were offered more than food and shelter. They had to be removed to other homes at the Pope's expense. This and other misfortunes that befell during his papacy were said to have reduced him to a state of perpetual tears.

Benedict XIII (1724–30) scandalized the Church by leaving everything to his corrupt 'favourite', Cardinal Coscia. When he died, Rome rose up to the cry: 'Now let's go and burn Coscia.' So Clement XII (1730–40) put Coscia in jail for ten years and fined him 100,000 ducats.

Benedict XIV (1740–58) was known throughout Europe for his love of Rabelaisian stories. When he was still plain Cardinal Lambertini in 1739, he was visited by a French statesman, who wrote to a friend saying that the future pope had told him 'some good stories about girls' and that he had greatly enjoyed the Frenchman's stories of the debauchery of Cardinal Dubois and the French court.

The most intolerant pope of them all, Clement XIII (1758–69), ordered nude statues and paintings – including the frescoes in the Sistine Chapel – to be covered up.

Pius VI (1775–99) was offered the canonry of St Peter's at the age of thirty-six, but declined it because he was engaged to be married. However, with the consent of his fiancee, he entered the Church. She became a nun. He was an extremely vain man. 'In order to heighten its effect, he paid particular attention to the snow-white hair that framed his countenance,' wrote papal biographer Ludwig von Pastor. 'Some went so far as to suggest that he elegantly raised his long robe to one side so as to show his shapely foot. This betokened a serious flaw in his character which fitted ill his desire for fame. These weaknesses were severely criticised and exaggerated by the satiric Romans.'

He was deposed by Napoleon and forced into exile at Valence. His death was entered quite simply in the register there. It reads: 'Name: Citizen John Braschi. Trade: pontiff.'

18

Just say no

*O*n the face of it, the popes cleaned up their act at the start of the nineteenth century. The climate of public opinion was changing. Newspapers and scandal sheets had started up, so they had to learn to be a little more discreet. In the age of liberty and republicanism, they had also lost much of their power.

Pope Pius VII (1800–23) was forced to give his blessing to the marriage of ex-bishop Talleyrand to his long-term mistress. His papal secretary of state Cardinal Consalvi convinced him that it was the sensible thing to do. Napoleon himself had ordered Talleyrand to marry, to give his government a more respectable gloss. Consalvi himself was a layman. He told Talleyrand that, owing to his love of pleasure, he had had the moral delicacy not to become a priest.

Later Pius VII was forced to give Napoleon his divorce from Josephine. At the same time, he condemned bible societies as 'a most abominable invention that destroyed the very foundations of religion'.

Sixteen days after the death of Pius VII, fifty cardinals met in conclave to elect his successor. After twenty-six days of intrigues, disputes and briberies, Cardinal Annibal della Genga was proclaimed pope, under the name of Leo XII (1823–29). He was only sixty-three years old, which seemed to be a deviation from the rule of the cardinals, who generally elected one of the oldest among them, the nearest to the grave, giving the others a chance of the job. But della Genga was in very bad health, 'in consequence of his excesses in every kind of debauchery,' it was said. Indeed, Leo XII was well known to be a 'converted rake'. However, he had enough strength left to prohibit the selling of wine in Rome, and ban any woman's dress with a hemline above the ankles.

The new pontiff had been born in the diocese of Fabriano. He became a priest at the request of his father, Count Illario della Genga, but was plainly ill-suited for it. It is said that he was soon raised to the highest offices of the Church 'by intrigues with Roman courtesans and low services rendered to the offsprings of the incestuous Pius VI'.

Under Pius VII, he was sent to the Diet of Ratisbon to protect the interests of the Holy See. Afterwards he was ambassador to the court of Napoleon, where he distinguished himself by the basest flattery. And when Louis XVIII replaced the defeated Napoleon, he was delegated to compliment him on his elevation but 'disgusted the court with his despicable adulation'. On his return to Rome, it was said that 'he used all his influence under Pius VII to procure a restoration of the rack and other barbarous practices of the dark ages'.

As Pope, he restored the Jesuits – who had a bad reputation for scourging and debauching nuns – and reinstated the Inquisition. He even called on Ferdinand VII of Spain to perform an auto-de-fe and burn heretics at the stake, granting full indulgence to all those who co-operated or assisted at the barbarous spectacle. And, yes, he was another pope who put tin fig leaves on the naughty bits of classical statues.

In the 1840s, there were rumours concerning Gregory XVI (1831–46) and the great fortune of his chamberlain, Gaetanino, who was formerly his barber. His Holiness, it was said, showed great partiality for Gaetanino's wife and her seven children. She had an apartment in the Quirinal Palace, which had a communicating door through to Gregory's apartment. Rumour had it that Gregory was the father of Gaetanino's children.

It was also said that Gregory exiled a cardinal to the Legation of Ravenna in a fit of jealousy and that there were further scenes of domestic disquiet when a beautiful young nurse from Tivoli attached herself to the chamberlain's family and attracted the attentions of the Pope.

Gregory XVI was a great reader, a fan of the salacious French novels of Paul de Kock. He was also well known for living the life of an epicurean. He drank Orvieto wine and champagne. It was said that he got drunk every night. What is certain is that he tried to force Jews in Ancona and Sinigaglia to stay within the ghetto, banned them from having Christian nurses or servants or inducing Christians to sleep in the ghetto. Jews were also banned from sleeping outside it.

He set the Inquisition a rather unusual task. They were to track down anyone who made a pact with Satan to produce impotence in farm animals. Culprits were to be imprisoned for life.

Pius IX (1846–78) discovered that one of the reclining beauties on Pope Paul III's monument in St Peter's, the naked figure of Justice, was modelled on Giulia Farnese, Paul III's sister and mistress of Pope Alexander IV. Pius IX had a metal chemise put on her which was then painted to look like the original marble.

However, when he was expelled from Rome for two years by a Republican uprising, he sought sanctuary with Cardinal Antonelli, the son of a Neapolitan bandit and notorious for his love affairs, who became his closest adviser.

Pius was against bible societies and freedom of the press. More than 8000 political prisoners packed the papal jails during his reign. Nevertheless he became the first 'infallible' pope – by proclaiming himself so.

Pius XI (1922–39) wrote *Casti Connubii,* redefining Christian marriage and condemning contraception. The Catholic Church, he said, must 'stand erect in the midst of the moral ruin which surrounds her, in order that she may preserve the chastity of the nuptial union from being defiled by this foul stain'. Pius XI was plainly blessed with little sense of irony.

In 1932, he ordered German Catholics to drop their hostility to Hitler, and shocked Catholics around the world when he backed Mussolini's invasion of Abyssinia.

His successor, Pius XII (1939–58) was quick to condemn other people's sexual mores, but remained curiously quiet on the subject of the holocaust. He has been much criticized for not doing enough to help the Jews. His defence was that he thought condemnation would make things worse, but he could have done something about it. He was the one man Hitler feared, because so many of Hitler's troops were Catholic. However, he did condemn artificial insemination in any form and, in *Miranda Prorsus*, laid down strict guidelines for what it was permissible to depict on film and in other audio-visual media.

He had a close relationship with Sister Pasqualina, a German Franciscan nun, who was his housekeeper in Berlin, where he witnessed the rise of the Brown Shirts. He had seen the events that had led to Hitler's takeover from the beginning. In 1919, he had been papal nuncio in Munich when German communists declared the establishment of the short-lived Bavarian Socialist Republic as part of what they hoped would be Soviet Germany. His residence in Briennerstrasse was sprayed with machine-gun fire. When he phoned the Communist High Command to protest, he was told: 'Leave Munich tonight or you die.'

When he was recalled to Rome in 1929 to be made a cardinal, Sister Pasqualina accompanied him and served as his personal maid until the end of his life.

When he was just fourteen in 1895, the future Pope John XXIII (1958–63) wrote: 'At every time...I must avoid having dealings with, playing, or joking with women – regardless of what condition, age, or degree of kinship.' Two years later, he realized that, like it or not, was going to have to meet with women. He recorded that 'Women of every condition, even relatives or saintly persons, I shall meet with respectful reserve and avoid all familiarity, all gatherings and conversation with them, especially if they are young. I shall not raise my glance to their faces, remembering what the Holy Spirit teaches: "Do not look at a virgin, lest you stumble and incur penalties for her."' His namesake, the fifteenth-century Baldassare Cossa would have turned in his grave.

The second John XXIII's successor, Paul VI (1963–78), stamped down on artificial methods of birth control again in *Humanae Vitae* and countered renewed moves for a married priesthood in *Sacerdotalis Coelibatus,* which insists once again on the need for clerical celibacy. However, he did loosen up slightly on mixed marriages in *Matrimonia Mixta.*

He extended the papal commission on birth control and set the great contraceptive debate raging. Pius XII had already relaxed the position by allowing sex during the 'safe' period. Up until then, even this rudimentary type of 'safe sex' was condemned as mutual masturbation. Permitting the use of the so-called rhythm method of contraception – or Vatican Roulette, as it is known – abandoned the idea that sex was solely for procreation. It allowed that sex could be enjoyed as an expression of love or as a pleasure in itself – a grave sin in the eyes of former popes.

The liberals on the papal commission argued that if that method of contraception was all right, what was wrong with using condoms? And what was wrong with the pill for that matter? If the rhythm method was okay, so were the rest. All the laity on the commission held this view and four-fifths of the clergy were won over. But Paul VI would not stand for that. He said that ruling on contraception was beyond the competence of the council. What's more, he admitted to the newspaper *Corriere della Sera* that he found discussion of such things embarrassing. He alone would decide, and he was against it.

'Woman is a reflection of a beauty which transcends her, it is the sign of a goodness which seems to Us infinite,' he said. 'For Us, woman is a vision of virginal purity... She seems to converge naturally towards a unique and supreme figure, immaculate and sorrowful, which a privileged woman, blessed among all, was destined to become, the Virgin Mother of Christ, Mary... This is the plane on which We meet Woman.'

But the real problem with permitting the use of artificial contraception was a political one. For centuries, popes had condemned it, to permit it now would suggest 'that they condemned most imprudently under pain of eternal punishment, thousands upon thousands of human acts which are now approved'.

In *Humanae Vitae*, published in 1968, Paul VI condemns all use of contraception – 'before, or at the moment of, or after the sexual act' – as sinful, though a nod and a wink is given to the rhythm method. The danger of artificial contraception, Pope Paul points out, is that it reduces women in the eyes of men 'to being a mere instrument for the satisfaction of his own desires'.

John Paul I (1978) seems to have agreed, but he died in bed after just a month in office. Rumours of foul play circulated, especially as no autopsy was performed. Probably the most fanciful theory put forward was that he was murdered because he planned to revise *Humanae Vitae*.

The current pope, John Paul II (1978–) was a writer in his youth. He wrote some love poems and a play about marital love called *The Jeweller's Shop*. He may have known something of what he was talking about because, when he was a twenty-year-old student he was attached to a girl. But the 'attachment' was broken off after the death of his father and his recovery from two near-fatal accidents. He went missing during the war for three years and it was rumoured that he was married and widowed. In fact, Pope John Paul II claims he was secretly studying for the priesthood.

264

John Paul II has never backed away from *Humanae Vitae* and has written his own thoughts on human sexuality in *Love and Responsibility*, which was published in 1981.

He was a member of Paul VI's papal commission on contraception, but was mysteriously absent when the vote was taken on *Humanae Vitae*. However, on 12 November 1978, three weeks after becoming pontiff, he reprinted an article he had written earlier for *Osservatore Romano* called 'The Truth of the Encyclical *Humanae Vitae*'. In it he says: 'Every act of sex must be open to the transmission of life.'

Plainly John Paul II is a good man, which is lucky for Christendom but which means that his life is not half as colourful as those of some of his illustrious predecessors.

Bibliography

The Catholic Encyclopaedia, New York, 1907
Clerical Celibacy, Roman Cholij, Leominster 1989
Crises in the History of the Papacy, Joseph McCabe, New
    York, 1916
The Decay of the Church of Rome, Joseph McCabe,
    London, 1909
The Devil a Monk Would Be, T. Clifton Longworth,
    London, 1923
Encyclopedia of the Early Church, Angelo Di Berardino,
    Cambridge, 1992
Eunuchs for the Kingdom of Heaven, Uta
    Ranke-Heinemann, New York, 1990
The Female Pope, Rosemary and Darroll Pardoe,
    Wellingborough, 1988
The Gay Chronicle of the Monks and the Nuns, Joseph
    McCabe, Girard, Kansas, 1930
Gnosticism – its History and Influence, Benjamin Walker,
    Wellingborough, 1983

BIBLIOGRAPHY

The Gods of Generation, J.A. Dulaure, New York, 1934

Homosexuality and the Priesthood, edited by Jeanne Gramick, New York, 1990

History of the Inquisition of Spain, Henry Charles Lea, New York, 1907

History of the Catholic Index, Joseph McCabe, Kansas, 1931

History of the Popes, Dr Ludwig Pastor, London, 1949

A History of the Popes, Joseph McCabe, London, 1939

The Holy Blood and the Holy Grail, Michael Baigent, Richard Leigh and Henry Lincoln, London 1982

I Have To Tell This Story, Leon Hayblum, New York, 1995

Jesus, A.N. Wilson, London, 1992

Jesus the Man, Barbara Thieling, London, 1992

Keepers of the Keys, Nicholas Cheetham, London, 1982

Liber Pontificalis, Raymond Davis, Liverpool, 1992

Lives of the Early Popes, Thomas Meyrick, London, 1878

Lives of the Popes, Rev. Horace K. Mann, London, 1925

The Lives of the Popes, B. Platina, London, 1645

Nero, Miriam T. Griffin, London, 1984

New Catholic Encyclopedia, New York, 1966

Oxford Dictionary of the Popes, J.N.D. Kelly, Oxford, 1986

Pope Joan, Emmanuel Royids, translated by Lawrence Durrell, London, 1954

The Popes at Avignon, G. Mollet, Edinburgh, 1963

Popery, Cypriano de Valera, London, 1704

A Protestant Dictionary, Charles Wright and Charles Neil, London, 1904

Religion and Sex, Chapman Cohen, London, 1919

The Rise, Decline and Fall of the Roman Religion, James Ballantyne Hannay, London, 1925

Rome Before Avignon, Robert Brentano, University of California, 1990

The Roman Index of Forbidden Books, Frances S. Betten, St Louis, Missouri, 1909

The Roman Pontiffs, Henry G. Daggers, New York, 1845

Sacerdotal Celibacy in the Christian Church, Henry C. Lea, Philadelphia, 1867

Secret Memoirs of a Renaissance Pope, Pius II, London, 1988

Sex in the Church, Oscar Feucht, St Louis, 1961

Sex in History, Reay Tannahill, London, 1980

Sex and the Penitentials, Pierre J. Payer, Toronto, 1984

Sex and Race, J.A. Rogers, New York, 1940

Sex in Religion, G. Simpson Marr, London, 1936

Sexuality, Religion and Magic, Michael A, Kószegi, New York, 1994

Simon Peter, Carsten P. Thiede, London, 1986

The Three Popes, Marzieh Gail, London, 1969

The Trial of the Templars in the Papal States and the Abruzzi, Anne Gilmour-Bryson, Vatican City, 1982

A True History of the Lives of the Popes of Rome (with A Description of their particular Vices and Misdemeanours), H.M. and R.T., London, 1679

Chronological list of Popes and Anti–popes

The names marked in italic are anti-popes. Popes mentioned in the text are marked by an asterisk(*). Anti-popes have their numerals in brackets where they share the title with an official pope

*d. *c.*64 Peter the Apostle
*c.*66–*c.*78 Linus
*c.*79–*c.*91 Anacletus
*c.*91–*c.*101 Clement I
*c.*100–*c.*109 Evaristus
*c.*109–*c.*116 Alexander I
*c.*116–*c.*125 Sixtus I
*c.*125–*c.*136 Telesphorus
*c.*138–*c.*142 Hyginus
*c.*142–*c.*155 Pius I
*c.*155–*c.*166 Anicetus
* *c.*166–*c.*174 Soter
*c.*174–89 Eleutherius
189–98 Victor I

198/9–217 Zephyrinus
*217–22 Callistus I
*217–35 *Hippolytus*
222–30 Urban I
230–35 Pontian
235–36 Anterus
236–50 Fabian
251–53 Cornelius
251–58 *Novation*
253–54 Lucius I
254–57 Stephen I
257–58 Sixtus II
260–58 Dionysius
269–74 Felix I

275–83 Eutychian
283–96 Gaius
296–?0304 Marcellinus
306–08 Marcellus I
310 Eusebius
311–14 Miltiades
*314–35 Silvester I
336 Mark
337–52 Julius I
*352–66 Liberius
*355–65 *Felix II*
*366–67 *Ursinus*
366–84 Damasus I
*384–99 Siricius
*399–401 Anastasius I
*401–17 Innocent I
417–18 Zosimus
418–19 *Eulalius*
*418–22 Boniface I
422–32 Celestine I
*432–40 Sixtus III
*440–61 Leo I
461–68 Hilarus
468–83 Simplicius
*483–92 Felix III
*492–96 Gelasius I
*496–98 Anastasius II
*498–514 Symmachus
*498/9; 501–06 *Lawrence*
*514–23 Hormisdas
523–26 John I
526–30 Felix IV
*530–32 Boniface II
530 *Dioscorus*
533–35 John II
*535–36 Agapitus I
*536–37 Silverius
*537–55 Vigilius
*556–61 Pelagius I
*561–74 John III
*575–79 Benedict I
*579–90 Pelagius II

*590–604 Gregory I
604–06 Sabinian
607 Boniface III
608–15 Boniface IV
615–18 Deusdedit
619–25 Boniface V
625–38 Honorius I
640–42 John IV
640 Severinus
642–49 Theodore I
649–53 Martin I
654–57 Eugene I
657–72 Vitalian
672–76 Adeodatus II
676–78 Donus
678–81 Agatho
682–83 Leo II
684–85 Benedict II
685–86 John V
686–87 Conon
*687–701 Sergius I
687 *Paschal*
687 *Theodore*
701–05 John VI
705–07 John VII
708–15 Constantine
708 Sisinnius
715–31 Gregory II
*731–41 Gregory III
*741–52 Zacharias
752 Stephen
752–57 Stephen II
757–67 Paul I
767–68 *Constantine*
768–72 Stephen III
768 *Philip*
772–95 Hadrian I
*795–816 Leo III
816–17 Stephen IV
817–24 Paschal I
824–27 Eugene II
827–44 Gregory IV

827 Valentine
844–45 Hadrian III
844–47 Sergius II
844 *John*
*847–55 Leo IV
*855–58 Benedict III
*858–67 Nicholas I
*867–72 Hadrian II
872–82 John VIII
*882–84 Marinus I
*884–85 Hadrian III
*885–91 Stephen V
891–96 Formosus
*896–97 Stephen VI
*896 Boniface VI
*897 Romanus
*897 Theodore II
898–900 John IX
*900–03 Benedict IV
*903–04 *Christopher*
*903–04 Leo V
*904–11 Sergius III
*911–13 Anastasius III
*913–14 Lando
*914–28 John X
928–31 Stephen VII
928 Leo VI
931–36 John XI
936–39 Leo VII
939–42 Stephen VIII
*942–46 Marinus II
946–55 Agapitus II
955–58 Benedict III
*955–64 John XII
*963–65 Leo VIII
*964 Benedict V
*965–72 John XIII
*973–74 Benedict VI
*974–83 Benedict VII
*974; 984–85 *Boniface VII*
*983–84 John XIV
*985–96 John XV

*996–99 Gregory V
998–1001 *John XVI*
*999–1003 Silvester II
1003 John XVII
*1003–09 John XVIII
1009–12 Sergius IV
*1012–24 Benedict VIII
1012 *Gregory (VI)*
*1024–32 John XIX
*1032–44; 1045; 1047–8
  Benedict IX
*1045–46 Gregory VI
*1045 Silvester III
*1046–47 Clement II
*1048 Damasus II
*1049–54 Leo IX
*1055–57 Victor II
*1057–58 Stephen IX (X)
1058–59 *Benedict X*
*1058–61 Nicholas II
1061–4 *Honorius (II)*
*1061–73 Alexander II
*1073–85 Gregory VII
*1080; 1084–1100 *Clement III*
*1086–87 Victor III
*1088–99 Urban II
*1099–1118 Paschal II
1100–01 *Theoderic*
1101 *Albert*
1105–11 *Silvester IV*
1118–19 Gelasius II
1118–21 *Gregory (VIII)*
*1119–24 Callistus II
*1124–30 Honorius II
1124 *Celestine II*
*1130–38 *Anacletus II*
*1130–43 Innocent II
1138 *Victor IV*
*1143–44 Celestine II
1144–45 Lucius II
1145–53 Eugene III
1150–55 Julius III

1153–54 Anastasius IV
*1154–59 Hadrian IV
1159–64 *Victor (IV)*
*1159–81 Alexander III
1164–68 *Paschal III*
1168–78 *Callistus III*
1179–80 *Innocent (III)*
1181–85 Lucius III
1185–87 Urban III
1187–91 Clement III
*1187 Gregory VIII
*1191–98 Celestine III
*1198–1216 Innocent III
1216–27 Honorius III
*1227–41 Gregory IX
*1241 Celestine IV
*1243–54 Innocent IV
*1254–61 Alexander IV
*1261–64 Urban IV
*1265–68 Clement IV
*1271–76 Gregory X
*1276–77 John XXI
1276 Hadrian V
*1276 Innocent V
*1277–80 Nicholas III
*1281–85 Martin IV
1285–87 Honorius IV
*1288–92 Nicholas IV
*1294–1303 Boniface VIII
1294 Celestine V
1303–04 Benedict XI
*1305–14 Clement V
*1316–34 John XXII
*1328–33 *Nicholas V*
*1334–42 Benedict XII
*1342–52 Clement VI
1352–62 Innocent VI
*1362–70 Urban V
*1370–78 Gregory XI
*1378–89 Urban VI
*1378–94 *Clement VII*
*1389–1404 Boniface IX

*1394–1417 *Benedict XIII*
*1404–06 Innocent VII
*1406–15 Gregory XII
*1406–10 *Alexander V*
*1410–15 *John (XXIII)*
*1417–31 Martin V
1423–29 *Clement VIII*
1425–? *Benedict XIV*
*1431–47 Eugene IV
*1439–49 *Felix V*
*1447–55 Nicholas V
*1455–58 Callistus III
*1458–64 Pius II
*1464–71 Paul II
*1471–84 Sixtus IV
*1484–92 Innocent VIII
*1492–1503 Alexander VI
*1503 Pius III
*1503–13 Julius II
*1513–21 Leo X
*1522–23 Hadrian VI
*1523–34 Clement VII
*1534–49 Paul III
*1550–55 Julius III
*1555–59 Paul IV
1555 Marcellus II
*1559–65 Pius IV
*1566–72 Pius V
*1572–85 Gregory XIII
*1585–90 Sixtus V
1590–91 Gregory XIV
*1590 Urban VII
1591 Innocent IX
1592–1605 Clement VIII
*1605–21 Paul V
1605 Leo XI
*1621–23 Gregory XV
1623–44 Urban VIII
*1644–55 Innocent X
*1655–67 Alexander VII
*1667–69 Clement IX
*1670–76 Clement X

1676–89 Innocent XI
1689–91 Alexander VIII
*1691–1700 Innocent XII
*1700–21 Clement XI
1721–24 Innocent XIII
*1724–30 Benedict XIII
*1730–40 Clement XII
*1740–58 Benedict XIV
*1758–69 Clement XIII
1769–74 Clement XIV
*1775–99 Pius VI
*1800–23 Pius VII
*1823–29 Leo XII

1829–30 Pius VIII
*1831–46 Gregory XVI
*1846–78 Pius IX
1878–1903 Leo XIII
1903–14 Pius X
1914–22 Benedict XV
*1922–39 Pius XI
*1939–58 Pius XII
*1958–63 John XXIII
*1963–78 Paul VI
*1978 John Paul I
*1978– John Paul II

Index